BLOODY LANE

BLOODY LANE

MARTIN E. LEE

MATTHEW C. FLEURY

GARN PRESS
NEW YORK, NY

Published by Garn Press, LLC
New York, NY
www.garnpress.com

Garn Press and the Chapwoman logo are registered trademarks of Garn Press, LLC

Bloody Lane is a work of fiction closely based on history and geography. References to historical events, real people, or real places are used fictitiously, and are not intended to depict actual events or to change the fictional nature of the work, and all situations, incidents, and dialogues are products of the authors' imagination and are not to be construed as real.. Other names, characters, places, and events are products of the authors' imagination or are used fictitiously, and any resemblance to actual events, locales, or persons, living or dead, is entirely coincidental.

Book and cover design by Benjamin J. Taylor
Cover image by Geoff Kuchera/iStock.com

Library of Congress Control Number: 2015950366

Publisher's Cataloging-in-Publication Data

Lee, Martin E., 1950-
Bloody lane / Martin E. Lee and Matthew C. Fleury.
pages cm
ISBN: 978-1-942146-25-4 (pbk.)
ISBN: 978-1-942146-26-1 (hardcover)
ISBN: 978-1-942146-27-8 (e-book)
1. Antietam National Battlefield (Md.)—Fiction. 2. Murder—Investigation. 3. Historical reenactments—Fiction. 4. Right-wing extremists—Fiction. 5. Conspiracy—Fiction. I. Fleury, Matthew C. II. Title.
PS3612.E36 B66 2015
813—dc23

2015950366

There he is, just come out of the woods on the near side of the creek. Right on time, all got up in Union blue. Blue's a better target than gray, easier to see, especially at a distance. About 200 yards and heading in your direction, not a clue that this is his very last day on Earth.

The sun's almost up, hidden behind the knoll rising on the other side of the creek. Quiet. A hawk wheels overhead. It, too, is hunting.

Wait until he's below you, wait until he stops by the bridge. Check the rifle's action one last time, put a shell into the chamber, then close the bolt. One shot is all you get. One shot is all you need.

Now you have him in your sights. He suddenly lifts his head, turns his gaze in your direction. Not to worry, though. He's a hundred yards away, and between you and him is a thick curtain of trees and brush. No way he can see you. Probably thinking about the battle, about the rebels who held the same position that you hold now.

Get into position. Settle one knee into the hash of leaves and twigs and dirt. If you dig into it a foot or two, there's a good chance you'd find a Yankee minié ball, one of the thousands fired during the fight over the bridge. Ancient history, as far as you're concerned. All those young men. Now it's his turn to die.

Rest your elbow on your knee. Tuck the rifle stock against your shoulder, cradle the smooth wood of the barrel in your palm. The air smells of gun oil and damp grass. It's going to be another scorcher.

He's stopped, standing with his back to you, looking at the creek. Perfect. A hundred yards. No wind. Aim at the spot just to the left of his ponytail. He won't be needing that anymore. Won't be in need of anything except an undertaker. Good riddance, anyway you look at it.

Breathe. Finger on the trigger. Crosshairs centered on the back of his head. He'll never know what hit him. Breathe easy. Easy. That's it. Now squeeze.

1

Felix Allaben had just turned to the obituaries when the telephone rang. His first thought: Don't answer it. He wasn't expecting a call, and at the moment he didn't feel like talking to anyone. His daughter had phoned at 6:00 for her weekly debriefing from San Francisco, where she was staying with his brother. And his friends knew better than to call him on a Sunday evening, when it was his custom to sequester himself with the weekend papers – the Frederick Post and the Baltimore Sun – always in that order and always beginning with the obituaries.

He was settled in a roomy wicker chair on the garden patio, a tumbler of vodka and tonic close by one hand and the stack of papers by the other. Above the stuccoed wall at the far end of the garden the spires of Frederick rose into the pale August sky. The scent of honeysuckle hung in the air.

Pedro, Allaben's big black Labrador, lay in a heap at his feet. Pedro knew his master's ways; more than knew, he sympathized. With every bleat of the phone the dog answered a low growl. Six, seven, eight times. Allaben sighed in resignation. Slowly he got to his feet. The dog batted his tail against the flagstone. Allaben ordered him to stay, then trudged to the screen door.

He picked up the phone in the kitchen twilight. There was a

prickly silence; then, "Allaben? Is that you?"

He recognized the reedy voice at once. It was Sam Folliard.

"Yeah, Sam, it's me."

"Is this a bad time?"

That was just like Folliard – let the phone ring a dozen times, then ask if it's a bad time. Allaben never ceased to wonder how a man so contradictory could possibly have risen to an undersecretary's rank, even one as shadowy as his.

"I was out back," he said, "with the papers."

"I tried the cell, left a message."

"The cell's upstairs on my desk, Sam. It's Sunday."

If Folliard got the hint, he gave no sign of it.

"I suppose you've heard," he began.

No, thought Allaben, I suppose I haven't. What's more, he didn't want to hear. But Folliard was undeterred.

"It's Gwynn, that former colleague of yours. The whistleblower."

"Curtis Gwynn?"

"Found him shot at Antietam Battlefield."

"Is he dead?"

"D.O.A. Looks like homicide. TV's picked up the story but it's not in the papers yet. Happened this morning, early. A park ranger found him – Hal Snyder. Does that name mean anything to you?"

"Snyder? Yes, I know Hal Snyder."

Allaben heard the tap of the screen door. That would be Pedro. Two summers ago, Miranda had tied a length of rope to the handle and taught the dog to use it to open the door. That way she could go away to camp secure in the knowledge that he could come and go as he pleased. Miranda on her hands and knees, rope clenched in her jaws. See, Pedro?

The dog came ambling into the kitchen, nails clicking against the tile floor. He circled once, woefully eyed his master, then sat at his feet.

"Allaben? You still there?"

"Yeah, Sam, I'm still here. Funny coincidence – I just talked to Gwynn last week. He said he'd be taking part in the weekend's battlefield events."

Folliard waited a second. "And?"

"He called me, that's all. Wanted to reminisce, stroll down memory lane."

Not altogether true – Gwynn had hinted there was something more – but Allaben would keep his own counsel on that score, at least until he'd heard Folliard out.

"Who's handling the case, Sam?"

"I'm hoping you will." Folliard let this sink in, then went on. "Officially, it's ours. The body was found on Park Service property, and that makes it federal jurisdiction."

"Maybe so, but it's still kind of a stretch, isn't it?"

"It's close enough," said Folliard.

Allaben knew what that meant. If Folliard were sufficiently interested, he'd make it close enough.

"What's in it for you, Sam?"

"That's for you to find out. Right now the locals are running the show. Washington County Sheriff's Department."

"That's Wick Mallory's turf."

"Right. I talked to him an hour ago. Smoothed the way. He had nothing but good things to say about you. You practically walk on water, to hear him tell it."

Allaben watched the dog's flanks bellow and cinch. The clock in the study struck eight. He glanced at the window. The sky was turning indigo.

Folliard decided to interpret the silence.

"Problem with Mallory?"

Allaben pictured the sheriff's big, rugged face.

"He's a good cop, Sam."

"But …"

"But he likes the easy ones."

"Maybe this is an easy one."

"Then why call me?"

"Because I'm a worrier, Felix, and a worrier likes to share his worries. Maybe you'd like me to pull some strings?"

"Come on, Sam. You're already pulling them. What about Snyder?"

"Snyder's a big fan, too. I guess he heard about the Shenandoah case. He'll help you out at the battlefield. Anything you need. He knew Gwynn, or recognized him. And it's practically in your back yard. The usual per-diem, plus expenses. Interested?"

"Let me sleep on it, Sam," Allaben said. "I'll call you in the morning."

He sat for a while after he'd hung up the phone, staring at nothing. Night had come down and the kitchen was dark. The house settled into silence around him, the only sounds the steady pant of the dog, the idle drip in the sink, and the locust rhythm of his own thoughts.

Why the obituaries? Because they leave nothing unresolved, no loose ends. No miscellaneous details. The entire story – beginning, middle, end – boiled down to a few column inches of newsprint.

Everything in its place, each parcel – schooling, jobs, memberships, survivors – neatly tied up with a phrase. The inexpressible grit and grime of experience scrubbed away, consigned to the ghostly life that can only be read between the lines.

> Mrs. Rebecca Allaben died yesterday at St. Luke's Hospital in Baltimore. She was 37 years old. Mrs. Allaben succumbed to gunshot wounds suffered on April 22 in an armed robbery in Baltimore. Her husband, Felix Allaben, was also wounded in the attack. The district attorney's office announced this morning that murder charges would be added to those already pressed against the man alleged to have committed the assault, Ronald Gillespie, 17, of Baltimore.
>
> Mrs. Allaben, the former Rebecca Lacey, was born in Frederick on October 9, 1979. She was the daughter of the late Franklin Lacey II and Emily Heath Lacey. Mr. Lacey was from 1994 until his death in 2012 the president of County Federal Bank.
>
> Rebecca Allaben attended Frederick schools. After graduating in 1997, she spent two years in the Peace Corps, chiefly in the African nation of Sudan. Upon returning to the United States, she entered Johns Hopkins University, from which she graduated in 2004. She went on to earn a Master's degree and then a Ph. D. from Vanderbilt University.
>
> Mrs. Allaben joined the faculty of Hood College in 2008, and in 2013 became the Chair of the English Department. She resigned from that position in 2014, and at the time of her death held the title Professor of English Literature.
>
> Rebecca Lacey married Felix Allaben in 2003. Mr.

> Allaben, formerly a Lieutenant in the Baltimore Police Department and an investigator for the Justice Department, is now a private security consultant.
>
> Besides her husband, Rebecca Allaben is survived by her mother and a daughter, Miranda Allaben. A memorial service will be held on Saturday at 11:00 at All Saints Church in Frederick.

Six paragraphs, set in sturdy Times Roman. As intractable as the dates chiseled into the headstone.

The plot to the left of hers was reserved for him. Earth to earth, ashes to ashes.

If only it were as simple as that.

2

Allaben awoke on Monday morning to the thud of the newspaper against the front door. He'd fallen asleep on a sofa in the living room. His left hand hurt. It ached like it had a heart of its own, a broken one. The doctors said that it would always hurt – sometimes a little, sometimes a lot – and went on to warn him about relying too much on pain killers. But Allaben didn't mind the pain because the pain served him right.

He lay on his back and thought about Gwynn, about what a royal pain in the ass Curtis Gwynn could be. And about Sam Folliard, whose stock in trade was cunning. And about Wick Mallory and the good old days of baseball and beer. Mallory was wearing a sheriff's badge now.

Someone had shot Curtis Gwynn. Who? One of the cops Gwynn had fingered? One of the husbands whose wives he'd bedded?

And on Antietam battlefield, of all places. Why there?

He sat up and peered at his watch: 7:20. Far too early to call Folliard. The Stippetti establishment would be open for business, though. He hauled himself out of bed, shaved, showered, made some coffee. The cup and spoon were rattling in the kitchen sink when Pedro turned away from his empty bowl. Allaben grabbed the leash and headed for the door.

The day had broken hot and sticky. As he turned out of the alley onto Second Street, he glanced at the bank thermometer – already 77 degrees. Pedro stopped to sniff at the iron boot scraper at the curbside, then tugged at the leash. They set off at a brisk clip.

First past the stately Ramsey House, where Abraham Lincoln had visited a wounded Union general and had later addressed a group of Frederick citizens. Then past the carriage house and slave quarters of the Ross-Mattias estates, followed by the mansions themselves, one red and one white, but in every other respect mirror images of each other.

There were few obstacles to negotiate as they walked toward Ozzie's, only storekeepers hosing down the Court Street sidewalks, and well-groomed men and women, briefcases in hand, hurrying by. In an hour and a half their assistants would be bringing them coffee in offices in Baltimore and Washington.

Pedro turned right at Market Street, barked in satisfaction, and dragged Allaben through the open screen door into Stippetti's Tobacco Shop. A battered Coke machine leaned against one wall, racks of magazines against another. Newspapers lay stacked on a bench before the battered oak counter. Behind it was an array of tobacco products – cigarettes, cigarillos, cheroots, cigars, plug. A beam of light had found its way through the signs and notices that encrusted the window, picking out the relief on the corner of an ancient brass cash register and bleaching the knuckles on Ozzie Stippetti's gnarled hands. One of these slowly rose from the racing form spread before him to the unlit cigar clenched in his teeth.

"Morning, Pedro. And good morning to you, Lieutenant."

"Morning, Ozzie. Looks like another scorcher."

"Love the heat," Ozzie rasped. "Like butter on toast."

He reached behind the counter and produced a box of dog bones. Pedro promptly sat, eyes fixed on the prize. Ozzie shook one from the box. He studied the bone carefully, as if checking for defects, before tossing it to the dog. Ozzie was partial to animals, especially dogs and horses. Human beings he held in low esteem. Take it from Ozzie, only a fool bets on a biped.

"Yesterday," he growled, "the sixth at Pimlico, I come this close." He rested his thumbnail against the end of his nose and stretched out his index finger. "What's that – five inches between me and four grand? I could use four grand."

"You ought to come out to the ball park, see the Keys play," Allaben said in reply. "It's a lot less expensive than the ponies."

"At least the ponies look good when they lose," Ozzie retorted. "Who are the bums playing tonight?"

"Winston-Salem. Rod Hurley's starting."

Allaben picked up the Post. The Gwynn story filled a bottom quarter of the front page."Frederick Man Found Dead at Antietam Battlefield." He skimmed through the lead. The reporter didn't seem to know any more than he did.

"How about our friend Curtis Gwynn?" Ozzie asked. "Says he was got up in a re-enactor's uniform."

"Union blue, head to toe. Did you know him?"

"He came in once in a while. Liked the 'Havanas' even though they're rolled in El Salvador. Liked to spout off, too, especially about the Civil War." Ozzie pointed his finger at the ceiling and adopted an orator's stance. "The victory of Northern capital – wage labor over slave labor! Industry over feudalism!' Something like that. I didn't listen to much of it."

Allaben nodded. That was Gwynn to a tee. Never happier than when he was being contrary.

"Fact," said Ozzie, "I took him for a Southern sympathizer. Are you sure he was in blue?"

"So I've been told."

"Maybe the Blues pay better."

"Curtis Gwynn was not the type who could be bought," Allaben said.

"Could get himself killed, though," Ozzie replied. "He sure as hell picked the place for it."

Pedro shook his head to get Ozzie's attention, and Ozzie obliged with a second bone. He gave Allaben a sidewise look.

"Speaking of uniforms," he said, "I hear the Bruce battery is looking for someone to fill out the howitzer crew for the goings-on at the battlefield."

"You know I don't go in for that stuff, Ozzie."

Allaben did not disguise his irritation with Ozzy's gambit, the same one he took every year at the approach of the events commemorating the battle at Antietam.

Ozzie countered, "Me, I'd be out there hell for leather if it wasn't for my bum knee. Here you are, a walking Civil War encyclopedia, and you take a rain check every year. I just don't get it."

Allaben felt no obligation to explain himself. He knew that he probably couldn't have done it to his own satisfaction even if he'd tried. So he dodged with a fact that happened to be both true and convenient.

"I've got to fetch Miranda that day. She's coming home from California. No time for battlefield duty."

At the mention of Miranda, Ozzie sighed in concession. He

nodded at the newspaper in Allaben's hands.

"Can I inquire are you taking a professional interest in this Gwynn business," he asked, "or is this one of your hush-hush jobs?"

"I'm heading over there this morning."

Allaben fished some change from his pocket and counted out the price of the paper. Ozzie gave Pedro the once-over.

"You taking the mutt?"

"How's my credit?"

"You're not back by closing time, the dog's in hock."

With that, Ozzie took the leash and guided the dog behind the counter. By the time Allaben reached the doorway, Ozzie was once more bent over the paper and Pedro was sprawled on the floor, working on a second bone.

3

A photo of Gwynn accompanied the story in the Post. The newspaper lay folded on the passenger's seat, and Allaben glanced at it from time to time as he drove the twenty-five miles to Sharpsburg. He recognized the photo. It was the same one that had appeared in the papers when the corruption story broke, which would make it about four years old. Gwynn was in uniform, beardless, groomed to within an inch of his life – in short, a "before" picture.

Allaben hadn't known him then. It was only after Gwynn had left the department, hounded out for violating the code of silence, that Allaben had had anything to do with him. And then only because he'd been ordered to. The commissioner had asked him to talk to Gwynn privately, to find whether he was sitting on any more nasty revelations. It was a dangerous game at all three corners, a game which, when Allaben later thought on it, none of them could win.

Gwynn had called only last week. As usual, he hadn't wasted time with preliminaries. He came straight to the point.

"Hey, Lieutenant, someone tried to kill me today. Tried to run me down."

"Where?"

"Patrick and Bentz. I was heading for the Raw Bar."

"That's a tricky corner."

"Tricky, nothing. Trust me, this was deliberate."

"Did you get the plate?"

"You kidding? He had to be doing fifty. White Toyota. Camry, I think. The bastard almost took out a light pole. I was flat on my keister, which is how come I didn't see the plate."

"Did you report it?"

"What do you think?"

Of course he hadn't reported it. Gwynn was still a pariah to every police department within hailing distance of Baltimore. Which was fine with Gwynn, who was born to play the martyr. He thrived on persecution. Allaben had more than once seen fit to tell him so, and to remind him in a friendly way that in every martyr's garden there is a snake that goes by the name of Paranoia.

In any event, every officer Gwynn had fingered – five in all – had to be considered a possible suspect. Each would have to be checked out. That would mean legwork, lots of it. Maybe that could be left to Mallory and his crew?

Allaben followed a school bus into the parking lot at the visitor's center for the Antietam National Battlefield. At the information desk he learned that park ranger Hal Snyder had escorted the sheriff and coroner to the side of the creek. They would be waiting for him there.

He climbed to the observation deck atop the visitor's center to reacquaint himself with the lay of the land. To Allaben's eyes, the landscape before him, however serene in appearance, was not at all a pleasant thing to look upon. It presented an unsettling panorama that evoked the horrors of the battle that had been waged there. A pack of schoolboys, just liberated from the bus, swarmed over an artillery piece below. Beyond stretched a great green meadow, dotted with monuments, that gradually fell away toward Antietam Creek.

In the distance rose the saddle of South Mountain. To Allaben's immediate left stood the reconstructed Dunker Church, a humble white structure that had been a focal point in the battle's ferocious early morning fighting. A canvas tent was pitched near the church, with litters in plain sight and a crude ambulance wagon parked close by – the aftermath of the previous day's field hospital demonstrations. A handful of volunteers, some still in uniform, were breaking down the tent, taking away the lanterns, shovels, and the boards and the barrels that had served as operating tables, and boxing up medical supplies.

If there was anything remarkable about the set being dismantled before him, it was its workaday character, for Allaben knew that during the battle itself – not the re-enactment, but the one in which young men oozed real blood – the field hospital would have been a hellish scene, a nightmarish place of screams and groans and death-rattles. The wounded who were carted there would have been greeted by the ghastly sight of corpses piled waist-high in ragged heaps and then been tended by surgeons who worked feverishly to dress wounds, tie arteries, and set broken limbs.

Beyond this scene, perhaps half a mile away, was the infamous Cornfield; to his right, and at about the same range, the observation tower that marked the foot of the equally infamous Sunken Road. This crudely fashioned farm lane had seen carnage and bravery in equal helpings, a paroxysm of savagery rarely equaled in battles before or since. No wonder that those who had been witness to the slaughter there knew it by another name – Bloody Lane.

Burnside Bridge, where Snyder and the others would be awaiting him, was in the same general direction as the tower, but hidden from view and well over a mile away.

Allaben returned to his truck and drove to the lot overlooking the bridge. He parked beside a red-and-white Washington County Sheriff's Department cruiser, stepped out of his vehicle, and took a look down below.

Yellow police tape cordoned off the stairway leading down to the bridge. Antietam Creek flowed smoothly below. A swath had been cut in the grass on the far bank, and beyond a rail fence, now garlanded with police tape, a field of knee-high grass gave way to brush and thicket, which gave way in turn to a wooded hillside.

Downstream, three men could be seen standing along that bank. One of the men he recognized at once as Snyder – a six-foot-eight beanpole crowned with a ranger's hat is hard to mistake. Neither of the other two men was Wick Mallory, though the one in the pea-green uniform was presumably from the sheriff's department. The other wore a gray suit and a straw hat.

Allaben climbed down the stairs, crossed the stone bridge, and walked toward them. The creek drifted beside him, glinting silver and jade in the hot morning sun. Snyder stepped forward to greet him as he approached, leaving the other two men huddled in the shade near the bank of the creek. Snyder wrapped Allaben's hand in his own. On his face – bony, sallow, woebegone – gathered an expression of tongue-tied commiseration. Allaben knew what was coming. Snyder cleared his throat. On his breath, beneath a cloak of peppermint, lurked the scent of bourbon.

"I was awful sorry about your wife," he commenced.

"Good of you to say so, Hal. I appreciate it," Allaben replied, adopting a tone of stony resignation. Practice had shown him that this was the note most likely to spare him further condolence. But Snyder would not let it go so easily.

"Terrible thing," he intoned. "Terrible thing when a woman, an innocent … I just couldn't believe it, and that's the God's honest truth. Still can't."

What was Allaben to say to that? Ditto and amen?

"What became of him, anyway," Snyder continued, "the kid who did it?"

"Copped a plea. He's doing seven to twelve."

"Not much justice in that. Ought to fry him. I don't know what the world is coming to."

Allaben didn't know, either, nor was he much interested. Justice? Better minds than his had foundered on that reef. His wife was dead, blown away by a doped-up 17-year-old, and he had been spared, bloodied but alive, and that was all there was to it.

"All right, Hal," he said, "let's get down to business. Show me where you found Gwynn."

Snyder's face smoothed with relief. "I'll tell you this," he said. "When I first got here and I see they're both in full uniform – kepi to boots – I figured it was some re-enactors pulling my chain. Wouldn't put it past them. But then I see it's Irwin kneeling beside him, and he's not the sort that goes in for that stuff. Besides, there's something about a dead man says it can't be anything else."

He left off to introduce the other two men, who had drifted over from creekside. The man in uniform was indeed a deputy sheriff, Dan Thompson by name – abbreviated D.T. by his friends, as the deputy was quick to insist. Allaben put him at about 25. He was short and stocky, gone a little slack around the middle. In his eyes played the defiant swagger of a short cop. But he returned Allaben's greeting with a good-natured smile and shook his hand like he meant it.

"Where's Wick?" Allaben asked. "I expected to see him here."

"Sheriff sends his apologies. He got called to a meeting with some VIP." D.T. grinned. "Said you'd be surprised to learn you're not the only big shot he knows."

The other fellow was swarthy and lean, as tall as Allaben, which would put him at just over six feet. He eyed Allaben carefully from beneath the brim of his straw boater. His name was Griffith Laroux, and his title was Medical Examiner for Washington County, Maryland. He received the hand Allaben offered in his own, as cool and well manicured as a mannequin's, and gave it a perfunctory shake.

Snyder led the party about thirty yards up the creek bank to the point where the tree branches began to mingle overhead. Here, in mottled shade, the ranger pointed to a patch of fern-covered ground. A vaguely human form had been outlined on it with white spray paint.

The ranger started cautiously. "The victim was discovered here, face down and laid out just like you see it. The guy who found him – his name is Roger Irwin – says he didn't move the body or change its position. Just felt for a pulse, which there was none of. Investigation of the scene bore him out, right, D.T.?"

D.T. grunted affirmation. "No sign the body was moved. Just traces of Irwin. No reason to doubt him."

"Nobody else around?" Allaben asked.

"It was early," Snyder answered. "About six-thirty. Battlefield doesn't open until eight. I was out walking the grounds like I do every morning. I was out back behind the cemetery when I hear something – might be a gunshot, might not. Turns out it was. Sounds like it comes from over this way. 'Course it took me awhile to get here. I wasn't hurrying. Irwin passed me in his Jeep a couple of minutes before I reached the parking lot."

"Who is Irwin? What was he doing here?"

"Roger Irwin," Thompson answered. "Lives in Shepherdstown, across the river. Worked for the Navy. He's a re-enactor, a regular. Snyder knows him."

Allaben glanced at Snyder, who nodded corroboration.

"He and this Gwynn had a bet over some general fording the stream," Thompson explained. "Got into an argument Saturday night at Mansfield Tavern in Sharpsburg. I got called in there that night, matter of fact. Gwynn and Irwin were going to meet here early Sunday morning, walk Snavely Ford Trail, and may the best man win. Mac, the bar owner, called the sheriff's office. Gwynn was picking fights with all and sundry. Squabbled with Don Parker, too. That's the fellow owns Antietam Motors. Mac thought it might turn nasty. I was just up the street at the filling station, so I got the radio call."

"So Irwin shows up Sunday morning, finds Gwynn lying here, and is kneeling beside him when Hal comes on the scene."

"That's it," said Thompson.

"Irwin didn't hear the shot?"

"Says he didn't. He was still in his car."

"And you believe him?"

"I don't know why I shouldn't," Thompson replied.

Allaben changed gears. "What about the body?"

Laroux opened his notebook. "The victim is a white male, age 34 years," he began. "Apparent cause of death – gunshot wound to the head. Looks like the bullet entered about here." He put the tip of his index finger to the back of his head, just to the right of center. "I'll give you the details after the autopsy. In any event, death was instantaneous."

"Any ideas about the weapon?" Allaben asked.

"Judging by the damage it did," D.T. answered, "a rifle for sure, a big one, something that packed a punch. Not some small-ass .22."

"A hunting rifle?"

"Yeah, or a military weapon. We'll know more if we recover the bullet. I'm not too optimistic, though. Might have changed direction when it hit his skull. Could have gone anywhere."

"Did you turn up anything?"

"No shell casings, if that's what you mean," D.T. said. He pointed in the direction of the steep wooded bank that led to the parking lot. "Shot would've come from up there, unless the body was moved, which there's no reason to think it was."

Allaben nodded acknowledgement. He studied the spot where Gwynn's body had lain.

"Photos?" he asked.

"A couple dozen digitals," Thompson answered. "I took them myself. They're in the files."

"I'd like to see them."

"No problem. But you'll have to come to Hagerstown. It's rules," he explained, "unless the sheriff says different."

"I understand he was in a uniform – Gwynn, I mean."

"He sure was. Irwin, too. Union blue. Hats, all the trappings. Must cost something."

Allaben pressed on. "Anything in his pockets?"

"Currency – not much, maybe forty dollars. Loose change,

wallet, little notebook, maps, receipt. He spent the night at the Sharpsburg Arms, the B & B just off the battlefield," said Thompson. "He must've walked down here from the inn. His car's still parked there."

While Allaben mulled this over, the deputy drew a handkerchief from a pocket, lifted his hat, and mopped his brow. Laroux restored his notebook to a slot in his briefcase, then fidgeted with the clasp.

"Well," he ventured, "if there's nothing else, Inspector, I've got an autopsy to perform back in Hagerstown. The deputy's giving me a lift."

Allaben had no objections. Thompson and Laroux went ahead, while Allaben strolled back along the bank of the creek with Snyder.

"D.T. tells me you knew the guy," Snyder said. "Is that why you're here?"

"Yeah, Hal, I knew him. Not well, but I did know him. He was on the force in Baltimore when I was there. Got himself in trouble by turning in some bad cops. A lot of guys hated him. Good cops as well as bad. But that was years ago."

They had reached the footing of the bridge, and Snyder followed Allaben as he walked out onto it. They paused upon reaching the middle of the span. Allaben glanced upstream. He pictured Gwynn's body lying beside the creek, Union blue on fern green, blood seeping from a hole in his head. Gwynn still and lifeless, frozen in death, as timeless now as one of the stone soldiers who adorned the battlefield monuments.

Snyder drooped his long torso over the stone rail, resting his elbows on the weathered wooden coping. "Of course, I didn't know him at all," he said. "Oh, I'd see him from time to time at the reenactments – I recognized him when I got to the body – but he was just another one of these Civil War buffs, a dime a dozen around here." He paused. "It's kind of a shame, isn't it? Killing a man right here on the battlefield? Shows disrespect, if you ask me." He shook his head sadly.

He straightened up and followed Allaben to the foot of the bridge. Together they climbed the stairs to the parking lot. Snyder declined Allaben's offer of a lift.

"I've got to stick around, make sure the tourists don't trample over everything. Poole's coming by to relieve me at 10:30. Then I'll set up a desk for you at the administration building on Main Street. The one next to the cemetery."

Signaling his okay, Allaben ambled over to the nearby bluff overlooking the bridge. Gwynn's killer might well have positioned himself there, he thought, A thicket of leafy oaks and papaws were enough to hide him from view, should anyone have cause to look that way from below or from the parking lot. And the killer would have a clear line of fire. It would be an easy shot for anyone who could handle a rifle. He spent a few minutes scuffing through the mat of dead leaves covering the ground, but found no sign that anyone had been there recently. He'd leave the systematic search of the area to the sheriff's department. Unlikely that they'd find anything, but you never know. Killers can be careless, too.

Snyder was standing in the parking lot when Allaben returned from his reconnaissance. "Sure you didn't see anything yesterday morning, Hal? When you walked to the bridge, I mean. Just Irwin?"

Snyder shook his head. "Don't think so. I wasn't paying too much attention until I got to the bridge. Then a lot of police cars. But if something comes back to me, you'll be the first to know."

Allaben made him promise. "I'll probably be back some time later today. I'm going into town now, stop by Mansfield Tavern. Then I guess I'd better talk to Irwin."

He had opened the car door and was about to climb in when he caught sight of a young man walking in their direction from the upper end of the trail leading to Snavely's Ford. A teenager, sixteen or seventeen, lanky build, fair, close-cropped hair. He had on a pair of baggy black shorts and a gray T-shirt bearing the Frederick Keys emblem, a sneering eagle in a baseball cap. The boy paused as he came abreast of the two men, leveling upon each in turn a direct, even stare. Snyder nodded acknowledgment but said nothing, and the boy went on his way. Allaben followed his back as he steadily walked off.

"That's the Parker boy," said Snyder. "Likes to hang around here."

"Parker?"

"Yeah, his father's Don Parker, the one at the bar D.T. was telling about."

"Do you know him?"

"The boy? Only from here. They call him Donnie Junior. We've talked a couple of times. He knows more about the battle than I do. Strange in a kid that age, don't you think?"

Allaben was thinking about the Georgia riflemen who, from the cover of the woods beside him, had rained bullets on the Federals who tried to take the bridge on the morning of that bloody day in September, 1862. An excellent location from which to deal death, and as ideal a spot now as it was then. Allaben gazed down at the killing field – the narrow bridge, the low stone wall just across the lazy stream, and the open meadow beyond it.

He bid Snyder goodbye, promising once more to keep him posted, and started for town.

4

Lester Dawson sat facing the diner's entrance. Tucked into a booth that afforded the privacy he required, he took in the establishment in which he'd been waiting for the last twenty minutes. Pink and putty were its predominant colors, the 1950s its personality. But this was no retro version of a classic diner – it was the real deal. From the pungent odor of bacon grease and the droning of ancient air conditioners to the frayed Naugahyde stools that lined the Formica counter, Jimmy's Diner was neither hiding its age nor prettying up its looks. The same could be said of the two servers who patrolled the place, one of whom was presently standing over Dawson.

"Here's your coffee, hon. Fresh pot. And your 2%, too. Bring you something else – maybe one of our homemade blueberry muffins? They're Martinsburg's finest, you know. And the best in all of West Virginia, if you ask Jimmy."

Dawson slid his hat closer to the edge of the table top, clearing the way for the cup, milk, and sweeteners that "Dot" was placing before him. He politely declined the muffin, not by saying as much but by simply gripping his ample stomach with both hands while aiming a winning Dawson grin in her direction.

"Awww, got it, hon. I hear you," she responded, matching his grin while glancing down knowingly at her own girth. "Anyone joining you this fine September morning?"

In answer to his nod in the affirmative, she prepared a second place setting and padded off with a promise to return when his companion arrived.

Dawson turned his attention to his phone and a text that informed him that his expected companion was still a few minutes away. Tardiness annoyed Lester Dawson. He'd have to put the latecomer in his place.

He began to absent-mindedly twirl the hat, a tan Stetson with a silver buckle on its felt hat band. It was the kind of cowboy hat meant to signal wealth and status, though Dawson was no cowboy. He wasn't even from the West. He hailed from Covington, Kentucky, where the Dawson Trucking Company sign could easily be seen along the south bank of the Ohio, directly across the river from the "Queen City" of Cincinnati.

That trucking company had grown over the years from a small local concern into a regional powerhouse, earning him dollars, connections, and time to pursue other interests. And beginning with the election that bestowed upon the country its first African-American president, he began using all three resources to stir up a little trouble. All for a good and noble cause, a cause that he was advancing this very morning in a humble diner that served Martinsburg's finest blueberry muffins.

Just as he finished his coffee, the man he was waiting for

arrived. Dawson watched the man as he stood for a moment in the doorway, practically filling it, and followed him as he slowly made his way to the cashier, looking about for the clue that would tell him where to park himself. At last he spotted the hat. He nodded toward Dawson, made his way over and squeezed into the booth. He grinned first at his table companion and then up at the waitress, who'd returned with a pot of coffee, as promised.

"I'll take one of them coffees, darling," he drawled, "and a sweet roll if you got one."

Dot poured coffee for her new customer, then refilled Dawson's cup and hastened off. The two men waited in silence until she returned with the roll and a bowl filled with little pats of butter. Dawson had used the interval to size up the man facing him across the table.

He didn't fit the thin voice Dawson had heard on the phone. He was older than he'd sounded, and larger, too. This was a full-bearded, balding, bear of a man. He was stuffed into khakis and a plaid shirt, its distinguishing feature a small Confederate flag pin adorning its collar. From their conversations, Dawson had pegged him as a tough-talking zealot with a military background. He'd done well for himself with a string of barbeque joints. Dale Froeling had spoken for him, and that recommendation was good enough, too.

Dawson spoke first. "They call you Bull, right?"

"Yessir. Everyone 'round here calls me Bull."

"Well, Bull, I hope keeping me waiting is not how you guys do business 'round here. How can you expect me to rely on you when you can't even show up on time?"

"Sorry, Mr. …"

"Smith."

"Okay. Mr. Smith. It won't never happen again. I promise you," Bull said contritely.

Dawson cut him short. "Okay. You're here. Let's get down to it. This job I've picked you for – it's an opening volley. We're getting out a message, a challenge. 'Which side are you on? Are you going to be a friend or a foe?'"

"I like the sound of that, Mr. Smith. So will my boys." He pulled a handkerchief from a hip pocket and mopped his forehead.

"Then we'll follow up with something bigger," Dawson continued, "something that says loud and clear, 'Look out, America, we mean business.'"

This drew a grim smile from Bull.

"It'll get everyone's attention," Dawson went on, "especially the teary-eyed, race-blending liberals. Those bastards will be asking themselves, 'Am I going to get popped? Are the cops going to protect me?' Remember, those gun-control zombies don't carry and don't shoot. The coloreds sure as hell do – guns are the tools of the trade in the drug wars."

"Yeah, but we know how to take care of that lot," Bull put in enthusiastically.

Dawson nodded. Then he took a sip of his coffee, leaned in, and spoke more softly.

"Okay. Good. Now let's go over the plan."

It was a simple plan and talking it through went quickly and smoothly. When they finished, Bull bit into his roll, took a hearty gulp from his mug, and wiped his mouth from side to side.

"We got this, Mr. Smith. Just leave it to me. You won't regret trusting me with this mission."

"No changes. No speeding. No accidents," Dawson said in

reply. “Nothing to draw attention to yourselves. Tell your guys. And no word about this to anyone else. You don’t know me. We’ve never met.”

“Roger that,” Bull acknowledged. “It’s going to be a breeze, like lighting fire crackers on the Fourth of July. I got everything under control.”

Lester Dawson hoped that he had.

5

There was only one vehicle in the gravel lot in front of the Mansfield Tavern, a dusty, rust-trimmed pickup loaded with cinder blocks. It was noontime, and the sun had Sharpsburg to itself. Main Street was empty. So were the front porches that crowded the ramshackle sidewalks. Not a soul in sight. Nor so much as a quiver in the air until Allaben shut the car door. The metallic smack might have been heard in the next county.

It was certainly heard inside the tavern, for he had the attention of the four people who were its sole occupants even before he came through the door. Two patrons – young men in T-shirts and dusty jeans, work boots and baseball caps – sat at one of the dozen tables scattered between the entrance and the bar. Both had paused over their meatball heroes to give Allaben a not-so-furtive once-over. At the bar a shriveled old man had twisted on his stool, behind him an empty glass, while the barmaid, refill in hand, took stock of the newcomer.

A life-size wax effigy of the tavern's namesake, Major General Joseph Mansfield, stood at the far end of the bar. The general had fallen early in the battle of Antietam, struck down by a Rebel's bullet, and died the next day.

A glittering jukebox sat in a corner, an 8-ball pool table close by. The bar itself was a well-worn, homely affair. At the edge ran an inch-wide lip of brass, tarnished beyond redemption. It was as plain as the establishment it anchored, and as free of sentiment as the hand-lettered notice posted on the wall behind it – "No Credit. No Exceptions. No Kidding!"

The barmaid kept an eye on him as he approached, curious and at the same time a little mistrustful. The clientele of the Mansfield Tavern seldom wore suits and snap-brim hats. The old man had turned back to his beer and the keno game in progress on a monitor mounted behind the bar. But the girl was entirely unaffected in her interest. She was young – barely out of high school – stout, blond, plain. Allaben touched the brim of his hat. The gesture drew a shy smile in response. Her teeth were small and uneven.

"What's your pleasure?" she drawled.

"I don't believe we're acquainted," he said.

"Lilly. Lillyanne Burke is my full name. It's after my grandma. But in here I'm Lilly."

"Felix Allaben." He offered his hand. Hers was meaty and damp.

Allaben nodded toward the wax figure. "Didn't the general use to stand by the doorway?"

"Oh, Mac moved him over here when the old guy got all beaten up – lost the arm and part of his nose. Some of the fellas was … well, they was fighting and rumbled right over him. Didn't mean nothing by it. You can see where they done the repair."

Allaben studied the general's nose. A seam was indeed visible high on the bridge, as were a number of dents and nicks upon cheekbone and chin. The pigment in the waxen flesh had long since faded away. Framed by the whiter-than-white tint of the cheap wig and false beard, the death-mask pallor of the face appeared downright ghoulish.

"I understand you had an argument or two in here last Saturday night," Allaben said.

"No more than the usual," returned the girl matter-of-factly. "Sometimes it gets kind of rough, but Saturday was child's play."

"Never got past name-calling," sneered the old guy.

Allaben turned to him. "You were here Saturday night?"

The old man continued to stare at the keno game, as if his profile were all the stranger deserved.

"Simon more or less lives here," said Lilly. "More, now I think on it." She smiled at her own wit.

"Saturday's generally the most entertaining," Simon observed. "Fools will prove they're fools on a Saturday night. No different this time."

"Anyone especially foolish?" Allaben asked, returning Lilly's smile.

Simon turned to him, on his wrinkled face a look of deep skepticism.

"As if you didn't know," he said.

Lilly shrugged. "You're a deep one, Simon."

But Allaben had understood Simon's meaning very well. He reached into a jacket pocket and retrieved his credentials.

"That's quite a sniffer you've got," he said, displaying the badge first to Lilly, then to Simon.

"Already told it to the sheriff," he said. "Shouldn't have to tell him at all, seeing as how the deputy sheriff was here in the flesh, saw it all for himself. Those two should get themselves coordinated. Sheriff wanted to know all about Mr. Ponytail and the Admiral, and about Ponytail and the car dealer, too. Talking about fathers and sons. Carrying on about guns. Saying park rangers should carry 'em, what with all the violence you see on the news. Hey, a shooting right here on the battlefield. I told him everything I heard."

"'Simon has the memory of three,' as Mac likes to say," Lilly explained.

"Mac?" Allaben asked.

"MacKenzie Lamb. He's the owner."

"Was he here Saturday night?"

"He sure was, on account of Saturday's the busiest night of the week."

"Nothing gets by me, especially if it's in the foolishness department," Simon put in. "Mac's righter than right about that. And I told it all to the sheriff."

"But you haven't told it to me."

"Then you should get yourself coordinated, too."

The two diners had finished their lunches and were preparing to go. The one in the blue hat came ambling over to settle the bill.

"That's the usual eight seventy-five," said Lilly. Blue Hat counted out the money.

"Buy Simon a beer," he counseled Allaben. "His pump needs regular priming."

"Wasting your money," chimed in Red Hat, who was digging in a pocket for a tip.

"Simon goes hazy after he's had five or six."

"That means any time after noon," explained Blue Hat.

Allaben looked to Lilly, who nodded discretely. "Simon was here, though," she added.

"Sure as I'm a Christian," Simon added, "you pups never hear nothing for all your yapping. I'm a man who can drink *and* listen."

"At least you're half-right," said Blue Hat. And with that, he and his buddy headed for the door.

"Y'all take care of yourselves," Lilly called.

The door creaked open, let in a wedge of light, then creaked shut. Silence briefly reigned.

"They're regulars," said Lilly, by way of afterthought.

"They're skunks," Simon corrected.

A throttled roar issued from the lot outside, followed by a spray of gravel.

"That was uncalled for," said Lilly.

"Damned fools gonna drop those blocks," said Simon. "They ain't waitin' for Saturday night."

Allaben looked at his watch. He left ten dollars on the bar and ambled to a table that was tucked into a niche near the pool table. He pulled out his cellphone.

The Washington County Sheriff's Department answered after two rings. He gave his name and waited for Mallory to come on the line. Hagerstown is thirteen miles from Sharpsburg – so went his thinking – and in the wrong direction. Did Mallory owe him one? Or was it vice versa? Allaben was trying to recall whose was the last entry in the ledger of favors, a book close to the heart of every lawman, when the phone came to life.

"Felix! Where are you? You coming by?" Mallory's voice was mellow as a tenor sax.

"I'm in Sharpsburg, my friend, at Mansfield Tavern. Are you going to make me come up there?"

"Just so happens I'm going to be your way – I mean in Sharpsburg – tomorrow."

"Hal Snyder's got me set up in the park headquarters."

"Yeah. He told me all about it. Red carpet's out. The G-men get the VIP treatment."

"Speaking of VIPs, who's so important you gave me the brush-off this morning?"

"None other than Maryland's next attorney general."

"I suppose you mean Mason Greer?"

"You don't have to sound so happy about it."

"Just a reminder, Wick – first he's got to win the primary."

"Trust me, Felix, he's going to win. The country's singing a different tune, and Mason's all over the melody."

"I hear it's a toss-up."

"Yeah, well I got the inside dope."

"You thinking of going into politics?"

"Why not? A sheriff's already up to his badge in politics."

Allaben tried to picture Wick Mallory in a business suit. It wasn't easy to do. For as long as he had known him, Mallory had been in a uniform of one sort of another – first baseball, then Army, then sheriff's department.

"But first we've got this Gwynn case to solve," Mallory went on, "so I can go out in a blaze of glory."

"Are you sure you're okay with this arrangement, Wick?"

"You mean working with you? Hell, yes! We don't deal with a lot of homicides in Washington County, not this kind anyway. Just promise me you won't hold out on me, okay? I mean seeing as you're federal and seeing as how Gwynn and you are both alumni of Baltimore P.D."

Allaben let a second elapse. "I don't cover for anyone, Wick. Let the chips fall where they may."

"Then we're fine. What time tomorrow?"

"Two? At park headquarters?"

"You're on."

"Personal effects, statements, et cetera."

"You've got it. Who have you talked to so far?"

"Snyder, your deputy, the coroner. D.T.'s told you all about that."

"Yes, he did. Told me you and Snyder had a little private chinwag, too."

"Personal matter. Nothing to do with the case."

A pause. Then, "How are things, Felix? How's that little girl of yours?"

"Miranda's fine, thanks. And not so little any more. She's with my brother in San Francisco. Spending the summer there."

"Russell?"

"And his partner, Douglas."

A pause from Mallory; then, as if he didn't know what else to say, "I've never been to San Francisco."

"She's having the time of her life. Went to a Giants game last week."

"I haven't been to a ball game in years."

"Don't you miss it?"

"No, Felix, I don't. I played it out of me. You?"

"I take in a game now and then, keep up with Delvecchio. He still talks about that bat of yours."

"Say hi to him the next time you see him."

"I'll do that."

"And what about you?" Mallory went on. "How the hell are you doing?"

"I'm okay. One day at a time, just like they say on the cereal boxes."

Mallory decided to leave well enough alone. "It's the only way, I guess," he said. Then, changing the subject, "This Gwynn case – you got any thoughts about it? Any of your famous notions?"

"Nary a one, Wick. Only it's already giving me a headache."

"You know how it is in this line of work, Felix. A lot of headaches."

"Have the headaches got anything to do with your career plans?"

"They come with the job."

"That's what I mean."

Mallory snorted. "Okay, partner, you'll be the first one I call when I feel that mid-life crisis coming on. Meantime, let's get to work. I'd start with Irwin if I were you."

6

Shepherdstown lies four miles west of and across the Potomac from Sharpsburg. Allaben was there in ten minutes. He drove into the center of town, which is anchored by the campus of Shepherd University. It was a summer weekday and college was not in session, so the sidewalks were nearly empty. On a weekend afternoon in the fall or spring these same walks would be teeming with students, second-home professionals, and daytrippers from D.C., all cruising the galleries and emporiums that line German Street. Or having brunch at the Red Rooster. Or slurping ice cream cones in the shade of the art-house marquee.

He turned right at the four-way stop, following the directions given him over the phone by Roger Irwin. After two blocks, gentrified brick and stucco gave way to a stretch of humble wood-frame houses, each set off with a patch of sunburned lawn. These petered out after another quarter mile. The sidewalks came abruptly to an end, and the street turned into a country road. Exactly 1.7 miles from the turn at River Street he came to an old stone bridge spanning a brook. Fifty yards beyond the brook was an unsigned turn to the right. Allaben took it.

The road rose gradually through a stand of poplar and beech. From time to time he caught sight of the brook running below, headed for a rendezvous with the Potomac. In a few minutes, Allaben found himself on the rim of an open plateau. A big, white farmhouse was fixed in its center, like a knob on a casserole lid. A gray barn and a paddock flanked one side of the house and a three-stall garage the other. Shade trees towered near the house. Otherwise there was nothing taller than weeds between him and the person of Roger Irwin, assuming it was Irwin whom Allaben saw walking from barn to house.

The man stopped when he caught sight of the car. He shielded his eyes and followed Allaben's slow progress up the lane, which ended at the asphalt driveway before the garage. Two of the three stalls were closed. In the shadowy recesses of the third, Allaben could make out the tail of a Jaguar convertible. He pulled up behind it.

A brick walkway led from the house to the asphalt. The man stood before the doorway to the house and waited for Allaben. He was of middle stature, parade-ground straight, crew cut gone gray, blue-eyed, deeply tanned. He was dressed in a blue shirt and a pair of khakis loosely tucked into black riding boots. Allaben took the hand he extended.

"Allenby? I'm Roger Irwin."

"It's Allaben, actually. Felix Allaben."

Irwin did not apologize. "Any trouble finding the place?"

"None at all. The directions were flawless."

"That's partly vocation, partly avocation. Let's go in, get out of the sun."

He led Allaben into the house. It was cool and dark. They passed down a hallway before turning into a large living room. The far wall was all glass. Through it a flagstone patio and a glimmering swimming pool were visible. The room was sparely furnished – an oriental rug over a polished floor, a sofa and armchairs clustered around a coffee table, a walnut console against one wall, and a fieldstone fireplace set into another.

Irwin strode toward a door opposite the one they had entered. They had almost reached it when Allaben instinctively flinched as something swooped past the window, something large and bright. He turned in time to see a plume of water rise from the far end of the pool, and in the same instant heard a muffled splash. A moment later a woman in a blue swimsuit emerged from the near end. Her eyes were Asian and her hair was black, cut pageboy fashion. She was shaking water from it when she caught sight of the two men. Irwin showed her the palm of his hand in greeting. She grinned, turned, and dove into the water once more. Irwin glanced at his watch.

"My wife," he explained. "It's time for her laps."

He paused, as if to allow Allaben an opportunity to comment, then opened the door and ushered Allaben into a study.

"Make yourself at home," he said, "while I get us some ice water. Or would you prefer something stronger?"

Ice water was fine. He said so to Irwin, who promptly slid back a door set into a side wall and disappeared. Allaben turned his attention to the study.

In the center of the room was a mammoth L-shaped desk. An open laptop and a printer occupied the short leg. On the longer surface was a telephone, a magnifying glass, the June issue of *The Map Collector*, and a perfectly executed scale model of an aircraft carrier, one of a fleet of plastic warships docked about the room. An elaborate bookcase of mahogany and glass stood in one corner, atop it an antique sextant. Framed yellowing maps covered the walls.

The glass doors to the bookcase were locked. Allaben was peering through them at the spines of a two-volume, leather-bound edition of *The West Point Atlas of American Wars* when his host returned. Irwin set down a tray bearing a pitcher of water, two tall glasses, and two coasters. He poured the water, then motioned to a chair near the desk. He waited until Allaben was seated before taking his own. They faced each other across the desk. The aircraft carrier was now directly in front of Allaben.

"The *Intrepid*," said Irwin, "commissioned 1942." He sipped from his glass. "Were you in the service?"

Allaben shook his head. "I went from college into the Baltimore P.D."

"Me, I always wanted the Navy, especially the flattops," Irwin went on. "Dreamt I'd skipper one of these." He nodded at the model. "But I'm asthmatic, so I did the next best thing – worked for the Navy as an engineer. Built ports all over the Pacific – Vietnam, Philippines, Korea."

"You're retired?"

"I did well by the Navy. From time to time I do some consulting. Sense of duty, I guess. Don't need the money."

"So much for the vocation."

Irwin paused. "That's right. I said, 'part vocation, part avocation.' I'm impressed."

"I'm a good boy. I listen when I'm spoken to."

"I appreciate the warning. You're with Justice?"

"Freelance. With the Bureau of Investigations."

"I don't know how much help I can be," Irwin said. "I've already talked with Sheriff Mallory."

"You've given him a statement?"

"Full and complete. I have nothing to add to it."

"Did you know Gwynn?"

"We were teamed from time to time on the artillery demonstrations. In fact, we were battery mates on Saturday. Fourth United States, Battery C, in Richardson's Division, Sumner's Second Corps. I was the gunner. I aimed the piece and gave the order to fire. He was at the breech, number four on our gun platoon. He knew his cannon, I'll give him that. But he was a strange man – erratic, unpredictable."

"You said you barely knew him."

"You didn't have to know him very well to know that."

Allaben put his glass down on a coaster and leaned back in his chair. He studied the maps on the wall. "Are these the avocation?"

"Antique maps, especially of the Civil War era. But my hobby's turned and bit me."

"You're talking about the argument with Gwynn?"

"I wouldn't characterize it as an argument. It was a difference of opinion."

"I knew Gwynn. He had arguments, not differences of opinion."

Irwin looked at him carefully. "You knew Gwynn?"

"Years ago. He was with the Baltimore Police. So was I."

"Is that why you're here?"

"Coincidence."

Another hard look from Irwin. "Any theories?" he asked.

"Not yet," Allaben replied. "I'm still doing my homework."

"I gave a statement," Irwin reminded him.

"But I haven't read it yet. Besides, sometimes it jogs the

memory to go through it again."

He pulled a notebook from a jacket pocket and opened it to a blank page.

Irwin sighed, then closed his eyes and sat in silent concentration. When he spoke, it was with the deliberate, abstracted air of a man determined to anticipate and answer, in as few words as possible, all of the questions bound to be asked of him.

"Mallory told me that you know something about Antietam, so I won't bore you with background. Suffice it to say that Gwynn and I did not see eye to eye on the subject of Burnside's assault. Gwynn held that Burnside was an utter and criminal ass to have ordered all of his troops over that bottleneck of a bridge when there were perfectly adequate fords downstream. Gwynn had done some reconnoitering along the creek, you know, and had seen for himself. Well, I've been down that creek myself – several times. And think what you like of Burnside's abilities as a soldier – I'm no higher on him than most – the fact is, he really didn't have any practical choice. I grant that the reconnaissance was slipshod. I grant that Ambrose Burnside was an unimaginative, even hidebound officer. All the same, there was no other way he could cross his divisions and obey the orders he'd been issued – to storm the bridge, get a foothold on the west bank, and attack from there.

"But Gwynn wouldn't have it. So we agreed to meet by the bridge bright and early next morning, walk Snavely Ford Trail, and test his observations against mine. I drove over there Sunday morning, and I found him dead."

"Was the argument overheard?"

"Certainly it was. At least by any who wished to overhear it. For some people the battle is joined every day, almost with the same ferocity. He was one of those people. He was ranting. The deputy sheriff came in just afterward."

"What were you doing there to begin with?"

"A custom. Some of us get together during these re-enactments. Saturday night we were celebrating that afternoon's performance and toasting the upcoming medical demonstration. I was going to participate in that, as well. So was Gwynn. That's why we met – or were going to meet – at the creek near the bridge so early on Sunday morning."

"So it wasn't just you and Gwynn."

"No. There were some others. It was crowded. A Saturday night. I didn't know that Gwynn would be there. All of this is in the statement."

"But you did know Gwynn."

"As I said, I teamed with him a couple of times. He was mainly a Gettysburg man, one of those freelance guides who takes visitors around in their cars and pontificates."

"Was your wife with you?"

Irwin seemed taken aback. "I wouldn't take her to a place like that."

Allaben thought for a moment. "Did you notice an old man at the bar – wrinkled, toothless, big ears?"

"Yes. I guess I did. I'd forgotten about him."

Irwin paused a second, then went on. "You have to understand that Gwynn was taking on everybody that night. He wasn't drunk, I think, but he might as well have been. Browbeating everyone who came in range. Our little debate was a sideshow compared to the quarrel he had with that car dealer."

"What was that about?"

"I don't know. I was near the pool table and couldn't hear them."

"But it was you who last saw him alive."

"No," Irwin smiled at this sally. "It was I who first saw him dead."

"Did you hear the shot?"

"No again. It might have happened seconds before I got out of the car, or he might have been lying there for half an hour. He was still bleeding, so it couldn't have been much longer than that."

"What time was it when you arrived?"

"Seven-o-five exactly. I know because I was late. We were supposed to meet at six-thirty, but I had car trouble – a flat, actually. One of the rear tires on the Jeep. Must've rolled over something coming in Saturday night."

"And what time was that?"

"Before 11:00 I watched the news with Lin. It's all in the statement."

As if for punctuation, a soft rap sounded at the door.

"Here she is," said Irwin. "Ask her, if you like."

She had changed into a sleeveless white dress. Allaben stood. She studied him from the doorway.

"Ask me what?" Her voice was firm and precise.

"Mr. Allaben has been grilling me," said Irwin.

"Grilling?"

"Interrogating," Irwin explained.

Allaben stepped forward. "Felix Allaben, Mrs. Irwin. I'm investigating the death at Antietam Battlefield."

She took his hand. "Well, Mr. Allaben," she smiled, "I hope you got more out of him than I usually do."

Irwin looked at his watch. His wife took the cue. "Yes," she said, "I have to get back to the gallery. But I can't get out. I'm blocked."

Irwin came to the rescue. He turned to Allaben. "You're parked behind the Jag. Are we finished?"

"For the time being," said Allaben, "though I may have further questions once I've read the statement."

Irwin shrugged in resignation. To his wife he said, "Come on, darling. Let's get you unblocked."

She rewarded her husband with a smile of a radiance that seemed a trifle excessive for the occasion. She turned, presenting her back to the two men, then bent her head forward, as if in prayer. Irwin stepped up behind her. Deftly he fastened the dress's top button. A faint blush surfaced upon his tanned cheeks. Allaben wondered whether it stemmed from happiness or embarrassment, or both. Between husband and wife there is a game that only they can play.

Irwin pressed his fingertips against the nape of her neck to signal he was done. She did not turn, but walked straight off. The two men followed her across the living room, each self-consciously ignoring the languid metronome of her hips.

7

The two-lane highway between Boonsboro and Frederick overlays the roadbed of what was once the National Road, the route followed by General McClellan as he pursued Lee across Maryland. Allaben was traveling east, however, the direction opposite that of the long columns of gray and of blue that had marched this route to battle. Were he to have traveled this road late in the summer of 1862 – on the 14th of September, to be exact – he would now be meeting rank upon rank of men in blue – Indiana farmboys, Irish toughs from New York, New England idealists, and hardheaded Pennsylvania Germans.

Perhaps the most soulful of them sensed the dreadful carnage that was coming. But most would be thinking no further ahead than the end of the day's march and a camp dinner of hardtack and coffee. They had come ten miles from Frederick and had already been bloodied in a skirmish right here at South Mountain. They would be worn and weary, though not so footsore as the shoeless boys in gray who had already slipped across the Antietam.

Allaben was weary, too, and unsure of what to do next. He had come away from Shepherdstown with nothing but grounds for speculation. Perhaps there had been more to the dispute between Irwin and Gwynn than Irwin had let on. Irwin's wife, for example, even if she hadn't been in the tavern that night. Gwynn had been a shameless dog around women, especially attractive women. And Irwin had had opportunity as well. But for the time being all of this was so much conjecture.

And again at Sharpsburg, where he had briefly stopped on his way back, he had learned nothing further from Hal Snyder. The ranger had dutifully shown Allaben around his makeshift headquarters and then taken his leave, claiming duties elsewhere in the park. But when Allaben had pulled out of the driveway half an hour later, he caught sight of the tall ranger in the far corner of the cemetery, leaning against the high stone wall and staring out at the battlefield.

Allaben had considered turning up Pry Lane to visit McClellan's headquarters. From there he would have a panoramic view of the battlefield; but he had decided against it. McClellan had not gained anything by the position, and neither probably would he. Of course McClellan had gained very little by the famous Lost Orders, either. Lee's campaign plans, spelled out in the form of Special Orders 191, had been found in the Frederick grounds where Lee's army had last encamped. They tell McClellan that the Army of Northern Virginia is spread very thin, so thin, in fact, that he could destroy it piecemeal if he possessed the gumption to act upon the information that luck had delivered him. He could put an end to Lee's invasion, end the war then and there. But, McClellan, true to form, had failed to exploit his advantage.

"Easy for me to say," thought Allaben. He could think of an instance or two when as a detective he, too, failed to see what was plainly before him. Or had seen it too late. It had been just such a failure that had led to his own sorry reckoning with fate. That slip had cost him his wife.

Baltimore. They had driven there to celebrate Rebecca's release from the hospital, where she had spent two weeks being treated for "exhaustion," a euphemism for the state of depressive hysteria into which she had slid, as chronic bipolars will, after the latest manic binge. A Saturday afternoon. They had seen a play and afterwards had dinner. It was raining, misty, unseasonably cool. He'd parked the car in a quiet side street he knew from his days as a cop on the beat. They walked arm in arm through the drizzle, and were a few yards from the car – and from what might have been – when the world collapsed, shrunk in an instant like a punctured balloon.

"Hey, mister! You gonna help me out?"

Two kids, 15 or 16 years old, in baggy denim and hooded sweatshirts. One of them hung back, hard to define in the dusk, while the other got on with business. He kept his eyes on Allaben alone.

"We're in a hurry," said Allaben, trusting that a cop's tone of authority would spare him further nuisance.

"You ain't got time? That what you're telling me?"

"I'm a police officer."

"Then you know what this means." The kid pulled a gray automatic from the waistband beneath his sweatshirt.

Rebecca whispered, "Felix." She didn't have to say any more. Allaben knew what she meant – you're not a cop anymore. Don't be a jerk. Whatever you're thinking of doing, it isn't worth it.

"Help you out how?" he asked the kid.

"Give me your fat wallet, all your money, no foolin' around. That's how."

The one who'd hung back was shifting from foot to foot.

His head was rocking, too, very slightly, as if he were dancing to unheard music. His hands were buried in the sweatshirt pouches. A long curl of blond hair slipped into view, and from beneath the hood came a high-pitched voice: "Get the keys, baby, so we can go for a little ride."

Not a him, Allaben realized, but a her. Would a girl be carrying a piece?

But of course Rebecca was right. It, whatever "it" was, wasn't worth it. The rain began to peck at the sidewalk, the car, the brushed nickel of the kid's gun. Allaben reached for his wallet. Then came the shots, five of them, five distinct explosions.

One of them caught Rebecca in midstep. Down she went – crashed really, as she no longer possessed even the instinct to protect herself. Nothing remained to her at all except the eerie salute of life leaving her, a sound something between a sigh and a groan, the weary answer a woman makes when yet another impossible chore is asked of her.

He had been hit, too, though he was not immediately aware of it. He felt as if he'd been seized by some immensely powerful device, seized and held upright. Otherwise he could not account for the fact that he was still standing. And not only still standing, but turning to face the kid, turning in time to see the boy's cockeyed stare, see the rain bounce off his face like the sweat that flies from a fighter's face when he's been tagged a good one.

Then he had sat down beside his wife. Her hair had spilled over her face, curtaining one eye. The other was open. Allaben reached for her, wondering as he did so at the flourish of red that trailed his hand. It was then that he observed that a hole had been torn through his palm and this pain set in in earnest.

Anything else. McClellan and Lee. The Lost Orders. Burnside Bridge. Blue and Gray. Gwynn and Irwin. Then and now. Anything. Allaben concentrated on the road before him. The sky had darkened. It looked like rain. Five miles to Frederick, and already he was cruising through exurban sprawl – a tract of split-levels and another of town houses cheek to jowl with empty, swaybacked barns; fields once bristling with corn now planted only with billboards, rusting farm machinery on one side of the road, a sprawling car dealership looming on the other.

Allaben slowed down. This was not just any car dealer. Towering above the ranks of shining new Toyotas was a lozenge-shaped sign that read "Antietam Motors." He had passed this lot dozens of times and never so much as given it a second thought. Now he was of half a mind to look in on Mr. Parker, just to put a face to the name. And, come to think of it, to match the father to the boy he had seen this morning coming up from Snavely Ford Trail. The kid that Snyder knew. Donnie Junior.

But all of this could wait. Parker could wait, and so could the kid. It was nearly 5:00 and Ozzie would soon be leaving the store to have his dinner. From the crest of the hill at Braddock Heights, Allaben could just make out the church spires rising into an ominous-looking sky over Frederick. If he didn't get stuck in traffic, he would be home in ten minutes.

8

He drew up next to his house, parked the car, and walked straight to Stippetti's. Pedro emerged from behind the counter, sheepishly wagging his tail. This could mean only one thing – a dog with a guilty conscience.

"How many treats, Ozzie?" Allaben asked.

Ozzie deliberated a moment before answering, "Double figures. The dog's not a monk like you. He needs his nourishment."

Allaben studied Ozzie's ample midsection. Ozzie ignored the implied comparison. "Ain't like you're racing him," he said. "You ask me, this Popsicle stick could use some fattening, too."

He pointed a thick finger at a photo on the front page of the sports section of the Post. The picture showed Rod Hurley about to deliver one of his patented splitters.

The caption beneath the photo read "Strike three? Keys will send one-time World Series MVP Rod Hurley against Winston-Salem."

"I guess there aren't many Hurley fans at the Post," commented Allaben. "They're already writing the obituary."

"He's washed up," said Ozzie. "A lost cause."

"I like a lost cause," Allaben said, "one with all the hope wrung out of it."

"I hear they give him shots it hurts so bad."

"Not according to Delvecchio."

"Hurley wouldn't tell the manager, for God's sake!" Ozzie snorted.

Allaben shrugged. He didn't share Ozzie's cynical view, not of this matter anyway. Delvecchio would know, he was sure of that. But there was no point debating the point – Ozzie's convictions were his mat and his ring, and he would no more be budged from them than a sumo wrestler.

Allaben decided to walk up Market and home by way of Charles Street. The route would take him through Gwynn's neighborhood, and he could take a look at the place where he lived – or had lived. Once Pedro was satisfied that this was no mistake, but a deliberate detour, he was happy to play the scout, keeping in advance of his master as far as the leash permitted.

The sky had grown even darker. The air smelled of the storm to come. From time to time Pedro cocked an ear, listening for thunder. And when the first rumble sounded in the distance, the dog turned to his master, inviting him to reconsider this expedition. But Allaben paid no attention. They had covered six blocks and were approaching Gehring Street. He was walking at a quick pace, and the sultry air was taking its toll. His shirt stuck to his back.

At Gehring he turned right. The houses were all modest, two-story affairs of clapboard and shingle. There were a few cars parked in the street, more in the narrow asphalt driveways. A kid on a skateboard came rattling toward him, but at twenty feet veered down a driveway and hurtled into the street.

In a few minutes he was abreast of number 88. He stopped to study the house from the sidewalk. It was freshly painted, dark red with white trim, and set at the end of a long driveway. Behind the house was a two-stall garage. The driveway was empty. A stairway led to the second floor, where Gwynn had lived for the last three years.

House, yard, garage – all were trim and tidy. Someone had been at pains to keep the place shipshape. Certainly not Gwynn. Appearances had been of no consequence to him.

Was anyone at home? Allaben did not see any signs of life. Doors and windows were shut, the curtains drawn. Garage doors were down. A green lawn hose had been neatly stowed on a spool attached to the house. On the veranda two wooden rocking chairs sat empty and still. A folded newspaper lay near the door. He had been standing there a few minutes now, long enough to be noticed, should there be anyone inside who cared to notice. No face appeared at the window; nobody came to the door.

Allaben pictured Gwynn's face. It occurred to him that he had never seen fear on it, not even when Gwynn had good reason to be afraid. And there was more to it than mere bravado. Gwynn would do what he thought was right, and screw the consequences. Compromise? Not if he could help it. No wonder so many had given him a wide berth, crossed the street when they saw him coming, failed to return his calls. The question now was, Who had no longer been able to avoid him?

A breeze suddenly came up. He heard it rustle through the trees and felt it play over the back of his neck. He looked skyward. Heavy gray clouds were billowing overhead. From behind him came the sound of a bottle top being slowly unscrewed. He turned. It was the kid on the skateboard, rattling up the sidewalk and taking his time about it.

At number 86 the screen door opened and a woman appeared. A redhead in a halter and denim shorts. She stared at Allaben.

"You got business with the Prescotts?" she asked.

"Doesn't look like anyone's home."

"They're not," she explained. "Monday is their golf day down there at the Monocacy Links. It's senior-discount day. Only, you ask me, they're not gonna get in a full eighteen." She nodded skyward.

"As a matter of fact, it's upstairs I'm mostly interested in."

"You ain't the first one seems to be interested in that house."

"No?"

"Nope. A white car passed by a couple of times already today."

"A Toyota, was it?"

"I don't know one car from another. It wasn't no bus or truck. That's what I can tell you. Hey, what's with all the questions? You the police?"

"Sort of."

"Sort of how?"

"Federal government."

"Is that so?" She nodded toward Gwynn's apartment. "Of course, nothing that man got up to would surprise me."

Allaben removed his hat and ran a finger along the liner. "Did you know him?"

"No more than I had to. He used to watch me sunbathing out back. My husband caught him peeking once. Almost took a bat to him. That was before the divorce," she added.

She turned her attention to the boy on the skateboard. "Frankie!" she hollered. "You get yourself in this house this minute! It's gonna rain buckets."

Frankie came to a stop at the walk leading to the front steps.

He scowled at Allaben, then picked up the skateboard and trudged up the walk.

"Can I go on the computer?" he asked as he slipped past his mother into the house.

"You sure can, honey. Only close the door so I don't hear those games. I got a headache."

The screen door banged closed. Pedro tugged at the leash. The redhead stared up the street, then turned back to him.

"My name's Kate. Kate Boyd. If you want to, you can come up on the porch, keep dry," she said.

A heavy drop of rain smacked into his forehead and drooled down the bridge of his nose.

"No, ma'am, I don't think I will," he said, "thanks very much."

He replaced his hat, nodded goodbye, and started home. In a matter of seconds it was pouring. The sidewalk was a boiling sheet of water. At the corner he turned left, glancing back through a dense veil of rain at number 86. The door was closed and the porch was empty.

By the time he reached home Allaben was thoroughly soaked. Water drizzled from his hat and his shoes felt like sponges. He went through the garden to the back of the house and let himself in, leaving Pedro under the patio awning to dry off. Once he was inside, he slipped off his shoes and stripped to his underwear, deposited his belt and the contents of his pockets on the kitchen table, and carried the soggy heap of clothes to the laundry room.

He felt the air conditioning keenly when he returned to the kitchen. Goose bumps puckered on his arms. He retrieved a bottle of vodka from the freezer, poured a finger's worth into a juice glass, and drained it in one long swallow. It flowed like fiery syrup down his throat. He was tired but restless. It was six o'clock. He could catch the news, but he didn't want to watch the news. Pedro scratched at the door. Allaben plucked a can of dog food from a cupboard, opened it, and forked out the evening ration.

In the refrigerator there were two bottles of wine, a carton of milk, a can of coffee, condiments, a carton of eggs, a package of English muffins. He seldom cooked anymore, hadn't at all, in fact – excepting the occasional plate of eggs – since Miranda had left for California. He stared vacantly into the yellow glow of the refrigerator. The vodka had done its work. He felt warm inside and cool outside. He was hungry now. Should he call for Chinese? Mexican? Visit the raw bar? He poured himself another jigger's worth of vodka and downed that before returning the bottle to the freezer. He'd shower, then review his options. But first, he'd better check for messages.

He padded from the kitchen to the dining room. Dim light filtered through the curtained windows. The dining table needed dusting, though why bother? It was never used anymore. He and Miranda ate in the kitchen or, weather permitting, on the patio.

Miranda, now his and his alone to shepherd through the wilds of adolescence. Miranda, 15 going on 20 when she wasn't going on 10.

He crossed the dining room and opened the door into the hallway that connected the vestibule with the main stairway. Across the way was his office and, deeper into the house, the living room.

The phone was on his desk, a worn, old partner's model that had belonged to his father. There were five messages. He switched on the desk lamp, pulled a notepad from a drawer, and pressed the play button.

The first message was from Folliard, a routine "How's it going?" call. Numbers two and four were from Stuart London at the Post. Allaben had wondered how long it would take him to get in touch. He scribbled the number on the notepad. The third message was from Gene Delvecchio, calling to say that if the game tonight was called, Hurley was still going to start tomorrow night, as originally scheduled. "Orders from the front office. A lot they care about my rotation."

Last was an invitation from Carolyn Brandes. She was calling from the restaurant. She'd hired a new chef and he was cooking fish tonight. "Besides, I haven't seen you in ages. My table, eight o'clock. Be there?"

9

It was still raining when he got to Carolyn's. He made a dash from his car to the door and slipped inside, brushing rain from his hat and jacket. The bar was dark and quiet. All the stools were occupied, and the overflow stood in little clusters two and three deep behind the seated customers. There was no jukebox, no music, just the gregarious murmur of a saloon, now and then punctuated by laughter.

He made his way through the bar, nodding to a few familiar faces and shaking a hand or two along the way. A narrow corridor connected the bar and the dining room. Allaben paused at the entryway. A young man in a white sharkskin jacket stepped from behind a lectern and greeted him.

"Carolyn's in the kitchen, Mr. Allaben. She'll only be a moment."

Allaben declined his offer to show him to the table. He knew the way. The room formed a rectangle a little longer than it was wide. The longer walls were lined with booths, and on each side of the center aisle was a row of tables covered in starched linen. The room was half full. Carolyn's table was in the corner nearest the kitchen. Allaben was halfway there when she made her appearance, delivering some parting instructions as she came through the doorway.

She was tall and slender, verging on the angular. A curl of chestnut-colored hair had fallen over her forehead. When she caught sight of Allaben, she granted him a whimsical smile. In some people it's the mouth, in some the eyes that give them away. In Carolyn's case, Allaben decided, it was the latter.

She took him by the hand and led him to the booth. The table was set for two. He waited for her to slide in before he sat himself opposite her.

"I'm glad you've come," she said.

"I'm glad you invited me," he replied as he settled into the leather upholstery. The lamp in the wall sconce burnished the woodwork and glinted on the wine glasses. Her eyes were sea-green. He felt immediately at ease, as he always did in her company. Always did and always had, for they went all the way back to high school. She smiled again. If he weren't careful, he might even enjoy himself.

A blond waitress appeared. Carolyn turned to her.

"Pay him no mind, Linda," she said, nodding at Felix. "Just bring us two of the swordfish specials and a bottle of the Montrachet. And tell Jean-Paul to go easy on the salt."

Linda frowned. "He'll cuss me something awful just for 'presuming' an opinion. You know he will."

"It's not an opinion, it's an order," Carolyn smiled.

Linda looked dolefully at Allaben, as if in the hope that he would intervene on her behalf. Then she sighed theatrically and set off for the kitchen.

Carolyn turned her attention once more to Felix. "Jean-Paul and I don't quite see eye to eye on the subject of salt," she explained.

Before Allaben could comment, she put a finger to her lips. They sat silently. One second. Two seconds. Three seconds. Then came an alarming crash from the kitchen, followed by muffled oaths. The voice was very deep, very angry. Though he could not distinguish individual words, Felix could tell they were not spoken in English.

Carolyn smiled in bemusement. "God, he's stubborn," she said. "Every night it's another eruption."

"French?" asked Allaben.

"Maybe," she replied. "Maybe Belgian. Maybe Swiss. He won't say. Won't be 'predicted' – his word – by his place of birth."

Linda burst through the kitchen door, flushed with anger. She carried with her an ice bucket, a tripod, and a bottle of wine. Without a word she set the bucket on the tripod, then pulled a corkscrew from a pouch at her waist.

"I'll open it," soothed Carolyn, "and don't take it personally. It's me he despises. I'll talk to him later, I promise. Now sashay over to table six. The gentleman there's craning his neck so it looks like he's lost."

Linda did what she was told to do, leaving them alone. Allaben watched Carolyn open the wine.

"This chef must be something special," he ventured.

"You'll see. He's a royal pain, but he can cook like nobody's business."

She filled two glasses, then tucked a dinner napkin around the bottle and twisted it into the bucket of ice.

Felix raised his glass. "To you."

"Fair enough," Carolyn answered, lifting her glass in reply. "But," she added, "I think we should drink to you, now that you're back in business."

He studied her wry smile, wondering not that she knew but

how she had found it out.

"You forget, Felix. I know everything that happens in this town. This is where the news hounds come for lubrication. Stuart London was in earlier. He says you knew him."

"Knew who?"

"The guy who was shot, of course. Gunn."

"Gwynn. Curtis Gwynn. Yes, I knew him from Baltimore. He worked for me for awhile. The kind of cop who'd ticket a hearse. Holier than thou. Though he liked the ladies, especially married ones."

"A lot of reasons not to like him."

"Somebody needed only one reason."

"So it was definitely murder?"

He gave her a look that as much as said, "You know the rules."

"Okay," she conceded, "I get it. You're worried about my well-being because you're so awfully fond of me."

As a matter of fact, he was. For all he knew, the guy who pulled the trigger, if it was a guy, might be sitting in this room. That hefty cowboy in the fringed ivory jacket, for example, the one at the table opposite them, the one who toyed with his food like a man with a guilty conscience and whose sole dining companion was an oversized tan Stetson.

Carolyn had followed his glance.

"Don't know his name," she said in a low voice. "Some muckety-muck in the Greer campaign, I think."

That would explain the guilty conscience, Allaben thought – but then corrected himself. Someone in that position would probably have had his conscience removed long ago. Like an appendix, it served no useful purpose in a politician. And he should know.

How many times had he sat in a corner of his father's study, tucked into the chafed leather of a club chair – sat so quietly and for so long that his father and his father's cronies had forgotten he was there and therefore didn't trouble with euphemism as they parlayed and plotted and divvied up the spoils?

"Felix? Felix Allaben?" Carolyn smiled indulgently as he answered the summons to return to the here and now.

"Do me a favor?" she asked.

"If I can."

"Oh, you can, Mr. Allaben. Believe me, you can."

"Then tell me what it is."

"Simple – don't go all heroic. Okay?"

"I'm not the heroic type."

"Maybe not, but you are the stubborn and pig-headed and mulish type. You're as true as a compass. Set you on a course and there's no turning back."

"That could be a description of Gwynn."

"We can't talk about Gwynn, remember? Besides, you're a lot smarter than Gwynn. Nicer, too."

She studied her wine glass, then leveled her eyes on his.

"You haven't been in since Rebecca died."

Allaben shook his head.

"Regrets?" she asked.

"I haven't figured it out yet."

"For what it's worth, I don't."

"Don't what?"

"Have any regrets. Don't beat up on yourself."

"Sometimes life is punishment enough," he said.

Carolyn gave herself a moment to consider that proposition,

then asked about Miranda. “How is she doing, Felix?”

“It’s hard to tell. She doesn’t talk about it very much.”

“She’s her father’s daughter,” Carolyn observed.

“Her mother’s, too,” Allaben replied. “Now more than ever, if that makes any sense.”

“It does make sense.”

“I sent her out to California for the summer. Just so she could get out of the house. She’s with my brother – my brother who happens to be friends with Stuart London. Coming full circle here.”

Allaben was glad to turn the talk to business again.

“How did Stuart London know that I knew Gwynn?” he asked.

“You’ll have to ask him. I’d been thinking about you. Then Stuart comes in and starts asking questions. I didn’t know you were acquainted.”

“We do each other the odd favor. I haven’t seen him for awhile.”

“He’s got round as a barrel again. He didn’t have your cell, and I couldn’t give it to him because I don’t have it, either. You’ve got mine, haven’t you?”

He knew he didn’t have her number – he’d be too often tempted to call it – but he reached into his jacket pocket to pull out the phone and pretend to check. Only the phone wasn’t in his jacket pocket. It wasn’t in any of his other pockets, either, because he’d left it on the dresser in his bedroom.

“Here,” she said, offering him a pen and a restaurant card, “write it down. We’ll do this the old fashioned way. If I can just remember my own number.”

She tilted her head back and closed her eyes, lending Allaben the opportunity to admire her throat. She was wearing a simple white blouse. The top two buttons were undone, leaving exposed about thirty degrees of lightly tanned skin. Her hair folded like a sable scarf over her shoulder. He couldn't deny it, even if he were of a mind to – she was really quite splendid. And now he had her number and, regrets or no, no reason any more not to call it.

They had been an item in high school. And they'd been good together, been envied, been happily aware that they were well matched. They'd broken up in their senior year – he no longer remembered why – and then they had gone away to school, he to Baltimore and she to Boston.

They had kept track of each other, though, as if in anticipation of some unspoken eventuality, an eventuality that five months ago had come to pass. She could reel off the high and low points of his career, just as he could hers – college, globe-hopping; Amtrak to New York for a stab at modeling, a stab at theater, a stab at culinary school; back to Frederick and the Post; stringer and freelance photographer; marriage, a miscarriage, a reckless husband, therapy, divorce. Then she had scraped together everything she had or could borrow and bought a seedy tavern on the west side of town, a watering-hole for the Post crowd, and in two year's time turned it into Carolyn's.

Its namesake now sat across the table, waiting for something from him – he wasn't sure what. He glanced once more at her card and slid it into his pocket.

"Don't go and lose it now," she said. Then, as if to relieve him of an unnamed obligation, she turned back to business.

"I'm thinking about opening on Sundays."

"Again? You made a solemn vow."

"I could fill every table, Felix. Two seatings."

"I'm sure you could. It's the best place in town. But what about the vow?"

Carolyn had pledged when she'd opened the restaurant to keep it shuttered on Sundays. That way she could go at least one night each week without smelling of kitchen. And she had stuck to her pledge, though she was regularly pressed by customers and her accountant to reconsider the policy.

She stared into her wine glass, allowing him a three-quarter view of her eyes, then mused ruefully, "What am I going to do, sit home and watch TV?"

Allaben was about to deliver a rejoinder to this shameless piece of play-acting when Linda arrived with their dinners. In the bustle that followed – steaming plates laid before them, fish knives allotted, and pepper ground – the talk turned to the dish Jean-Paul had fashioned, a raft of grilled swordfish beached on a reef of corn and red-pepper salsa.

It was as delicious as it looked. They ate hungrily, now and then trading notes about the preparation of the dish. When they had finished, Allaben asked Carolyn to convey his compliments to the chef.

She set her face in a baleful glare, lowered her voice and rasped, "Je crâche à ton gout misérablement bourgeois!" then unscrewed her face and added, "Which I translate as, 'Take your compliment and stuff it.' You haven't earned the right to venture an opinion. Jean-Paul's a brawler. Go toe to toe with him a couple of times, then he may hear you out. We've had our share of donnybrooks, believe me."

Allaben emptied the last of the wine into their glasses. Carolyn ordered him a sorbet, then excused herself for a moment while she visited other tables. He watched her work the room, the soul of grace and charm. What in him would amount to affectation was to her second nature. She was at home.

Which is where he probably ought to be. Pedro would be pacing by now.

"Besides," he said in answer to her exhortations to stay, "I'm a working stiff again. I've got to get an early start tomorrow."

He stood. She caught his hand.

"But you haven't told me anything about the case. And that won't do. I've got a reputation to uphold."

"Next time."

"What time is 'next time'?"

"Tomorrow. I'll take you to a ball game. The Keys are in town for a couple of games. They've made the playoffs. You can yell at the Bleacher Creature, win a prize."

"How am I going to pry anything out of you at a ball game? You'll be stuffing your mouth with peanuts or cursing the ump."

"They don't sell peanuts at the ball park anymore."

"I'll bring some."

"Make sure they're salted. Salt flavors the beer, especially if it's flat."

She shook her head as if to say it was time to put this little game behind them. Her hand still held his. "Sure you won't stay?"

He lifted it her hand, bowed ever so slightly, and kissed her wrist. The smell of her flesh almost changed his mind.

10

The rain had stopped, and by the time he reached his house the night sky was beginning to clear. He stood in the quiet garden and studied the heavens. Handfuls of stars were sprinkled across the broad black slate overhead. Here and there he detected a cluster that vaguely suggested a figure, but he was no good at constellations. The only ones he could identify for certain were the Big Dipper and Orion, and neither was presently in view.

He studied the back of the house, not so stately as the neoclassic façade that faced the street. The house was one of the oldest in the city and had been in his family for so long that it had come to be known as Allaben House. Generations of Allaben judges, bankers, and politicians had been born, had entertained, and had died within its precincts. The last to breathe his last in Allaben House was Felix's father, Charles Allaben, one of Frederick's richest and most illustrious citizens.

Now the house belonged to Felix Allaben. If he were of a mind to, he could sell it and move with Miranda to New York or Rome or Rio, or to San Francisco, where his younger brother lived. Or not sell it – deed it to the Frederick Historic Society. Let them make a museum of it. It was not as if he needed the money. His father had seen to that, bequeathed the house and the lion's share of the estate to his eldest son. Because Felix had come home and married and given him a grandchild. While Russell had done none of these things, and never would.

But Allaben had been to New York and Rome and Rio. Interesting places, all of them – definitely worth the visit – but not his idea of home. And yes, he'd returned to Frederick and married Rebecca and fathered Miranda. But he hadn't done any of these things to please his father. He'd done them because he wanted to. He had his own reasons for staying.

The house had fit Rebecca like a glove, the dazzling white variety that from finger to forearm graces a debutante. Rebecca came from the same stock as he, the prosperous and well-connected gentry of Frederick. She knew how a table should be set, how to reprimand the help, how to smile in mock disapproval when a guest at the dinner table – a colleague in the English faculty who'd drunk too much bourbon – said something outrageous, how to firmly but discretely rebuff that same guest when he tried to grope her beneath the starched ivory linen of the table cloth.

She was beautiful, she was refined, she was generous and smart and irreverent. She knew she was too good to be true, and was only too happy to let you in on the joke – once you had earned her trust and been allowed to slip past the veil of her good breeding. Allaben's father had adored her.

But then one day Allaben had come home from work to find the leavings of a luncheon party on the table. The flustered maid tried to explain: "Mrs. Allaben said I'm not to touch it." He had gone upstairs, found his wife in bed. "It's not worth the candle, husband," she'd said. His first thought was that she was "in character." Her specialty was 19th century English literature, and from time to time she amused herself by assuming the style and the diction of the period. But his first thought was wrong. She was not amusing herself. She was keeling before the wind of dementia, a wind that would turn typhoon and send her spiraling, eventually, into the maelstrom.

The second time Rebecca was hospitalized, tucked away in a discrete haven just outside Silver Spring, Allaben had driven his daughter to the shore for the weekend. Two and a half hours in the car, and neither had said a word about the calamity that had befallen them – wife-and-mother absent without leave. Finally, because he was the grown-up, Allaben had dragged the matter to the surface, like an angler reeling in a catch he wasn't sure he wanted to see.

They had sat side by side in beach chairs, bare feet kneading the sand, sunglasses to protect them, both against the sun and the uncomfortable sight of each other's eyes. Like her mother's, Miranda's were an almost otherworldly shade of blue. A stiff onshore breeze chased strings of dried seaweed up the beach. The sea rumbled and hissed.

"Your Mom's going to be okay, sweetie. She just needs to rest."

"Is it like shell-shock?" Miranda was studying the First World War in school.

"In some ways it is. The stress is so great that the mind just seizes up. It just can't cope any more. It's a medical condition. She was probably born with it. But it's manageable with the right meds and with our support. The doctors will treat her, we'll all take good care of her, and she'll be fine."

He had prayed she wouldn't ask the obvious questions: "What stress?" Or, even worse: "Do I have it, too?" There would be plenty of time for those questions, and for evasions from those questions, once normalcy was restored. He was trying to think positively, to be a rock for his daughter and an anchor for his wife. Steady at the helm. But as he lay awake at night in the beachfront motel room and listened to the crash of the surf, he could see nothing but shipwreck ahead.

His reverie was broken by an inquiring scratch from inside the kitchen door. Ever vigilant, ever faithful Pedro. Puzzled, no doubt, by this erratic behavior. It was not like his master to leave him alone in the evening, much less return at this hour, when uppity cats were making their rounds and the bang of a car door was a sound to reckon with.

Allaben gave the dog a reassuring pat as he let him out. The kitchen was dark and still. He stood inside the doorway, watching a shadowy Pedro sniff around the perimeter of the garden. From upstairs came the faint drone of an air conditioner. Bed. Sleep. One day into the case and he was bone tired. He opened the refrigerator, pulled out a bottle of water, unscrewed the top. The grate of aluminum on glass put him in mind of the kid on the skateboard – he'd have to see about getting into Gwynn's apartment, the former tenant of which was at this moment tucked into a refrigerated drawer in the Washington County Morgue. Flat on his back. A cadaver. A dead fish. And, once again, Allaben's responsibility.

He let Pedro in. A little breeze drifted in from the garden. Honeysuckle. What was the scent Carolyn had been wearing? Should he have asked? No telling, though, where asking might have led. Probably, after another bottle of wine, straight to her bed. Again.

Every husband is allowed to stray once, isn't he? Just one time, after sixteen years of faithfulness? One night out of 16 x 365 nights, give or take a few, since he'd pledged to remain forever faithful to his beautiful bride, Rebecca. A night when, not for the first time

– not the first time by any means – his beautiful bride lay sedated in a hospital bed. A night when on the spur of the moment he had stopped by Carolyn's for a drink, just for the hell of it, nothing more in mind than a reprieve from the drudgery of playing the dutiful husband to a bipolar wife, a reprieve from heartsickness and worry and demoralization. A night when it happened that Miranda was away on a school expedition. A beautiful night in April.

Why *had* they broken up?

Carolyn would remember, he was sure. But he'd never asked her, even on that night five months ago, when, lying side by side in the drugged aftermath of lovemaking, he could have asked her anything.

Three days later, Rebecca had been released from the hospital, and Allaben had driven her to Baltimore to celebrate with a show and a night out.

And now he could recite her obituary.

The clock in the study struck twelve. It was Tuesday. Pedro followed him through the dining room. At the foot of the stairway, Allaben paused. The doorway to the study was open, and through it he saw that the red light on the answering machine was blinking.

Listen now or save it for tomorrow? What if Miranda had tried his cell – the one he'd left upstairs – and then called the land line?

He padded to the answering machine. One message.

"Where the hell are you?" There was a long pause. "That was the sound of me thinking. It's Wick Mallory, nine-o-five p.m. and I want you to call me as soon as you get this. I don't care what time it is. Damn it, Felix. It's Hal Snyder. He's dead. A ranger found him by Bloody Lane on the battlefield. Antietam again. What the hell's going on here?"

11

Lester Dawson could smell Jimmy's Diner well before he entered it. It was 10:30 on a sweltering Tuesday morning. Dawson wondered how many gallons of coffee and how many pounds of bacon had already been served in the four hours since the diner opened. As he walked through the doorway, he saw that his dining companion was already present, sequestered in a booth in the rear of the diner. Dawson smiled at Dot, who'd recognized him as soon as he'd entered, and made his way to where Bull was waiting. The diner was half empty. None of the booths nearby were occupied. That was good.

"Smack on time and ready to rock and roll," Bull declared by way of greeting, then added, "*That's* how business gets done 'round here, Mr. Smith. I even ordered my sweet roll already. Hey, you always wear that hat? With the blast furnace outside?"

"Always," Dawson answered as he placed it on the seat beside him. "It keeps off the sun."

Before Dawson and his Stetson could settle in, Dot was on

them. Coffee pot in one hand, she placed Bull's order before him with the other, and directed her attention to her new customer. "Welcome back, mister cowboy. What'll it be today? Couple of eggs, maybe? Some flapjacks? And you already know about our muffins."

"Just coffee, please," Dawson responded, waving off the menu suggestions. In fact, despite the ice-cool demeanor he usually presented to the world, Dawson's stomach was today in knots – and with good reason. Not only Bull's operation, but another one presently in the planning stages, might be in jeopardy. Caution was the word of the day. Cancel came in a close second.

He waited until the waitress was out of hearing range, then directed a keen stare at Bull, who today was sporting a too-tight black t-shirt that read *Bulldog Barbecue* in large red letters over a flaming grill. Dawson imagined it was the same shirt that Bull's employees would be donning at that moment in all four of his restaurants. Soon they'd be sweating like Bull, who, despite the air conditioning, was swabbing his neck with a napkin. There was no sign of any Confederate pins or other cheeky attention-getters on him this time.

"You heard the news from Sharpsburg?" Dawson began.

"You mean the dead guys on the battlefield? Yeah, I heard. But it don't change nothing, does it?"

"Oh, I beg to differ," Dawson said sharply. "It changes my comfort level. And it should change yours. Don't you know what it means that a second man died there? It means the place will be swarming with reporters and cops again. We've already got a federal agent on the case and all the resources he's got behind him. We don't want the damn feds snooping around, do we?"

"No, Mr. Smith, I suppose we don't," Bull replied with what

sounded to Dawson like an awfully cavalier tone. "We just got to be extra careful now, don't we? And I, Bull Markham, am the soul of caution. Three combat tours and not a mark on me."

Dawson was decidedly not reassured by the bravado. "Look, Bull," he warned, "I've been advised that your guys were behind the open-carry debacle at that ball field in Lynchburg in July. That was bad business all around."

"Those fellas just took it on themselves to put their sidearms on display for all to see. I didn't have nothing to do with it," Bull objected.

"Put their guns on their hips and accidentally shot someone."

"The key word there is 'accident'. They was acting on principle."

"This job you and me are lining up, Bull? I've got to know the guys you've recruited aren't gun-toting cowboys like those clowns."

"They ain't," Bull replied defensively. "The guys I've picked out are the best."

"The best," Dawson repeated.

"The best means the best. Guys from my old command. They've all been in it pretty deep. They're for real. No worries on that score. Fact, one of them says to me, 'If the Taliban can do it, why can't we? Ain't we got the courage of our convictions?'"

"None of them ever seen around Frederick, I trust?"

"No way. One's from Michigan, likes taking it to the coloreds. The other guys hail from the Sunshine State."

"We need guys who are cool under pressure, Bull, guys who can think on their feet. No itchy fingers, no hotheads, no loose tongues."

"Guaranteed, Mr. Smith. I vouch for these boys. I'm going to get in on the action myself. Hey, it'll be like old times. And compared to the special operations they've been through, this will be child's play. You just relax, Mr. Smith. We got this."

Bull signaled to Dot with a raised cup, then went back to his sweet roll.

Lester Dawson shifted in his seat as Dot returned with his coffee, and then sat motionless while she refilled Bull's cup. When she'd left them, he returned to the task at hand. "Appreciate the advice, Bull, but I'll take a deep breath when I know there's no federal agent looking up my butt. I'll relax when it's time for relaxing. Meantime, let's get down to business, shall we? Did you pick up a flag?"

"A beauty. Big, too. Got all thirteen stars. Easy search online."

"Good. Now talk to me about explosives. Have they been shipped? Are they safely stored?"

"Affirmative on both counts," Bull replied quickly. "Everything's in place. Been working through your PRL contact over there. In fact, we just unloaded ..."

With an abrupt wave, Dawson stopped him mid-sentence. "Lower your voice," he directed. "Good, all right," he continued. "Now let's go over the plan, slowly, one more time. Start at the beginning. Pretend I'm hearing it for the first time."

12

Allaben learned from Mallory that Hal Snyder's body had been removed to the Washington County Morgue, where it lay in a refrigerated bunk beneath Gwynn's. Therefore, the ranger he spotted as he approached the observation tower at the foot of Bloody Lane could not possibly be his woebegone friend. Or even his ghost. This one, though decked out in the same olive-green Park Service uniform, was much shorter and fatter than Snyder.

All the same, it was very strange. Here he was again – a different location, it was true, but the same battlefield, the same broiling sun, and except for the ranger, the same cast of characters. Laroux and D.T. stood in the shadow of the tower, the former studying the shine on a well-polished shoe, the latter busy with a ball-point pen and a notepad.

It was the ranger who first noticed Allaben, piping up with an eager challenge.

"Inspector!"

Allaben waved acknowledgment.

"Inspector! We await you."

This greeting earned an undisguised sneer from Laroux and a stoical grimace from D.T. A peculiar sound, something between a snort and a sigh, sounded in the near distance.

The ranger marched forward, right arm extended, like a portly tin soldier. For a fat man he was remarkably swift. Allaben hadn't time to formulate policy before the ranger was upon him, testing his command of bureaucratic protocol.

"Poole, Inspector. Theodore Poole. Of a long line of Pooles in Civil Service. I believe, Inspector, that in the prevailing circumstances I am answerable only to you."

Allaben took the plump hand offered him. Poole grinned with satisfaction, burying his bright blue eyes in pillows of flesh. A sheaf of sandy hair, parted just above his left ear, was combed over a shiny pate. Beads of sweat trickled down his temple, trembled at the fold of his jaw, dropped onto his soggy collar. He pulled a handkerchief from a hip pocket and swabbed his face. Then, as he recalled the reason they were gathered, the smile disappeared.

"It's a tragedy, Inspector – nothing less," he intoned grimly.

Laroux had elected a suit of gray seersucker. He seemed not to notice the heat, which even in the shade of the tower was beginning to curdle the still morning air. D.T. offered Allaben a subdued greeting, his eyes hidden behind a pair of sunglasses.

"Where did it happen?" Allaben asked.

D.T. pointed to the south side of the tower.

Allaben walked around the base, Poole in tow. On the cement path a crude outline had been drawn in chalk, a gush of dried blood at one end. Snyder had landed in a formless heap. It was only the silhouetted foot that gave away the figure as a human being's. Allaben looked up. It was a long way to the top.

As if reading his mind, Poole said, "Eighty feet. He must have been pushing fifty miles per hour at impact. Right, Doc?"

Laroux had quietly joined them.

"However fast," he said, "it was fast enough. Broke his neck."

"Head first?" Allaben asked.

"Probably not. One of his legs and half of his ribs were broken, too. Leg, then side, then head. All in an instant, of course. His heart stopped maybe a second or two later. That blood drained from his nose. Not much, as you can see."

"Who found him?"

"I did," answered Poole.

"What time?"

"About eight-thirty. The second time."

"The second time?"

"I was here about 7:00 too. Hal stuck around after hours, especially here. I stopped by for a chat, climbed all the way up, but he made it plain that my company wasn't welcome. He could be like that sometimes, a little distant."

"Did you see anyone else?"

Poole shook his head. "No one to see. Sometimes people come in to walk Bloody Lane. It's easy – all they have to do is step over the chain at the roadway. But I didn't see anyone last night. I walked back to headquarters and worked on my monograph – a comparison of the accuracy of smoothbores and rifles – and I knocked off about eight. I locked up, went to my car and saw Hal's was still in the lot. He's never that late. So I started looking around. Found him here. Dead. Poor, unlucky fellow."

"Then what?"

"I called the sheriff."

Allaben turned to D.T. "Where is Wick, anyway?"

D.T. gave the thumbs-up sign. It took Allaben a second to decode its meaning.

"Up top?"

"He's brooding," Laroux explained. "We're to leave him be – do not disturb."

D.T. shrugged a glum "What can you do?" in confirmation.

Inside the tower it was dark and cool. Allaben started up the narrow metal stairway, which zigzagged toward the observation platform above. He was not keen on heights. Don't look down, he told himself, and was at once annoyed with his own infirmity.

As he neared the top the air began to stir, and when he emerged from the stairway, he was greeted by something like a breeze. Mallory stood at the stone parapet, his arms crossed before him. He was hatless. His graying blond tussled hair couldn't hide the bald spot that crowned the top of his head. Next to his left foot sat a wide-brimmed ranger's hat. Mallory's own Stetson was perched on the stone railing. He gave no sign that he was aware of Allaben's presence, but continued to stare – absently or absorbed, it was impossible to say – at the shimmering vista before him. It was only when Allaben had crossed the platform and stood beside him at the rail that he acknowledged that he was not alone.

"You're a lucky guy, *Inspector.* Ted Poole's answerable only to you."

"All in a day's work, Wick." To Allaben's mind, Theodore Poole – however pompous – was beside the point.

"Kick fatso where it hurts – that's some work I'd like."

"What's got into you?" Allaben asked.

"Two dead in as many days – that's what's got into me. I never liked this place."

"You think there's a connection?"

Mallory bent over and lifted the ranger's hat resting by his foot.

Beneath the hat was an empty bottle. When full it had contained a pint of bourbon.

"Found this just as you see it. You knew, didn't you?"

"Didn't everyone? A serious drinker can't hide it – not for very long, anyway."

Mallory frowned. "Does his wife need to know?"

"About the bottle? Depends on how you read it. Did he fall?"

"Sure he did. What else?"

Allaben took a quick peek below, then stepped back a pace. The soles of his feet tingled.

"The trouble with coincidence, Wick – any coincidence – is that it turns the odds into also-rans. I mean, it wouldn't be a coincidence if it weren't so damned improbable."

"No evidence of a crime, except suicide is still illegal in Maryland. The kind thing here, as I figure it, would be death by misadventure – the damned fool got drunk and fell off the tower, which is what happened, anyway. And that way the widow collects."

"What's Laroux have to say?"

"He'll listen to reason. What does he care whether Hal jumped or fell?"

"Or was pushed. She'd collect if it were manslaughter, too."

"What are we talking here, Felix?"

"What about Poole?"

"No way."

"We can't rule it out," Allaben said half-heartedly.

"No way Poole pushes Hal Snyder off the tower, Felix."

"Just rule him out for me, will you, Wick? So we don't have to think about him as part of the mix."

"Okay, Inspector. Whatever you say. But you know what happened here just as well as I do. Hal was up here watching the sun go down, thinking sad but happy thoughts. He emptied the bottle. Maybe he heard something. He leaned over. That's all she wrote."

"What was the bottle doing *under* his hat?"

"Who knows? Maybe he put it there?"

He probably *had* put it there, Allaben admitted to himself. Snyder had left the bottle under his hat – God knows why – in the messy and inscrutable way that the dead leave riddles for the living.

Mallory sighed. "All the men who died here. Why one and not another?"

"It's a battlefield question, Wick. *The* question."

"You mean one that doesn't have an answer."

"Not an easy one."

Mallory looked carefully at Allaben. "Sorry, Felix. I wasn't thinking."

"It's all right. I'm not so tender as I used to be."

Together the two men surveyed the landscape of cornfield, pasture, and hay that rolled away toward Antietam Creek, its course here and there detectable as a shadowy cleft in the sun-bleached distance. Bloody Lane, however, was right below them. Allaben pointed to it.

"Wick, did you know that survivors of the fight down there reported that bodies were piled and packed so close together that they formed a gory carpet? Men could walk the road without touching the bloody ground if they had a mind to."

"No, I didn't know that," Mallory replied. "All I know is that this damn place isn't good for anything but dying."

"There was plenty of that – dying, I mean – done here that day. A lot of bleeding and gasping and groaning. A third of the Rebels hunkered down in that road were killed or wounded. Maybe 2800 boys in all."

"It sounds more like a slaughter than a battle."

"It was a slaughter. The boys in blue, they were just kids, most of them. Raw recruits – newbies – who'd never shot a rifle in anger, never mind been shot at. Screaming, cursing, crying. Even laughing in hysteria. The noise was horrific, and some of the fighting was close in – savage."

"How come you know so much about it?"

"I was a history major. American history, especially the Civil War."

"I didn't know that."

"I was going to go to grad school. But I changed my mind."

"You could've wrote a book."

"There are books aplenty, Wick. Americans still can't get enough of the Civil War."

"Not so surprising, is it? D.T. likes to say that to this day we're all of us Yankees or Rebels."

Allaben shrugged, then nodded toward the lane. "Those kids who fought and died down there weren't thinking about North or South, slavery or abolition. If they were thinking about anything at all, it was staying alive. But D.T. is right, in a way. For a lot of us, the War has never ended. This tower? For some it stands for the defeat of an insurrection and a hateful way of life. For others, the defeat of a glorious rebellion and a honorable way of life."

Mallory fingered the brim of Snyder's hat, then observed, "Well, I'll guarantee you, Inspector Allaben, that Hal Snyder wasn't thinking such deep thoughts when he was up here last night."

A few moments passed as the two men stared, wordlessly, at

the mantle of sunburned grass that covered the sunken lane. The silence was broken by a deferential call from below.

"Inspector?"

"It's that jackass underling of yours," Mallory grumbled, "getting ready to answer to you."

Allaben edged nearer the parapet and leaned over to acknowledge the ranger, then drew back.

"Inspector?" Poole insisted. "Am I needed here any longer? I'm due to give a tour at ten."

"All right. That's all for now, Poole," Allaben called back. "Thank you."

In a moment the ranger could be seen waddling briskly in the direction of the visitor's center, his bald pate shining in the sun.

"Felix," Mallory said, "I've got Gwynn's things in my car. Also the reports you asked for. Still no sign of the bullet. Not much to go on in terms of crime scene."

"I'm thinking in terms of motive."

"Okay, partner, how are we going to divvy this up?"

Allaben had anticipated the question. He'd phoned Folliard before leaving for Sharpsburg. Folliard had greeted the news of Snyder's death with silence. At length he said, "Concentrate on Gwynn."

"Snyder hears the shot and finds Irwin with Gwynn's body. Two days later, he's dead."

"You've talked to Irwin?"

"Yesterday. The timing's not right for him. If it was the shot that Hal Snyder heard, it couldn't have been Irwin."

"If …"

"We'll never know for sure, not now. One of these days I'll retrace Snyder's walk from the cemetery to the Bridge. But the whole thing makes more sense if it wasn't Irwin. I should find out where he was last night, though, just for the hell of it."

"Don't get distracted, Felix," Folliard had said. "I'm not arguing that there's no connection between Gwynn's death and Snyder's – I'm not in a position to say – only that it's Gwynn's you should look into first. Don't forget – it's my nickel."

So be it. Allaben would obey orders, for now. He would leave Snyder's death to Mallory, which was the same thing as leaving it as an accident. He turned to Mallory.

"You check up on Poole, Wick. I'm going to talk to the others who were at the bar on Saturday night."

"You're giving Irwin a free pass?"

"No. Would you take that story at face value – and a flat tire, for God's sake? A story that can only be corroborated in part, and that part by his wife?"

"Word is, he's a spook."

"Irwin?"

"Ex-C.I.A., supposedly. A few of them retire here. You know that. Buy an old house and play the gentleman farmer. Of course, even if he is – and I don't know one way or the other – doesn't make him a more likely suspect."

No, thought Allaben, it didn't – but weren't the waters muddy enough already? He made a mental note to call Folliard again.

"And as for the others," Mallory went on, "besides Irwin's statement, all we've got to go by right now is what the barmaid says and the wisdom of that barfly, Simon. One of us should go back and talk to them again. Because that knucklehead D.T. didn't write it up at the time. Just returned his bottom to the car seat and drove back to the filling station – and a girl there he's courting. All of this is between you and me, Felix. I had him cook something up and back-date it soon as I found out."

So D.T. was in the doghouse. That explained the rueful demeanor.

A flock of birds rose up from beyond a hillock to the east, cawing in protest at some unseen intruder. Allaben watched them hover over, then reclaim the turf they had just abandoned. He checked his watch: 10:15. Though he stood too far from the parapet to see them, he knew that a sulking D.T. and an impatient Laroux must be waiting directly below. The breeze had died away. It was getting hotter by the minute. Allaben had had enough of the tower. He walked to the stairway.

"Come on, Wick," he said, "let's have a look at Gwynn's things."

But Mallory didn't budge.

"Hang on," he said. "About this one-time colleague of yours. I suppose you know that Gwynn liked to chase tail."

"Sure – anything in a skirt. Why? Are you thinking about Irwin's wife?"

Mallory turned from the parapet.

"Felix," he said, "you're going to find some things out about people I know, and I'd just as soon you started the finding out from me. So you just listen for a minute while I fill you in with some background of a private nature."

13

Snyder had been as good as his word. In the annex to the administration building he had arranged a makeshift office – an old metal desk and a vinyl-covered chair, a battered file cabinet, a fan, a telephone. A yellow Post-it was stuck to the desktop – "See me. Hal."

Allaben dropped his hat on the desk. Gwynn's personal effects were laid out before him, together with two oversized manila envelopes. One bore the evidence stamp of the Washington County Sheriff's Department. The other was inscribed with the emblem of the office of the Washington County Medical Examiner.

The latter contained a copy of the autopsy report and a dozen color photos. No surprises. Gwynn had died of the gunshot wound, no ifs, ands, or buts. The only point of interest in the whole document was Laroux's note, under the heading "Scars and/or Distinguishing Marks," that the deceased bore a tattoo on the inside of the right forearm. Allaben looked through the photos again. Sure enough, one of them showed a coiled snake, head raised and ready to strike. It was rendered in gray, with a red outline.

There was no air conditioning in the annex. Allaben had set the fan to oscillate, and every twelve seconds a surf of clammy air washed over him. He had opened the window to air the room out.

Through the window he could see the fieldstone wall surrounding the National Cemetery. Yesterday, Snyder had stood at a corner not ten yards away, staring out at God knows what. Probably at nothing, thought Allaben. From long experience he had learned the futility of idle conjecture. Still – "See me" about what? Where to find the key to the file cabinet? Or something he forgot to tell me about?

He tucked the note into the breast pocket of his shirt and turned his attention to the inventory arrayed on the desktop – mechanical pencil, plastic change-purse, wallet, map, miniature calculator, keys, wristwatch – excepting clothes, all that had been found on the body of Curtis Gwynn.

Allaben tested the mechanical pencil; it worked perfectly. He pulled the chrome stopper from bottom of the barrel but found nothing inside but extra leads. The watch was a cheap digital model, three minutes slow.

Two maps – the standard-issue Park Department brochure available to tourists at the Visitor's Center and a dog-eared, much folded and refolded depiction of the battlefield circa September, 1862.

He squeezed open the red plastic change-purse. A gush of copper and silver clattered onto the desk – $1.44. Together with the cash found in his wallet, that brought to a grand total of $43.44 the sum of money found on his person. Not that robbery – the garden variety stick-up, anyway – was likely to figure in this piece of nastiness.

Keys: one set to Gwynn's vintage Camaro, still parked at the Sharpsburg Arms, where he had spent the night, and another set to his apartment.

That left only the wallet, a brown leather billfold that had been recovered, according to the manifest, from the victim's right hip pocket. Allaben lay it open and methodically removed everything that could be removed: driver's license and registration; bank card, credit cards, library card; cards for voter registration, Social Security, and Selective Service; a plastic calendar given away by The Sojourner Shop, where Gwynn had been employed for the past two years.

There were a number of business cards tucked into an inside sleeve. Among them, two were of special interest.

One, from the inn, was stapled to a credit-card receipt and a hand-printed bill, both of which confirmed that Gwynn had paid in full for one night's stay. The B&B was situated near the battlefield grounds only a quarter of a mile from the Observation Tower. Allaben had stopped by before coming on to his makeshift headquarters. A quick search of Gwynn's car had turned up nothing. The proprietor had checked his records. Gwynn had booked the room six months in advance, and he had called to confirm the reservation a week before the date in question. In the proprietor's estimation, Mr. Gwynn had proved a model, if ill-starred, guest.

The maid, too, had formed a good impression of him. He had left the room in good order and left her a generous tip. She had not seen him depart on Sunday morning, but it must have been early. A private man, she guessed, not one for breakfast-table banter with strangers.

The second card was inscribed "PGP Realty." Of passing interest, perhaps, that a man who presumed to no more than a second-story apartment should carry a realtor's card in his wallet. More interesting to Allaben were the three lines of print at the lower left corner – the name of a licensed agent, an office telephone number, and a mobile number. If he were to call either number, he would be connected to Senior Vice President Pamela Parker.

And if Pamela Parker couldn't be reached at either number? Not to worry. If need arose, the bearer might turn the card over and try the number scrawled in ink on the back. Allaben had it on good authority – the sheriff of Washington County himself – that the number would connect him with the personal cellphone of the lady in question.

14

Allaben did not expect to care very much for Mr. Donald Parker, though he was prepared to admit that he could name no reason for this bias other than the fact that Parker, it seemed, was a cuckold. What of that? So were many another. As he pulled into the lot at Antietam Motors, Allaben reminded himself that a good cop is content to parlay with individuals. Only amateurs yearn for types.

He was barely out of his pickup before a salesman lit upon him. When Allaben informed him of his business, the young man, who sported a blue-and-gray "Fair Deal!" badge, aimed a finger at a one-story box of vinyl and glass that stood at the far end of a long row of gleaming new cars.

Two white sedans were parked beside the building, each pulled up before a sign that read "RESERVED." As Allaben drew nearer, he could make out the Toyota emblem on the tail of each car. Both bore dealer plates. As he approached the front door Allaben spotted, taped to the glass, the same Antietam Anniversary poster he had seen at Ozzie's. Another sign below it advertised a $9.99 firehouse pancake breakfast for that same weekend.

The building was as spare and unassuming inside as it was out, the only concessions to decor the red, white, and blue of the stars and stripes and the red, white, and gray of the stars and bars. These had been pinned side by side over the only two interior doorways in sight. Most of the floor space was devoted to a warren of cubicles, each equipped with a desk, chairs, and a computer terminal. A few of the cubicles were occupied by sales associates and their customers, haggling over prices or arranging payment terms. Apart from the messages piped over a P.A. system, however, the atmosphere was remarkably quiet, even subdued.

Allaben asked for Parker's office and was pointed toward the door beneath the stars and bars. As he drew near he could hear a noisy argument in progress, an argument that his knock brought to an abrupt halt. There was a moment of silence. Then the door flew open, and a young man swept past him – the same young man he had seen on the battlefield Monday morning – the empty-eyed Parker boy. Not so empty-eyed this afternoon, though. On the contrary, brimming with fury. The boy showed no sign that he even saw him, much less put face to memory. He stalked to the nearest exit, the same door through which Allaben had entered the building, and with a resounding bang slammed it shut behind him.

Allaben slid cautiously through the doorway. The office appeared to be empty. Narrow slats of sunlight filtered through the window blinds. Desk, chairs, file cabinets, a mammoth TV set.

A car engine sputtered just outside the window, then roared to life. As if lured from the deep by the throaty incantation, a figure slowly rose from behind the desk. Clutching an object that in the dim light Allaben took for a book, the man stepped to the window and drew the blinds, just in time to see the white Toyota peel from the lot and fishtail onto the highway.

"Damned kid!" he muttered. "When is he going to learn?"

"Learn what?" Allaben asked.

The man did not seem at all surprised by the question. He turned to study his visitor. "Learn the ways of adults," he said, "like live and let live, judge not lest ye be judged, one hand washes the other – things of that nature. Otherwise you go crazy." He carefully placed on the desktop the object he had held in his hands. It was not a book but a framed photograph. A part of the glass overlay was missing.

Allaben thought it was time to clarify the situation.

"I'm Felix Allaben."

"And I am Don Parker. I've been expecting you." Parker leaned over the desktop to shake Allaben's hand, then wearily deposited himself in the swivel chair, pointing as he did so to a chair opposite him.

Parker was a tall, big-boned specimen of middle-aged decline. Everything about him was a little slack, from the wattles of flesh forming beneath his chin to the argyle socks collapsed at his ankles. His features were regular, even handsome, but huddled-looking, as if cramped by the bloated expanse of his face. A wave of yellow hair swept back from his forehead. He had probably been quite a looker as a youngster – the fair-haired big man on campus who inspires crushes in girls and envy in boys – and no doubt relished his advantage, as immodest as he was vain. He leveled a pair of lazy blue eyes on Allaben, then – his self-possession fully restored – treated him to a toothy smile.

"I'm all yours, Inspector. Fire away."

"Was that your son?"

"Yes. Don, Junior. Do you have children?"

"A daughter."

"Teen?"

"She's fifteen."

"Then you know what they're like. Who can understand the teenage brain? Half finished, half – the bigger half – unfinished. Idealistic as all get-out. And don't get me wrong – that's fine, as far as it goes. But, God, they can be so sanctimonious!"

He paused, as if awaiting an "Amen." But Allaben declined to jump on that bandwagon. Miranda might be called many things, but sanctimonious was not one of them. Nor idealistic, for that matter. She was as hardheaded, as practical, as down to earth as they come.

Parker picked up the photo and turned it to Allaben.

"A good-looking kid, if I do say so myself. Takes after his mother. He's just got some growing up to do," he added.

It was a studio shot, head and shoulders against a royal blue drop. The boy was as fair as his father and his eyes were as blue, but the shape of his mouth was quite different, fuller and wider than his father's. Jaw and brow were stronger, too. It was a face that, unlike his father's, would age well.

Allaben turned his attention from the photo to Parker.

"Was that one of your cars he took off in?"

Parker nodded. "Yes. I keep a couple on hand."

"You use them as well?"

"Sure. One of the perks. You're not shopping, are you, Inspector? I've got to ask, or I wouldn't be the best damned car salesman in Maryland. Tell you what, you're not going to find a warmer welcome or fairer deal than what you'll get right here at Antietam Motors."

Allaben shrugged off the hype. He was sure that if Robert E. Lee rode up on Traveler, he, too, would be treated to the same pitch.

"I'll settle for some straight answers."

"Wick Mallory was right," said Parker. "'No small talk,' he says, 'and no beating around the bush.' No reason we can't get acquainted first, though. You can never know too many people – that's my philosophy."

"And you want to do what's right."

"Frankly, it's in my interest to do what's right. I've got my business to think of. And my family. To say nothing of my reputation. I've worked hard, given of myself. I'm a joiner, Inspector. A booster. Ask anyone."

Parker waved at the wall of plaques, testimonials, and photographs bearing witness to his civic-mindedness.

"I believe in giving back to the community," he went on. "I've done well by my neighbors. It's only fair that they do well by me. You don't stay in business fifteen years by short-changing your customers. And there's nothing un-American about profit, Inspector."

One of the pictures hanging on the wall caught Allaben's eye. He got up for a closer look. Parker paused to allow Allaben to study the photograph, then offered an explanation.

"Yes," he remarked, "me and Wick Mallory. We go way back. That's my wife standing between him and my brother-in-law, Mason Greer. I'm sure you recognize Mason. That picture was taken last June at our high-school reunion. Twenty years since we graduated. We haven't done too bad for a bunch of small-town kids. Wick's the county sheriff, my wife's got her own real-estate firm, I run the biggest dealership in the region, and Mason's running for attorney general!"

"You went to school together?"

"We sure did. In the same class. Wick was a year behind us, with my wife."

"I know. He told me this morning."

A guarded look passed over Parker's face.

"Did he?"

"That and a lot of other things. What about your brother-in-law? See much of him?"

"From time to time. I help out with the campaign – fund raising, introductions, that sort of thing. Can't be too far out in front about it, you know. Some of my customers are Democrats. You aren't going to drag him into this, are you? I've got nothing to do with it, and neither does he."

"What else did Wick tell you – I mean besides letting on that I don't care for beating around the bush?"

"Told me to tell you the straight truth just like I told it to him."

"About the murder of Curtis Gwynn?"

"What else? Here's the truth, A to Z. I didn't shoot him. And, before you ask, I don't know who shot him, either. Yeah, I got into an argument with him at the tavern. That's public knowledge. So what? Am I going to shoot the son of a bitch because I don't see eye to eye with him over who gets to carry guns? About freedom to make a buck on good land that's just sitting there for tourists? Or over whatever did or didn't happen on that damn Antietam Battlefield? That's crazy, Inspector. All I know is my conscience is clear. I don't have any trouble sleeping at night."

Allaben let him relax for a moment, let him think the worst part was over with. Then he asked, "How about your wife? Is she a good sleeper?"

A guttural sigh escaped from Parker.

Allaben pressed on. "Where were you Sunday morning?"

"At home. In bed. Until seven-thirty or so. I was here on the lot at 9:00."

"Your wife can vouch for that?"

A pause. "Sure."

"You don't sound too sure."

"Maybe it's your hearing."

"I didn't have any trouble hearing Wick Mallory."

Parker sighed again. "Okay, Inspector, I give up." He put up his hands to signal defeat. "You've found out about my wife and Curtis Gwynn."

Allaben said nothing. He waited for more.

"I suppose it does look bad," Parker continued in a resigned tone. "Jealous husband murders wife's lover. But it's not like that. Not at all. It's a mutual agreement, you see, an understanding that Pamela and I came to a few years ago. We're grown-ups, Inspector. It's only natural to be attracted to others, especially after seventeen years of marriage. What isn't natural is to deny normal, healthy physical needs just for the sake of stale custom. Jealousy is not part of our relationship."

Parker paused, as if deciding whether to add a gloss to his explanation. Allaben waited.

"You've got to understand something about Pamela." He paused again. "She's not had an easy time of it. We had three great years – as happy as larks. Then Donnie came along. It's been up and down ever since. I used to think it was post-partum depression, but post-partum doesn't last fifteen years. She's unhappy. She drinks too much. I don't like it, but that's how things are, Inspector. What am I going to do? She's my wife, so I cut her a little slack."

All of this came out of him as if by rote. It had the tinny sound of self-serving oratory, committed to memory and dragged out whenever the situation called for it. And Allaben wasn't buying any of it.

"So it was okay that your wife was fulfilling a normal, healthy, physical need with Curtis Gwynn."

Parker's face pinched. He looked like a child contemplating a spoonful of medicine. "Like I say, we have an understanding. What's good for the goose is good for the gander. And for your information, I didn't know about Gwynn – not until recently, anyway. I never traded a word with him before Saturday night. Ask Pam, if you like. She'll tell you the same."

"What did you argue about?"

"At the tavern?" Parker's voice lifted. He was happy to change the subject. "About property development. Gwynn was going on about the sanctity of historical sites, how there ought to be an absolute ban on development of land – even the tiniest speck of dirt – where men had fought and died. One of those pie-in-the-sky Civil War fanatics."

"And you don't hold by those principles."

"Of course not. And neither does my wife, by the way. We see eye to eye on that. It's downright backward to enslave progress to sentimental notions about history. We've got to live in the present, not in the past."

He shifted in his chair and made a show of studying his watch.

"Did your son know about him?"

"About Gwynn?" He stared out the window. "I don't think so."

"I'll have to ask him."

"Good luck. The only thing I can get out of him is contempt. I'm not pure enough, virtuous enough to suit him. Just ask. I'm sure he'll be happy to tell you all about my shortcomings."

"I'll be talking to your wife, too."

Parker snorted grimly, as if weary of being called upon. "Talk to whoever you like. I'd like to get back to my business. I really would."

"Where is your wife right now?"

"I don't know, Inspector. Where's yours?"

Allaben was upon him so quickly that Parker hadn't time to wipe the smirk from his face. It lingered there in idiotic contrast to the shock in his eyes. He retreated into his chair, waiting for the blow to land. Allaben hovered over him, enraged as much with himself as with the cringing oaf before him. What was he thinking? He knew better than to allow a smug lout like Parker to get under his skin. He had overreacted, plain and simple, and now would have to find a way to salvage the situation.

But Parker was too flustered to call the bluff. Instead he slowly raised his hands in a feeble gesture of surrender.

"I was out of line," he said. "It was uncalled for, totally, and you're right to take me to task for it."

Allaben straightened up. His fists relaxed. A moment passed. Parker was encouraged to try a sheepish smile.

"Do you know what the worst part is, Inspector? I was hoping we could be friends. Wick thinks the world of you, says I should introduce you to Mason. And now I've gone and forgot myself. God! What you must think of me."

He indulged himself with a rueful shake of the head, as if to punctuate his confession. But Allaben wasn't in a forgiving mood, so when Parker raised his eyes, now full of penitence, the only blessing he received was delivered by Allaben's back.

15

The game was already underway when Allaben and Carolyn arrived at the ballpark. They had missed the top of the first. As they walked down the concrete stairway to their seats behind the Keys' dugout, the visiting team was taking the field. It was the Winston-Salem Warthogs, presently the fourth seed in the Carolina League playoffs, meeting the Keys on their home turf. The kid on the mound was a stocky right-hander whom Allaben had never seen before.

How was Rod Hurley doing? So far, so good, judging by the scoreboard. He'd allowed no hits and no runs. There had, however, been an error. Which may very well have been committed by the unseen party on the receiving end of the chewing-out that Gene Delvecchio could be overheard delivering inside the dugout.

Manny Klein, who doubled as pitching and first-base coach, stood twenty feet away, intently studying the pitcher. With chaw-swollen cheek, skinny frame, and brawny arms akimbo, he looked like a grizzled Popeye. Turning to investigate the cause of a ruckus in the stands – it was the Bleacher Creature up to some fan-pleasing prank – he caught sight of Allaben. By way of acknowledgment he pinched the brim of his hat, cupped the back of the neck, touched right hand to left thigh and then left hand to right elbow. It was the third sign that counted – right hand to left thigh meant bunt.

The communication must have been noticed by Delvecchio, for in the next instant the manager was out of the dugout and searching for its recipient. Delvecchio did not care for being kept in the dark about anything. He wasn't happy unless he was fully in command, fully informed, fully obeyed.

Why, then, did he torment himself with a job the very nature of which must deny him on at least two of these counts? In the first place, 19-year-olds are by definition uncontrollable; and in the second, it's the front-office people, the guys in the suits, who ultimately call the shots. The frustration of his position seemed to be weighing especially heavily upon him tonight. It was with a liverish frown that he greeted Allaben at fence-side.

"This ain't a job for a man of religion, Felix," he grumbled. "I swear to God the game of baseball's going to drive me from the faith."

"It's the cross you must bear, Del. Here, say hi to Carolyn."

"Nice to make your acquaintance," Delvecchio allowed. "I believe I had the pleasure of dining at your establishment." He nodded in Allaben's direction. "Can't you do better than this guy?"

"Probably, but he has good seats. And I'm glad you liked your dinner."

"Liked the dinner, didn't like the check. But what the hey? Hurley's agent was paying for it."

"So, Del, who's the kid on the mound?"

"Name's Ortiz. You can see he's got good breaking stuff, but word is he can't field worth a damn. We're going to test him right off. Anyway, Ortiz is the least of my problems. It's that damned Hurley."

"Looks like he started okay."

"Just wait," Delvecchio said. "He was lucky to get out of the inning. He's not going to make it, not this way, which is what I try to tell them in Baltimore. He's got to learn to throw some off-speed stuff. 'Pitch him,' they say, like they never heard me – which is par for the course. 'We're in a pennant race,' they say, 'in case you forgot. We've got to see what he can do.'"

Delvecchio and Hurley did not get on. And Delvecchio wasn't the stoical type, not the sort who grins and bears it. He'd let you know if he was ticked off, whether you were a hotshot kid just out of high school or the winner of a Cy Young award. With Hurley, of course, he'd had to restrain himself a little, cut the guy a little slack. Here was a pitcher who had three times won 20 games or more for the Orioles, and might do it again if his shoulder stayed cobbled together and he could master a couple of junk pitches.

But Hurley was a cool customer, self-absorbed and aloof. He took little interest in Delvecchio's counsel – or anyone else's, for that matter – and neither his erstwhile talent nor his indisputable numbers were sufficient, in the manager's eyes, to make up for his complete indifference to the playoff fortunes of the Frederick Keys. Hurley was a champion and had the ribbons to prove it, but given a choice Delvecchio far and away preferred the young pups who, for all of their shenanigans, still sweated for love of the game.

Allaben was inclined to be more charitable. He had been a pitcher himself, one-half of the locally renowned Allaben-Delvecchio battery – and furthermore was, like Hurley, a southpaw. He was prepared to understand and forgive the obnoxious extremes of the breed – the high-strung prima donnas and the sullen despots of the pitching mound. Though, as he viewed it, Hurley was neither, just a single-minded but damaged athlete desperate to stay in the game.

But Allaben did not have to jockey for turf in the locker room with him, as Delvecchio did. And in any event, this was not the time or place to pursue the matter. That could wait until after the game. The kid on the mound was finishing his warm-ups and Bobby Van Dorn, the Keys' leadoff hitter, had tossed away the rosin bag and was strolling toward the batter's box.

"Are we still on for Chesapeake's?" Delvecchio asked.

"Ten thirty," said Allaben. "See you there."

"God willing," sighed Delvecchio, and promptly disappeared into the dugout.

Allaben asked Carolyn if she was ready for a beer.

"As long as it's cold."

With that, Carolyn returned to her seat and Allaben marched up to the concession to fetch the beers and some popcorn. When he turned from the counter, he bumped into two young men arriving to place their orders. He'd zigged, but they'd not zagged. Apologies all around, and only an inch of one of his beers spilled. Allaben sidled up to the nearest condiment stand, deposited his tray next to the mustard dispenser, took a long look at the backs of the two young men, and checked his pockets – wallet still in place, nothing missing.

The engineered collision was an old pickpocket standby. Allaben had more than once consoled a victim with "Don't blame yourself, ma'am" or "It can happen to anyone, sir." But not to him, not an ex-cop, not if Allaben could help it. Call it a terminal case of street jaundice – he'd take no chances.

He'd no sooner returned to his seat and handed Carolyn her beer than Ortiz offered his first pitch, a heater that whistled by the batter's knees – strike one. The next two pitches were curves, both outside and low. Allaben watched Manny Klein give the signs. When Ortiz started his windup for the next pitch, Van Dorn squared around. The pitch was a low fastball. Van Dorn laid down a perfect bunt, a dribbler to the third-base side of the pitcher's mound. Just as Delvecchio had observed, the flailing finish to Ortiz's delivery left him unprepared to field it. By the time he managed to bare-hand the ball, Van Dorn had scooted safely to first. Manny twisted toward the stands, found Allaben, and cranked out a theatrical wink.

Van Dorn moved to second on a fielder's choice, but there was left stranded, as hitters three and four popped up and struck out respectively. Music flooded the ballpark – a honky-tonk number by Merle Haggard – and the Bleacher Creature capered atop the visitor's dugout.

The murmur of the crowd rose up into the balmy sky, which had darkened to purple above the aura of the stadium lights. It was bat night, and thousands in the sell-out crowd raised their free, official Frederick Keys bats as Hurley registered a strike-out or when, in the bottom of the second, the Keys' catcher knocked one over the 7 pin in the Urbana Lanes sign in left-center.

The Warthogs did not often face pitchers of Hurley's caliber, and for the first three innings he had managed to awe them into submission on the strength of his reputation. He threw only hard stuff – his fabled fastball, slider, split-finger. But their second time up, the Winston-Salem hitters began to notice that although those fastballs were coming from no less fabled a fireballer than Rod Hurley, they weren't rising or dipping as much as they had seemed to before. Their cleanup hitter knocked one out of the park. And just to show that that was no fluke, so did the next.

The second clout drew Manny Klein from the dugout. He

lumbered to the mound for a consultation with Hurley and then trotted back, watering the path with jets of tobacco juice.

Allaben later learned that Klein's counsel had been succinct: throw some curves. But take his heater away and Hurley was effectively disarmed. If a pitcher cannot intimidate, then he must baffle, and Hurley had never learned cunning – had never needed to, until now. He tried the curve, but it was no good. Another walk, followed by back-to-back doubles. Hurley did not put up a fight when Delvecchio came out to relieve him. He put the ball squarely in the manager's hand and strode stone-faced into the dugout. There were no boos. In the quiet that absorbs the resounding thud of failure, a solitary fan was heard to sing out, "Hang in there, Rod! You still got it!"

At least the game had a happy ending. The Keys came back to tie it in the eighth, and in the ninth won it with a perfectly executed squeeze bunt. There was a jingling of keys at the finale, and then the crowd filtered out of the stadium, well pleased with the team, with the outcome, and with themselves. Allaben and Carolyn stayed put. It would be awhile before Delvecchio could get away, and they could enjoy the tranquil evening's stillness together.

"Sure you don't want me to drive you to your place?" Allaben asked.

"The restaurant can get along without me for another hour. I've been checking my phone – no emergencies."

"You could come along, if you like."

"To Chesapeake's? Thanks very much, but this is obviously a 'guy' thing."

"More a custom than a thing. And it's his turn to pay."

"Next time, you and Del will come to Carolyn's – my treat."

"Only if they win?"

"Perfect. We'll start a counter-custom."

In a matter of moments they had the stands to themselves, or nearly so – the cleaning staff were soon at work sweeping and swabbing seats and concrete. Meantime, the groundskeepers policed the field, tamping down divots and raking the base-paths. Just as they finished rolling out the tarp to cover the infield – thunderstorms were forecast for late that night or early the following morning – the banks of stadium lights went dark.

16

The parking lot had been full when Allaben and Carolyn arrived for the game, so he'd had to park his truck a hundred yards away from the stadium entrance, on a strip of grass that held the spillover. Now the lot was nearly empty. The lights barely reached the grass, and the trees that separated it from the nearby highway cast his truck even deeper into shadow. It was dark, so dark that he did not see the figures standing next to his truck until he and Carolyn were twenty feet away. Three men, two leaning against the cab, the third on the opposite side, head and shoulders visible above the truck bed.

Allaben wondered if number three was taking a leak.

He gripped Carolyn's shoulder. His meaning was clear: stay put. Then he walked slowly to the driver's side of the truck and stopped a few feet short of the door. He turned back toward Carolyn to make sure she hadn't got it into her head to back him up – she hadn't. He turned again to the scenario before him. The two men didn't move. Allaben calmly studied them in turn. He'd seen them before. These were the two he'd bumped into just hours before at the stadium concession stand. They'd probably been frisking him. And they hadn't left the ball park empty handed, either. Each held a Frederick Keys souvenir baseball bat.

The first was young, stocky, crew cut. A tight-fitting T-shirt bulged over his belly. The second was in his thirties, lanky, with long, stringy hair. Both reeked of beer.

"This your truck?" the first one asked.

Allaben nodded. "Yes, it's my truck."

"Could it be I seen it in Sharpsburg this morning?"

Allaben didn't answer. He glanced at the window. The door was still locked, which meant the taser and the pepper spray were probably still in the glove compartment.

"I bet my buddy," Number One went on, "that it's this truck and no other. Ain't too many trucks like this to be seen in Sharpsburg. No wonder, too. Sharpsburg's hard on trucks. No telling what might happen to a high-class truck in Sharpsburg. And this one here's a beauty."

He slid his hand along the fender. Allaben casually put his right hand in his trouser pocket. He found the key. Which button locked and which unlocked?

"No less than he deserves," Number Two drawled.

"How's that?" asked Number One, who was busy sizing up Allaben's companion.

"She's a beauty, too. Just look at her."

Number One snickered. Allaben had had enough.

"Get out of the way."

"Hang on there, Felix." The third man had come around the back of the truck. Allaben had never seen him before. This one leveled a hard look at Allaben's pocket.

"What is this? Get the hell away from my truck," Allaben demanded.

"Just hold your horses, and I'll be happy to tell you." Number

Three stopped in front of Allaben. He looked anything but happy. Grim, purposeful, set on a thankless task – all of these – but certainly not happy. "But first," he continued, "give up on whatever you got in that pocket. We know you ain't armed."

The two men stood eye to eye. Number Three was an inch shorter, twenty pounds heavier, and ten years younger than Allaben. He wore a short-sleeve shirt. He was well groomed, self-possessed, precise.

"I'm a Federal law officer," Allaben started.

"I know you are," Number Three replied. "I am too, in a way. I've even got a badge. Here, I'll show you."

He pulled up his sleeve. Tattooed high on his right shoulder was a coiled snake, its head reared and ready to strike.

"Who are you?" Allaben demanded again.

"I've already told you as much as you need to know on that score, Felix. Now listen to me carefully, and then you can be on your way. Okay?"

Allaben weighed his options. None was very attractive. Number Three took his silence as acceptance of terms.

"Good," he said. "You've got some sense." He nodded toward Carolyn. "And you've got to think about your date. I could have my two friends here beat you to within an inch of your life. Believe me, they'd be happy to do it. But I'm not going to do that. Instead I'm going to let you off with a warning. Call it a professional courtesy. This time only, Mr. Felix Allaben. No more of your meddling, though. Understand? This Sharpsburg business is nothing to you. Just leave it alone. Because next time …" he nodded toward Numbers One and Two, "Well, let's just hope there isn't a next time."

For the first time Allaben heard the cars streaming by on the highway beyond the trees, not fifty feet from where he stood. Good citizens, most of them, going about their law-abiding business. So near and yet so far.

Number Three gazed vacantly at Allaben, as if reviewing a mental checklist. Apparently, the review was satisfactory. There was nothing more to say, so he set off for the parking lot. Numbers One and Two followed after him. Number Two was waving his bat. Allaben watched them go, relieved and seething at the same time.

The trio had gained thirty yards when suddenly Number Three stopped. He pivoted to face Allaben and called out.

"Forgot to tell you. We left you something to remember us by. Driver's side."

Allaben waited until they were across the parking lot, then walked to the other side of the truck. Something dripped from the door. A puddle had formed on the ground. All three of them must have unzipped and let go. No mistaking that smell. It wasn't beer, but it surely once had been.

17

Allaben watched the tail of the truck disappear into the shadowy froth of the car-wash. Carolyn stood beside him in the service station's vapory light. She put her arm around his waist. He'd barely said a word since they drove out of the stadium parking lot.

"Are you okay?" she asked.

"Hmm?"

"Come on, Felix." She gave him a little nudge. "Talk to me."

"I didn't like that little 'incident', Carolyn. I didn't like it one bit."

"Of course you didn't like it. What was there to like? But there was nothing you could do. Three against one. And they had bats."

"It bothers me that I can't figure it out."

"Figure what out?"

"What they were after."

"I thought they made it pretty plain."

"I'm not so sure," Allaben said. And then, as if just now remembering she had been there to witness it, "But I'm truly sorry you had to see it."

"Do you have any idea who those guys are?"

He gave her a grim smile. "I thought they were friends of yours."

"Be serious, Felix. It was scary."

Yes, the confrontation had been scary, though he'd never really expected it would escalate beyond hard looks and bluster. No. If it was scary, it was because he could not square Number Three's warnings with a plausible motive for them.

He mulled over the problem as he drove Carolyn to her restaurant in his spanking-clean truck through the darkened streets of Frederick. He didn't believe for a minute that the party or parties who engineered the confrontation really expected him to turn tail and withdraw from the case merely on the strength of their threats – unless Allaben was meant to read more into them than a threat against himself.

A groan from Carolyn interrupted his ruminations. She showed him her phone, which was lit up with a text message.

"Jean-Paul just bawled out a customer for daring to return a dish."

"You'll be there in a couple of minutes."

"What am I going to do with him?"

"Give him an ultimatum?"

"Probably do no more good than the one the snake guy gave you."

"Snake guy?"

"The one with the snake tattoo."

"You saw it?"

"Yes, and could tell that it meant something to you."

Allaben asked himself whether he should confide to her that Gwynn bore the same tattoo. No, he decided, not until he *did* know what it meant.

"You're not saying anything, Felix," Carolyn went on. "Does

that mean I should forget what I saw?"

He nodded. "For the time being, yes."

Allaben turned the truck into the parking lot at the restaurant and pulled up near the entrance. A last rivulet of carwash bathwater streamed down the windshield. Carolyn slipped her phone into her shoulder bag and opened the door. She took half a step, then pivoted to say goodbye through the open window. She smiled, and a shudder of heat coursed through him. Maybe, he thought, he should own up to the fact that he wanted her? He started to speak, but she leaned throuh the window and pressed her fingers against his lips.

"It's okay, Felix. You can trust me. Just watch out for snakes."

Chesapeake's was crowded and noisy. Allaben scanned the tables in the back until Delvecchio's craggy face came into view. He was tucked into a booth far from the bar's entrance, a spot that would spare them the distraction of all the coming and going between the barroom and the street.

Allaben made his way to the table and slid into the seat opposite Delvecchio, who looked to be about half-way through the two dozen Blue Points he'd ordered for them. Down went an oyster, chased by a long swig of beer. One side of his face, the one closest to the window, was lit blue from the neon beer sign beside him. The beer had failed to wash the gloom out of Delvecchio. His team had rallied to win in the ninth, but Rod Hurley had been touched up for two home runs.

"What took you?" he asked.

Allaben answered with a succinct account of the confrontation in the parking lot.

"A snake tattoo, you say?"

Allaben borrowed a pen from a passing waitress. He drew a coiled snake on a napkin and pushed it in front of Delvecchio. The manager stared at it. He shrugged.

"That's it? No lettering?"

"Just what you see here – gray snake, outlined in red. One of the guys was wearing it. He made sure I noticed it."

"Well," Delvecchio sighed, "it doesn't mean anything to me. Sorry I can't help you." He sent a crafty look at Allaben. "What do you care if he's got a snake tattooed on his arm, anyway? Got anything to do with that business at Antietam?"

Allaben smiled back at him. "That's for me to know and you to find out."

He dipped an oyster in red sauce and gulped it down.

"What good's knowing you if you won't ante up once in awhile? Don't I give you the inside scoop? Besides, I'm paying tonight. So, come on – fair's fair – what's the story with those two dead guys?"

"Right now, Del, all I know is that the first one, Gwynn, was shot with a large-caliber rifle. The ranger is more problematical. Might have fallen, might have jumped, might have been pushed. All we know for sure is he died from the fall."

"I can't say I knew Curtis Gwynn, but I knew of him."

Allaben did not try to conceal his surprise.

"*You?* How?"

"The Fish & Game Club. The one I belong to. He was a member. Joined late in the spring. I'd see him there now and then. Not the joining type, if you ask me."

"You mean your club?"

"I mean any club. He seemed out of place. Kept his distance.

There was something off-putting about him. Also, I hated that ponytail of his. It's funny, you find all types at the club, but they all want to be there. With Gwynn, I don't know why he bothered."

"How's it work? Do you have to be put up for membership?"

"Supposed to be. But a thousand dollars will do just as well. Or, now that I think of it, if you're someone the clientele would want to rub elbows with, like a Major League baseball star. Then you just might get a temporary membership. Gratis, no doubt."

"Rod Hurley? Really?"

"Really. And why not? Country boys and guns, you know. The guy's bound to miss his buck hunts. Hell, I wouldn't be shocked if he were there right now."

"Well, Gwynn was no baseball star. Any idea who put him up?"

"Not a clue."

"How would I find out?"

"The membership secretary. Calvin Moore is his name. He'd be able to tell you."

Allaben gazed out the window. There was a question forming somewhere. He was as absorbed in locating its source as in the words with which it would take shape. It came to him in the same instant that he realized he was staring at the intersection where Gwynn had almost been run over two weeks before.

"Del," he ventured, "the car dealer, Don Parker. Is he a member?"

"Sure. I see him and his wife there. And the guy on the posters, Mason Greer, our next attorney general. I hear he's Parker's brother-in-law. Don't see much of him since the campaign heated up. But he used to come quite a lot. Jeez, Felix, it's a small world. Pull a name out of the hat. Try me again."

Allaben went silent for a moment while he chewed on this news. His ruminations led him to another speculation, even airier than the last.

"Roger Irwin. Is that a name you know?"

Delvecchio looked at him carefully.

"Upper-class type? Asian gal for a wife?"

Allaben nodded.

"You're batting a thousand, Inspector. What kind of hat are you pulling them from?"

"You're in it, too."

"And so are a lot of others."

Allaben thought this over, then returned to his inquiry. "All right, Del. One more time. Tell me that Hal Snyder was a member, too."

"The ranger who fell off the tower? Sorry, Felix. You just crapped out. I never heard of Snyder before all of this."

"How often do you go?"

"How's this work, Felix? You're the only one who gets to ask a question?"

"It's the way it works when you've got answers and I don't."

Delvecchio sighed and went on. "During the baseball season, maybe once a month. More often in the fall and winter. Meetings are every other week. You talk fishing and hunting, compare notes, swap stories, drink whisky. Shoot skeet sometimes. Manly stuff."

"No womanly stuff?"

"It's coed, but the women don't generally show up except for the matches and the social events."

"Ever see Irwin's wife there?"

"I'd see her at dances and the competitions once in awhile.

She'd root for her husband. From what I've heard she isn't big on the outdoors."

"What do you hear about Pamela Parker?"

Delvecchio allowed himself a wry smile. "They say she likes indoor sports."

"Who does she like to play with?"

"You know how it is, Felix. Four or five beers and people start saying things. For example, that she sleeps around. Is this true? Who knows? They might exaggerate. Or they might've got it wrong. Or they might have it in for somebody. They might even think Don Parker's only getting what he deserves."

He paused, but only for a second, which was all the time it took to see the next question coming at him. He raised his hand to head it off.

"No names, Felix," he insisted. "None asked and none given."

Allaben wondered if Del's might not be among those names not given. He was unattached – never married – and therefore under no obligation to deceive, the same as Gwynn had been. And he possessed a sort of brusque vitality that some women found very attractive. A one-night stand? It wasn't at all out of the question. But, he remembered, who was he to talk about one-night stands?

"Got anything else to tell me, Del?"

"I read you like a book," said Delvecchio, studying Allaben's face. "No. I haven't enjoyed the lady's favors. And I wouldn't tell you if I did."

From the point of view of logic, the disclaimer made no sense. Allaben was about to tell him so, just to irk him, but Delvecchio had had enough of this line of inquiry.

"So how about it, Sam Spade?" he demanded. "You going to

tell me why you're so all fired up about the Fish & Game Club?"

"Curtis Gwynn is dead. Roger Irwin shows up minutes after the shot. Don Parker argues with him the night before. You tell me 'no names,' but this morning I heard the name Curtis Gwynn connected to the name Pamela Parker. Gwynn, Irwin, the Parkers – all members of the club."

"But not Snyder."

"No. Not Snyder. Or not as far as you know. We'll check, of course, but I don't expect to find his name on their rolls. Still …" he trailed off.

"And that's it?" Delvecchio asked. "That's all you've got? I'd better light a candle for you."

Both men were silent for a time, each drifting into his own thoughts. Delvecchio had a game tomorrow – two, in fact. The team was traveling to Myrtle Beach, and he still had scouting reports to look through. He polished off his beer and dug in a pocket for his wallet. Allaben still stared out the window.

"Hey, Felix. How's the hand?"

It ached, Allaben realized. It ached like hell. Now his attention was drawn to it he saw that he was flexing it – probably had been for awhile. He often did that when it acted up, often, as now, without being aware of it. A tight fist, as tight as if he were going to hit something, then splay the fingers wide. It didn't so much dispel the ache as dilute it, spread it over the length and breadth of his hand. Let the hand rest for a moment and the pain would once more condense, gravitate to the palm, and there, just east of the lifeline, settle beneath the scar of puckered flesh.

As a barometer his hand was unreliable. It hadn't troubled him at all the day before, despite the humidity and the downpour. Today it was a different story. Old-timers say they can feel it in their bones when rain or cold is on the way. The bullet that had torn through Allaben's left hand hadn't so much as touched a bone. And he didn't know if it was going to rain or not. But something was going to happen, something extremely unpleasant. Of this he was certain.

Delvecchio hailed a waiter and asked for the check, then turned to Allaben. "That Carolyn's a looker," he declared. "About time you got out."

"Don't start, Del."

"I'm just saying."

"I'm just saying, too."

"You need someone to call the pitches, someone you can trust."

"Is that an offer?"

A faint blush rose on Delvecchio's cheekbones. "You and me go way back, Felix. I got a right to worry about you."

"Funny you should say that," Allaben replied. "Because everybody in this case goes way back, except Gwynn, and he goes way back with me."

"Small town rules. You play against people you know. Anything else you want to take off me?"

"Yes, one more question," Allaben replied. "Guns. Do they keep guns at the club?"

Delvecchio's face reflected the glow of the streetlight. "It's a gun club, isn't it? Yes. A couple of gun cases – locked, for your information. Steward keeps the only key. Some antiques on display, Civil War rifles and revolvers. Can't be fired, I think. And members can keep hand guns in their lockers, which must be locked, too."

"Do you keep one there?"

"Yeah, I do. A shotgun and a couple of pistols. More convenient that way. Pain in the neck hauling them back and forth. Now what do you say you leave the tip? Least you could do, seeing as how I threw you so many fat ones."

18

It took four rings for Lester Dawson to snatch the correct cell phone from his desk drawer and answer it. The call, from former state senator Dale Froehling, was expected. He'd been waiting for it for the better part of the day.

"You're a tough man to get hold of, Dale."

"Well, you're not the only busy man these days. I got a campaign to get up and running, and this has been a heck of a week – a banner week, to tell the truth. Thing is, we just dug up some dirt about my opponent."

"Like what? Caught her in a lover's nest with her girlfriend's girlfriend?"

"Something like that. We're working out how best to use it."

"Can I be of assistance?"

"You sure could, Lester, and I'll be damned if there haven't been times I'd wished you were right here. So, tell me, how's it going with Bull Markham? Tough bastard, no?"

Dawson paused before he answered. Tough? Yes. Reliable?

Hard to tell.

"He's a cocky son of a bitch. I'll give you that," Dawson said. "A little rough around the edges for my sensitive nature. And the fiasco at that ballpark in Lynchburg, well, that gave me pause. But my gut says he's more dependable than not. And he's certainly champing at the bit. Appears to have some kind of private army thing going."

"Bunch of Iraq cronies. He's done some work for us before and, aside from that minor league stadium mess, no complaints. Yeah, I suppose he wouldn't make too many pals at a Harvard Club social, but he's a straight shooter. He thinks like we do."

"He sweats. I'm wary of sweaters."

"Aren't we all? Now, Lester, bring me up to speed on that, uh, other thing. You know what I mean."

"Hold on." Lester Dawson poured himself a couple of fingers of the single malt he'd evacuated from a desk drawer. He took a small sip. "Still doing my due diligence there. Moving ahead, but cautiously. The cat's still deep in the bag – no one but our inside guys knows a thing about it. It's a game changer, Dale. And, for now, I'm keeping Bull Markham and his foxhole buddies out of it."

"Makes sense, Lester. Now tell me about Mason Greer. How much does he know about what's on the horizon?"

"Nothing. And I intend to keep it that way. He's got his hands full, what with those battlefield deaths in his backyard during his campaign. The local sheriff isn't getting anywhere is what I hear. Plus there's this federal agent pain-in-the ass on the prowl. Trust me, Mason is best left out of this."

"I do trust you. Can't let anything come back and bite him. The less he knows, the better, as they say. And, by the way, I see that his polling numbers are real encouraging. Looks like a happy ending's in store there. Kudos to you, my friend, you must be pushing all the right buttons."

"I try, Dale."

"Keep me in the loop."

"Count on it."

19

Allaben still slept on "his" side of the bed. It was a king-size bed, so a good share of it went unoccupied. He had tried planting himself in the very middle – had even gone so far as to erect a levee of pillows to keep him there. All for nothing. Invariably he awoke to find himself in his accustomed berth, as if deferring, in the habit of sleep, to the ghost of his wife.

As a pup, Pedro had been permitted to sleep on a rug at the foot of their bed. Allaben had not approved of this practice. It did a dog no good to be coddled in such a fashion. But he had bowed to the wishes of Rebecca, who could not bear the mournful cries sent up by the castaway from his lonely isle downstairs.

"Let him cry," Allaben had advised. "Two nights and he'll be over it."

But Rebecca couldn't abide two minutes of his keening, never mind two nights. Thus she and Pedro had got their way.

And so, when Allaben awoke on Wednesday morning, he found himself face to face with the Labrador, whose coal-black muzzle rested on the margin of the bed not a foot away from his own.

"What time is it?" Allaben mumbled.

Pedro wagged his tail. He knew a rhetorical question when

he heard one.

It was 9:15 when they returned from their morning walk. At 9:45 Allaben was showered and shaved, at 10:10 breakfast was cleared away, and at 10:15 he was parked at his desk. He stared at the phone. He had left a message for Folliard the night before. It was time to call Washington.

Folliard wasted little time on pleasantries.

"I got your message, Felix. I've made a few calls this morning."

"What do you have for me, Sam? Is Irwin CIA?"

"Right forest, wrong tree."

"FBI?"

"Bingo. Irwin's under contract – something to do with monitoring the lunatic fringe."

"I thought that was your territory."

"My territory's bigger than that," Folliard replied. It was not a boast but a statement of fact.

"Do you know him?" Allaben asked.

"I know the name. Might he have been keeping an eye on Gwynn?"

"I don't know why. Gwynn was a loner. I can't picture him with passwords and secret handshakes."

"I'd check into it, Felix."

"I'll tell you this, Sam – someone's keeping an eye on me."

In a few words Allaben described the incident in the parking lot of Harry Grove Stadium.

Folliard listened in silence, then asked, "A coiled snake?"

"Yes, as in 'Don't tread on me.' Does it mean something to you?"

"No, but you probably should look into that, too."

"Irwin didn't own up."

"To what? That he draws a check from the Bureau? That you're on the same side? You know how the game works, Felix."

"I learned it from you."

"Then let me remind you. In this business, there is no same side."

"Is that why you're interested in Gwynn?"

"He was killed on government property."

"Come on, Sam. Level with me."

"You just do your job, Felix. And keep me posted."

At the same instant that Allaben hung up the phone he heard a car door slam. Someone had pulled into the driveway. Allaben glanced through the window of his study in time to see a woman in sunglasses striding up the brick path to the front door. In the driveway behind her sat a sleek white Lexus, polished to within an inch of its life.

Allaben waited for her knock before he opened the door. The woman stared at him through the screen-door mesh. He was sure he had never seen her before, but when she removed the glasses he knew who she must be. There was no mistaking those eyes.

"Mrs. Parker?" he ventured.

"Yes. I'm Pamela Parker," she replied. Her voice was low and syrupy.

He pulled open the screen door and she swept by him, then paused for directions.

"This way," he said. "We'll talk in the study."

She took a seat in one of the two armchairs, crossed her legs, and pulled a large embroidered handkerchief from her purse. She was dressed all in white – tailored suit; purse of patent leather;

heels; strand of pearls at her throat. Allaben looked for and found a wedding band on her left hand. She sat silently, coolly studying him as he took the measure of her.

The room was awash in morning sunshine, but she did not shrink from the unsparing light. She had no reason to. Blond hair, tinted butterscotch, eyes the same prepossessing blue as her son's, and a figure ample where it ought to be. "Ripe" was the term that came to mind. Plainly, no expense had been spared in fending off time's oily advances. Though she had to be pushing forty, she might, to the casual observer, have passed for ten years younger. Except, perhaps, in the eyes. Though as remarkable in color as her son's, they were lackluster in comparison, as if years of hard usage had worn the shine from them. She gazed at him steadily, waiting for his invitation to unburden herself.

Allaben felt himself under no obligation. He was at heart a gentleman of the old school, but this was business. So he crossed his left leg over his right and said nothing, trusting that silence would work in his favor. It did. She gave a start when the mantel clock struck the half hour, and then, as if that single chime were her cue, she began.

"You have a daughter, Inspector. And I have a son. So you understand that if I appeal to you, it's as one parent to another? Not for my own sake. I'll tell you everything you want to know. But Donnie is sensitive. He feels things deeply, and he gets to brooding. I don't want him mixed up in this. He knows more about life than is good for him already. Sometimes the truth asks too high a price. Sometimes it isn't worth it. This is one of those times, Inspector. I don't want you asking him questions. Ask me the questions. There isn't anything you're going to find out from him that I can't tell you."

The handkerchief was crushed into a wrinkled ball. Allaben counted to five. His turn.

"All right. Where was your son on Sunday morning?"

"Home."

"You're certain?"

"Yes. I looked in on him when I got out of bed. I didn't hear him come home Saturday night. Sometimes he stays with friends."

"You were with your husband at the bar in Sharpsburg."

"Yes. It's Don's kind of place, and from time to time I do play the dutiful wife."

"You saw Curtis Gwynn there."

"I saw him. I didn't speak to him. He and Don got into a shouting match. I kept out of it."

"What was the shouting about?"

"Something about land development. My husband's usual tirade against preservation. I didn't pay much attention."

"You knew that in reality it was about something else."

She shrugged. Allaben tried a different tack.

"What about your husband?"

"What about him?"

"Where was he?"

"Sunday morning? At home. With me."

"Are you sure about that, Mrs. Parker?"

"What's that supposed to mean?"

"Your husband didn't seem so sure."

"What did he say?"

"Didn't he tell you?"

A little color showed through her make-up. "I suppose you're paid to think the worst."

He ignored the observation. "Can you be certain that your son was in the house early Sunday morning?"

"Back to my son again? I'm as certain as *I* need to be."

"He didn't know Gwynn?"

"I don't think so. Look, I didn't check in on him. He stays up later than I do – a lot later. I haven't tucked him in in years. But he's a good kid. Stays out of trouble, does his school work, always has a job. I love my son. Lord knows I haven't been the world's best mom. But I do love him dearly. And he knows that I do."

"About what time was it when you checked on him that morning?"

"Oh, I don't know. Maybe 9, maybe 9:30. Look – when I got up, he was there in his room."

Late enough for him to have been to the battlefield and back, Allaben thought. But he kept the thought to himself, and changed the topic.

"What were your relations with Gwynn?"

Pamela Parker glanced away for a moment, and then, as if preparing for something unpleasant to drop into her lap, smoothed the handkerchief over her knees.

"I met him at the gun club one night. He made a pass, which I ignored. A day or two later I walked into the shop where he works on North Market Street. The owner is looking for a larger space. And there he was. Curtis, I mean. One thing led to another. We met maybe a dozen times over two and a half months."

"When was the last time you met?"

"Last week, Thursday. And that would have been the last time even if …"

"If he hadn't found himself unavoidably detained. So you

broke it off?"

"Yes. The truth is, a little of Curtis went a long way."

"And your husband?"

"We have an understanding, Inspector. He's told you about it. I don't ask him, and he doesn't ask me."

"Understanding or no, it's nothing to me, Mrs. Parker. It's none of my business. What I do care about is who knew what. So let me ask you again, point blank. Did your husband know about you and Curtis Gwynn?"

Allaben waited. It was like pulling teeth.

"Yes," she admitted. "I don't know how he did, but he knew. We quarreled. He was furious. Don't ask me why. He wouldn't explain. Only it was ditch Curtis or else. And Curtis wasn't worth making a stand for. So I let him go."

"How did Gwynn take it?"

She tugged at her skirt. "How would you take it, Inspector?"

As he considered the question, the phone on the desk rang. It was Wick Mallory.

"Felix," he said, "I've got news about Hal. Turns out we've got a witness. I just talked with him myself. Hey, pardner! We're beginning to get someplace."

20

It was nearing dusk when Allaben returned to Frederick. The wet street glittered with the tail lights of the car in front of him. The drizzle that had begun as he left for Boonsboro in the morning had gone on all day. The drive back had been punctuated by the beat of windshield wipers. Back and forth, back and forth, like a tireless semaphore. He allowed himself the observation that the windshield was not unlike the case.

Hal Snyder's death had probably not been murder. Or at least there was now some evidence that there had been no foul play. A sweep of the wiper, and the spatter of Hal's blood no longer need obscure the picture. Unless there was more – or less – to the evidence than there seemed to be.

Early in the morning D.T. had taken a call from the father of a teenage boy who claimed to have seen something at the observation tower at Bloody Lane. D.T. had passed on the news to Mallory, who had in turn called Allaben. In recognition of the fact that the youth had come forth voluntarily and because the family was known to D.T., Mallory had agreed to interview the boy in his home in Boonsboro rather than summon him to the sheriff's office in Hagerstown.

There were two very conspicuous police cruisers parked in the driveway when Allaben arrived at the address Mallory had given him, a small frame house at the edge of the village. A wooden scroll inscribed "The Browns" was fixed to the front door of the house. D.T. opened the door and let Allaben into the living room, where the three members of the Brown household sat in stoical silence on a couch of faded plaid. The room smelled of a long sickness. Between father, a sallow stick of a man, and mother, not so haggard but far from robust herself, sat the young man in question – fresh, pink, and brawny – the picture of health and vigor. The two who bracketed him seemed far too old and far too feeble ever to have been his parents. Which, in a sense, they were not. For Allaben had soon learned that the boy – his name was Jeremy – had been adopted as a toddler.

The introductions and background out of the way, Mallory invited Jeremy to tell his story just as he had told it to D.T. Jeremy had proceeded to do just that.

Monday evening he and a friend – it was a condition of Jeremy's testimony that she remain nameless – had driven to the battlefield, parked his car along the side of Route 34 just east of Sharpsburg, and strolled to Bloody Lane. There they had turned onto a dirt road that was off limits to the public, one that led to a privately owned farm within the battlefield grounds, and in a moment were out of sight of anyone – a park ranger, for example – who might happen by on patrol. Their object was a wooded knoll about a hundred yards distant from the tower. From their hideaway they could see its top. Jeremy had checked his watch upon gaining the hill: 7:05. He remembered it exactly because his friend was to be home by nine o'clock sharp, which meant they had a little less than two hours to smoke the joint he had tucked in his pocket, pick up some ice cream, and return her to a vigilant daddy's safekeeping.

They had been halfway through the joint when they first noticed two figures at the top of the tower, figures that even at that distance they had recognized as rangers. The hats had given them away. Besides, who but rangers would be so bold as to climb to the observation deck and show themselves to the world after the park had closed?

The next time he looked, about five minutes later, he saw only one hat: one ranger.

Of course, Jeremy could not be absolutely certain whom he had seen. The distance was too great. But they had seen no one else near the tower. And hadn't it been a ranger who had died? And hadn't that ranger been Hal Snyder?

The fall – or jump, for the latter still could not be ruled out – they hadn't witnessed. Nor could they say for sure how much time had passed when he first noticed that no one was up there anymore. Jeremy had given an estimate of no more than ten minutes. They had heard nothing – no shout, no cry, no scream. And for the half hour or so that they had stayed after last seeing him they had noticed no one else in the vicinity. The next day Jeremy had learned of the ranger's death and put two and two together. It had taken another day to muster the courage to tell his parents what he had seen and how he had come to see it.

Allaben pulled into his driveway. He doused the headlights and turned off the radio. The rain pattered on the rooftop of the cab and flowed in rivulets down the windshield. He sat and thought about Jeremy Brown's story.

He believed it, to begin with. So did Mallory and D.T. The kid had no reason to lie – not about what he had seen, in any event. What he was up to with the girl was a different story. She would have to be questioned privately to see that her story squared with his.

Okay, they had been smoking pot. So what? Brown's account agreed in every part with such circumstantial facts as were known. The chronology was right; it squared with Poole's account. And there was no physical evidence, no signs of a struggle, for example, to suggest that anyone else had had anything to do with Snyder's death.

The kid had seen Poole and Snyder standing at the top of the tower, and no one else – end of story. It seemed therefore that the ranger's death could be dismissed as in any way related to Gwynn's. Though that dismissal did nothing at all to clarify the focus of Allaben's case. On the contrary, it returned him to where he had begun – less one material witness and/or suspect.

His stomach grumbled. Pedro would be famished, too. Allaben donned his hat, pocketed the car keys, and made a dash for the front door.

After he'd fed the dog, Allaben turned to his own needs. He poured himself a glass of wine and rustled up some eggs. He ate at the kitchen table while he glanced through the evening papers. The Gwynn story had moved inside, where it stood shoulder to shoulder with the follow-up to Snyder's. Then he turned on the TV and watched a couple of innings of the Orioles-Yankees game, a blow-out that the Orioles were winning 10 to 2. He turned off the TV, then walked to the door and stuck his head outside. The rain was tapering off, so he took Pedro out for a walk.

When he came back in, he checked on the game again. It had begun to rain at Camden Yards, and the score was now 14 to 2. He switched to the 11:00 news, and, when that was over, killed another hour with a Mexican soccer match. At 12:45 he headed up to bed, tired but not sleepy, with Pedro bringing up the rear.

The phone rang just as he reached the top of the stairway. He had a book in one hand and a glass of water in the other. The answering machine was on. And it was late. All the same he stood and listened. The machine clicked on, the recording played, the message tone sounded. He could not make out the words, and he didn't recognize the voice at first. It was a woman's, but not Carolyn's, not Pamela Parker's. Where had he heard it before? Then he remembered – Gehring Street, halter top and cutoffs. He put down the book and the glass, drummed down the stairs, raced to the desk, picked up the phone.

"Hold on," he said. "I'm here."

The voice on the other end waited. When he turned off the machine, she started again. "It's Kate Boyd, Mr. Allaben, from Gehring Street. I know it's late and all, but something's going on over there."

"Over where?"

"Next door, at 88. I just seen someone coming down the stairs from his apartment. I don't believe he wanted to be seen. He was real careful and quiet. I'd never of known but I happened to be in the bathroom to get Frankie some aspirin and I looked out the window."

"Are there lights on?"

"The whole house is dark."

"Did he see you?"

"Don't think so. Should I call the police? I remembered you were interested in the guy, and I've got your card right here. So I called you."

"I'm coming right over. Leave the police to me."

"How long?" she asked.

He did some quick calculations. She seemed strangely calm, but he did not want to keep her waiting.

"Give me a few minutes. Keep the doors locked, and stay inside."

"They say that in the movies," she observed. "Just get yourself over here."

21

He made it in ten minutes. He drew up to the curb, got out of the truck, and walked briskly up the walk to the house. The porch light was on. She met him at the doorway, dressed in bathrobe and rubber sandals.

"Everything okay?" he asked.

She nodded.

"Frankie's asleep. And it's quiet as the grave over there."

"All right. You sit still. I'll go check the apartment, then come back here."

She looked at him doubtfully. He showed her his watch.

"I'm going to take this nice and easy, Mrs. Boyd. So be patient. Fifteen minutes. Then you can start to worry. Worry for five minutes, then call the police. And don't forget to tell them I'm up there. Now turn out the light and get back inside."

He stood on the darkened porch for a moment, studying the house next door. No lights, no signs of life. He slipped from the porch and crossed the driveway. Allaben's gut told him that the house was empty. Nevertheless, it occurred to him as he reached the foot of the stairways leading to Gwynn's flat that he didn't have his gun.

He did have the keys, however, though he only needed one

of them. The top lock – the deadbolt – was unlocked. In the dim light he could not tell for sure if it had been forced. The bottom latch, which only needed the door to close in order to do its work, was still locked. Allaben found the key to it and quietly let himself into the apartment.

The smell of fresh paint overlay the stale odor of cigars and old upholstery. Yes, Gwynn had been a cigar-smoker – hence his acquaintance with Ozzie. Allaben stood stock still, listening as if his life depended upon it, while his eyes adjusted to the dark. He heard nothing at all, not even the false silence of someone in hiding. As the room materialized around him he saw he was in the kitchen, and that directly opposite him there was a door that led to windows on the far end of the apartment. Through the windows set above the sink to his right he could now make out the midsection of the maple tree that bordered the sidewalk.

He felt along the wall for the light switch, found it, snapped it on. A ceiling fixture spread a waxy yellow varnish over the room. He looked around – no evidence of fresh paint. Directly beside him and against the wall stood a dining table of dark veneer. Three chairs were tucked into place around it. There was no other furniture in the room. Allaben crossed the cracked linoleum floor to the sink and turned on the tap. Water gurgled from the faucet. He opened the refrigerator. It was practically bare but still running. Likewise the gas stove. No one had troubled to inform the utilities that they had lost a customer.

He then treaded self-consciously through the doorway. To the left was a short hallway, with a door set into each side. One opened to a large bathroom furnished with a free-standing porcelain tub. Allaben peeked behind the shower curtain that encased it. No one shouted "Boo." No surprises, either, in the bedroom, which was as spare and as drab as a one-star motel. Obviously, Gwynn did nothing in here but sleep and entertain Mrs. Parker. And perhaps stare out the window, which provided a discrete but ample view of the upstairs windows of the house next door – and of its backyard, too, if you didn't mind a little craning. Just now there was nothing of much interest to look at, however. Kate Boyd was following his instructions to the letter.

He glanced at his watch: 1:07. Kate had another five worry-free minutes, more than enough time for him to satisfy himself that there was no trespasser on the premises besides himself. A thorough search, in the company of a representative of the Frederick Police Department, could wait until tomorrow.

The living room was the largest in the apartment. A faded red carpet covered the floor. For seating, there were a threadbare sofa and a lumpy armchair. A desk was set against one wall, its surface awash in paper. Against another a scaffold of brick and plank had been raised as a makeshift bookcase, each of its five tiers jammed with books, magazines, and file boxes.

Allaben switched on the desk lamp and fingered casually through the papers, a miscellany of junk mail, unopened bills, checking statements, and handwritten notes and memoranda. The top right-hand drawer, the only one that might have held papers, was slightly ajar. Had Gwynn left the desk in this condition? Or had someone entered the apartment and rifled through it?

Nothing else in the room – or in the apartment, for that matter – bore any sign of a search. The book cases were crammed but not disheveled, and he saw no flagrant gaps in their ranks. He crossed for a closer look. Outdoors magazines, Civil War periodicals, half a dozen file boxes. It would take hours to go through all of it. And Allaben now had only two minutes before Kate was formally scheduled to begin worrying. There were books, too, easily a hundred or more – a handful of paperback thrillers and a smattering of dog-eared volumes of political philosophy, but by far and away the largest share of them on Civil War subjects.

For the most part these were popular accounts of this or that battle, general histories, standard biographies, personal memoirs – in short, the sort of titles one would expect to find on the bookshelves of any student of the War. But cheek to jowl with these were a few rare specimens, too. For example, a calfskin-covered, oversized edition of E. P. Alexander's *Military Memoirs of a Confederate*. What would Gwynn be doing with a book like this, a book that would do Irwin's library proud, a book that might cost hundreds of dollars? Allaben carefully pulled it from the shelf and lifted the front cover. He was looking for an inscription, a book plate, a receipt – anything that would speak to its pedigree. But he found nothing except the price, which had been lightly penciled on the fly cover: $125. Gwynn's pockets weren't that deep.

He was about to restore the book to its place when he noticed that something had been pressed into its pages. Tucked between pages 190 and 191 he found a manila-colored envelope, roughly six by nine, clasped at one end. Inside it were pamphlets, a newsletter titled "Klan Watch," newspaper clippings, and a smaller, white envelope.

Allaben paused to consider the protocols, then made up his mind. He packed all of its contents back into the manila envelope, closed the clasp, folded it lengthwise, and stuffed it into his jacket pocket. He replaced the book exactly as he had found it, then stood for a final survey of the room. Everything appeared to be in order. He went to test the windows that overlooked the roof of the porch below. With agility and strength someone could mount the roof and enter the flat through them. The windows were shut but not locked. Allaben locked them.

Now he had to hurry. He turned and was headed for the kitchen when he distinctly heard a click and, an instant later, a loud puff. He stopped dead in his tracks, praying that the sounds didn't mean what he feared they might. Booby trap? For an instant he was back at the police academy. The ghost of Curtis Gwynn smirked at him. Then the kitchen exploded. Allaben only managed a sidewise glance at the brilliant flash that followed, for he was already flying backward, stunned, trying in his confusion to understand how he'd been slammed to the floor.

When he came to, he sat up, then tried to stand, but his legs wouldn't support him. The kitchen had gone pink. Smoke was ducking under the top of the doorway, swirling in billows of nasty gray over the ceiling above him. He did not so much see the fire as hear it, a violent chattering vortex. And it was coming his way. He felt its advance on his face and his hands. It seemed impossible that it could have so quickly got so hot. How long had he been out? Again he tried to stand, and this time remained upright, wobbling like a drunken man. The room was filling with smoke, and breathing, ordinarily the simplest thing in the world, was already becoming a dreadful chore.

Allaben knew a thing or two about fire, knew that he must act now if he was to survive, that in seconds the fire's lethal gases would poison his judgment and leave him defenseless, then insensible, then dead.

There was only one way out. He stumbled toward the windows, fumbled with the lock, and with an immense effort drew up the sash. The inrush of damp night air confused him. He hesitated. Was this truly deliverance or a deadly trick? Whom was he asking? He dared not turn to face the malevolent creature behind him.

"Jump!"

It was Kate Boyd, pleading with him from the middle of the lawn below. The maple trees behind her were flickering orange and green.

"Jump!" she screamed. "For God's sake, get out of there!"

He heard sirens in the distance. He could barely stand, much less jump. All the same, he hoisted himself onto the sash. A whoosh sounded and glass shattered behind him. From sash to roof was a drop of about a yard, from roof to ground another four. Allaben wasn't a gambler, but he had to like those chances. With a final shove he pitched himself out the window.

22

Allaben spent the night in Frederick County Hospital, where he was treated for smoke inhalation and assorted bruises and lacerations. He looked a lot worse than he felt. He had told the doctors so, arguing for his release. He'd call Ozzie for a lift home, or Delvecchio, or they could call a taxi for him. But the doctors insisted that he stay overnight for observation. There was no sign of hemorrhage, but they couldn't entirely rule out the possibility of internal injury. After all, he had tumbled from a second-story window, rolled like a hedgehog down a porch roof, and plummeted a dozen feet to the ground. Luckily, he had been met not by cement but by a muddy flower bed.

He had talked to a detective from the Frederick Police Department shortly after he had been shunted from emergency room to a private room, and he had been permitted calls to Ozzie and to Mallory before a baleful nurse had stuck a needle in his arm. In minutes he was in another galaxy, as far from trouble as a pharmaceutical magic carpet could carry him.

When he came around early the next morning, still groggy with sedatives, he did not understand where he was. Nor did he very much care. Worry seemed pointless, even foolhardy. He lay on his back, staring in fuddled satisfaction at the shadowy ceiling, vaguely pleased with his lot. Wherever he was, he was safe.

It was a different story when he awoke again three hours later. He ached everywhere. Daylight streamed onto his bed, glinted on the guard rails. He lifted his arm to check his watch and was surprised to find it gone. In its place was a white plastic bracelet. Not that the watch would have done him much good – he couldn't bring anything closer than his feet into focus.

Besides his own, there was one other bed in the room. It was empty. But Allaben was not alone. A voice gave notice that he had company.

"About time," the voice said.

He sat up. Stiff and sore, yes, but he could work through it. Carolyn was sitting in a vinyl armchair near the doorway, dressed in a sleeveless striped shirt and blue jeans. A newspaper lay folded in her lap. The sun was fully upon her. She seemed to glow.

"Carolyn?"

His voice fluttered; he sounded like a bad recording of himself. He was not completely sure that he wasn't dreaming, that it was really her and not a narcotic image he'd conjured up. What would Carolyn be doing here? Not that she wasn't welcome. On the contrary, her smile – whether honest flesh or apparition – was good medicine. He felt better already.

"You don't look so bad for someone who got caught playing with matches. How do you feel?"

"Like the matches got the better of it."

"Can we talk?" she asked.

"As long as you do most of it," he wheezed.

She came to the bedside and poured water into a plastic cup. He took it and drank, then held out the cup for more. She misread the request in his eyes. "I told you, Felix," she said, "that nothing happens in this town without my getting wind of it. Stuart London picked up the fire on the police scanner. He got there just as they were loading you into the ambulance."

"And he called *you*?"

"Earlier this morning. It never hurts to have a newspaper man in your debt. He told me about your adventure. Do you want me to read the story?"

He was vaguely aware that the question she'd answered wasn't the one he asked, but he didn't press her. Instead he fumbled for a button and slowly leaned back. The bed rose up to meet him halfway. Carolyn read from the back page of the paper:

> A man was injured and a retired couple were left homeless by a suspicious fire that raged through a house on Frederick's North Side late Wednesday night. The blaze, which gutted the two-family dwelling at 88 Gehring Street, was first reported at 1:25 A.M. It was brought under control an hour later, according to fire officials. The injured man, whose identity has been withheld by the police, escaped the conflagration by jumping from a second-story window. He was admitted to a local hospital. The owners, Mr. and Mrs. Evander Prescott, were not at home when the fire broke out. Police located the Prescotts in Bethesda, where they have been visiting their daughter and her family. The Prescotts occupied the first floor of the house, which fire officials describe as damaged beyond repair. The second floor of the house was until last week the home of Curtis Gwynn, who was found murdered at Antietam Battlefield on Sunday. Police officers confirm that arson is suspected in the

> Gehring Street blaze. A formal investigation into the cause of the fire will be conducted by fire marshals with the assistance of city detectives.

Carolyn folded the newspaper and returned it to her lap. Allaben lay silently, staring at her vacantly. He hated hospitals, hated the memories – Rebecca committed again, Rebecca medicated again, Rebecca restored and released again. And finally, in Baltimore, Rebecca lost to him for good.

"Penny for them," Carolyn interrupted.

"I'd have to give you change," he replied. His voice was stronger. "But for starters I'd like to know who I have to thank for keeping my name out of the papers."

"The sheriff from Washington County, right? You called him last night."

"Yes. But I don't remember asking him to do that."

"Well, that was Stuart's guess. You can ask the sheriff yourself. He's going to be coming by in a little while. He called from Hagerstown about half an hour ago."

"What time is it?"

"Ten-thirty."

"How long have you been here?"

"Long enough. Somebody's got to keep an eye on you. The things you get up to!"

"More like getting down to."

"Did your life pass before your eyes?"

"No, but Miranda's did," he answered.

"You're really worried about her, aren't you."

"I don't know how to help her."

"You love her. She knows that. And that helps."

"Maybe I should send her to a therapist."

"She probably wouldn't want anything to do with that"

Allaben shook his head in confirmation. "Like father, like daughter. Tolerance for pain – it runs in the family."

"It's not a virtue, Felix."

"Does she know I'm here?" he asked.

"You left very clear instructions that no one should be called." Carolyn pulled a cellphone from her bag. "Here," she said, "call her."

"She's not up – it's 7:30 in California. Anyway, I'm checking out of here."

"The doctors might have a thing or two to say about that."

"The patient might have something to say about it, too. I'm fine. And Pedro needs to be walked and fed. Probably sitting by the back door, ticked off, with his legs crossed."

Carolyn studied him carefully.

"I'll go over there, take care of the dog for you. I'll just swing by on my way to the restaurant. And you could stand a little feeding, yourself," she said.

"I don't think there are any Jean-Pauls on the premises."

"Maybe there is something to be said for Jell-O and yogurt, after all."

"You've done enough just by being here. I'll be fine. Wick Mallory will drive me back to my place. Don't worry about me."

"But I do worry about you."

"Why did we break up?"

"Allaben House."

He was as surprised at his question – it had popped out unbidden and unplanned – as he was at her answer and how quickly it came. As if she'd been pondering the question, too.

"My house?"

"I knew I'd never live there."

"We were eighteen years old."

"Old enough."

"Why didn't …" he began, but then left off when an orderly entered the room with a dry mop and began swabbing the floor. Allaben wasn't sure whether it was relief or frustration he felt at the interruption. Allaben House? He knew he couldn't leave it at that.

"So you worry about me?" he asked.

"I told you I do."

Allaben thought for a moment.

"All right. Come to the ballpark with me Sunday. We can worry together. Game starts at four. Rod Hurley's pitching."

"Come to the restaurant afterward," she said, "and you've got a deal."

Mallory turned up half an hour after Carolyn had taken her leave. He shifted from foot to foot, hat in hand, while nurses and doctors observed the check-out protocols. At length, Allaben was formally released into the sheriff's care, and minutes later they were driving away from the hospital.

Allaben's house was only ten minutes away. Five of those minutes they passed in small talk. Then, just as they reached Bentz Street, Allaben remembered that his truck was still parked on Gehring, where he'd left it the night before.

Mallory turned right at Bentz, then left at Church, and cruised toward the North Side. The police radio squawked from time to time, but Mallory paid it no mind. He sat sprawled behind the steering wheel, right hand at one o'clock, left elbow crooked out the window, sunglasses keeping his eyes secret. Allaben bathed idly in the muggy air funneling through the windows, a tonic to the chemical freeze of the hospital wards.

"You grew up here, didn't you?" Mallory asked.

"Same house I live in now."

"Why did you come back?"

"From Baltimore? I don't know – this is as good a place as any."

"For what?"

"To think things over. It was either Timbuktu or back to where I started from."

"I'd have chosen Timbuktu."

"Do you know where Timbuktu is?"

Mallory pondered. "Not a clue, Felix. But for sure it's a long way from here."

"You don't have to go that far to get a long way from here," Allaben said.

"Farther than Hagerstown. Take my word for it," Mallory replied. "That's why I've hitched my wagon to Mason Greer's star. The man's got his finger on the pulse of this country. With the economy in the crapper and Washington toadies and Wall Street freeloaders doing diddly-squat about it, Mason's got an opening. You watch, before you know it, he'll be going national. People like his step-up-to-the-plate attitude. Get the whiners and the regulators and the hustlers out of the way and take care of business like Americans used to. That's his thing. And it resonates. It resonates with me and a lot of folks like me."

"You've got your eye fixed on bigger things."

"Sometimes you have to take chances. Big ones, sometimes.

When I was a kid, I thought baseball would be my ticket to the big time. Didn't work out that way."

In his mind's eye, Allaben watched the young Wick Mallory clout a fastball over a center field wall, and heard again the awed gasp of the crowd.

"You know, Felix, it's all about high school," Mallory continued. "No, I take that back. It's about the first couple of years after high school. I'm talking about the ones who stick around – not you guys, the ones that go off to college. It's like musical chairs. Turn around and there's one less place for everyone to sit. So you grab it, before someone else does. Push him out of the way if you have to. No one around telling you to play fair anymore. No coaches to smell the beer on your breath or yell at you to stay off the weed."

"You could hit it a mile, Wick. No question about that."

"Best not to dwell on what might have been," the sheriff replied. "Water under the bridge, and nothing to be done about it."

"Otherwise you go crazy," Allaben said.

"Or soft," said Mallory. "But I am ambitious," he went on. "Nothing wrong with that, is there? I've worked hard. I want to get ahead. I'm not like you. I would have hated you in school. Everything was easy for you, wasn't it?"

"Sure," Allaben replied. "I was the one voted most likely to fall out a window, sprain an ankle, and get his eyebrows singed."

Mallory chuckled. "Why do you do this job, anyway? You don't have to work. And don't you dare tell me that you do."

Allaben gave the question due consideration. "Because," he said, "to quote a French poet, work is less boring than pleasure."

"Hell, Felix. What do the French know about work?"

"It's the diplomatic corps you're destined for, Wick. I wouldn't waste my time with law enforcement if I were you."

"It's hard, nasty work – unless you've got a desk job. And who want's that?"

"I don't like to see the bad guys get away with it," Allaben said. "For me, it's simple. Get the guy who did it and keep him from doing it again. Usually simpler said than done. It's frustrating, but you keep at it until you figure it out. Because what else are you going to do? And you know as well as I do that you don't always figure it out."

"Or you figure it out but don't have the evidence to put the guy away," Mallory added.

He turned onto Gehring Street and pulled up behind Allaben's pickup, which was parked before the walkway leading to number 86, just as he had left it. Allaben was mindful of his debt to a certain resident at that address. He had phoned from the hospital and got Frankie, who told him that his mother had left for work. That left Allaben with the better part of the day to figure out how to thank Kate Boyd for helping him save himself.

On the lawn before number 88 rose a low barricade of maimed furniture, waterlogged bedding, singed rugs, jagged pieces of wall and ceiling. Allaben slipped through a gap in the ring of debris and limped through a garden of broken glass. When he came to within a few yards of the front porch he stopped and looked up at the window from which he had jumped. Through the scorched, empty frame he could see a patch of gray sky. The roof over the living room had collapsed.

Mallory came up behind him.

"You were lucky, Felix."

"There was a funny smell – like wet paint."

"Fire marshal is sure it's arson but doesn't know yet what was used for accelerant. It went up awful fast, even for a torch job."

"What about the owners?"

"The Prescotts? It looks like they're clean. The Frederick boys will take a look at their bank records, finances, and so on. It's not my turf. But this doesn't look like an insurance job to me."

The two men stood in silence, surveying the woeful ruin. The coat of red paint had blistered and peeled at the house's upper reaches, revealing a discolored undercoat of white. Pools of water stood on the porch. The front door had been smashed in; it hung askew on its hinges, the entryway barred by an X of police tape.

Allaben pointed to a muddy gouge in the flower bed, which lay in a flattened shambles.

"That must be where I landed. Scored a 9.8, I hear."

Hal Snyder had plummeted eighty feet onto a slab of unforgiving concrete. By comparison his own date with gravity had been a picnic.

"You don't remember the fall?"

"No. In fact, I can't remember much of anything that's happened in the last couple of days."

"It'll come back to you."

The doctor had told him the same thing. And Allaben knew that both doctor and Mallory were right. But it left him uneasy, this odd sense of vacancy.

"This morning," Mallory went on, "I talked with the cops who brought you in last night. One of them interviewed the woman next door. Not much to go on. No way she'd be able to identify a suspect."

"So now we've got Frederick County mixed up in this mess."

"No more than we want them to be. You figure there's some link between the battlefield and the fire?"

"Don't you?"

"I don't know what to think anymore. Curtis Gwynn was a pain in the ass, I guess. But he was small potatoes. What could a guy like that do to earn himself a bullet in the head and his place torched?"

"Maybe it wasn't what he did, Wick. Maybe it was what he was about to do."

"Are you talking about Pam Parker?"

"She might explain the bullet, but not the fire. The affair, if that's the right word, was over."

"Did she tell you that?"

"Yeah. And I believe her."

Mallory shrugged. "Women."

"What about them?"

"I wish I knew."

The inscrutable nature of women? Allaben saw nothing to be gained in pursuing that line of thought. "It's the fire that puzzles me," he said.

"Maybe it was meant to distract us."

"It's a pretty risky distraction."

"You know as well as I do. If it's done right, arson ain't that risky."

"Does Donald Parker have the wits to do it right?"

Mallory took a moment to consider.

"Yeah, Felix, but Don Parker's lazy. Shoot the guy that's screwing your wife. End of story. No need to get fancy."

Allaben shrugged skeptically. If Donald Parker were to be believed, jealousy could be ruled out as a motive, even if he could not be ruled out as a suspect. Although it could be fairly asked,

Allaben reminded himself, how many husbands really mean what they say about their wives? Or, he added as an afterthought, could say what they mean?

23

Allaben drove himself home. Mallory followed him until they reached Braddock Street. There he flashed his lights by way of send-off, and turned onto Patrick, which would take him to the highway and to Hagerstown. They had arranged to meet at Sharpsburg on Friday morning. In the meantime, both would ponder how best to proceed with the investigation, its knotty contours now blackened by arson.

He unlocked the door, picked up the mail, and walked straight to the kitchen. He tossed the mail on the breakfast table and then poured himself a glass of ice water.

Next he put Pedro on the leash and took him out so he could do his business. He waved to a neighbor. The churchbell rang 2:30.

Back in the house, he climbed upstairs slowly and stiffly and just as slowly and stiffly got into the shower. In 15 minutes he was dressed, still sore but in clean clothes. No shoes, no socks. The bedroom floor felt cool and firm. He studied his face in the mirror as he brushed his hair. Tired, stern, critical.

Time to call Miranda. He wasn't looking forward to it, but sooner or later she'd find out about the fire. Better sooner and better that she learn it from him.

She answered with a laugh.

"What's so funny?"

"I'm playing Scrabble with Russell. He's trying to convince me that *unxius* is a word."

"Is it in the dictionary?"

"No. But Russell says he's a higher authority."

"Miranda, I've got some news for you."

Her tone changed instantly. "Are you okay?"

"I'm fine. I had a little adventure last night."

She didn't say a word while he gave her a censored account of the fire and his escape from it.

"You were in the hospital?"

"I got out an hour ago."

"You're home?"

"Yes. I'm in the kitchen."

"And you're okay? Honest?"

"A little banged up. Otherwise, none the worse for wear."

"Who's looking after you?"

Here was a chance to introduce Carolyn to the narrative. Miranda would probably find out about her sooner or later, too. But no, he was too tired.

"I don't need looking after."

"You should've called me."

Through the big kitchen window Allaben could see a squirrel scamper along the branch of the mulberry tree out back. Squirrels don't fall, he thought. Unless they're shot, he thought.

"I'm calling you now, aren't I?"

"You know what I mean."

"I didn't want to wake you up. Didn't want to worry you."

"What do you think you're doing now? You know something,

Dad? It's not easy being the daughter of Felix Allaben."

He heard a voice – his brother's – just behind his daughter. He heard her say, "He's okay," heard his brother say, "That's what he always says. Ask him if anything's broken."

"Miranda, tell my brother that he can rest easy. A few bruises. Nothing serious. I jumped out a window, that's all. Thing is, it was a second-floor window."

"Very funny, Dad."

"You'll see me the Friday after next, sweetie. See that I'm not fibbing."

"Call me later – just so I know you're still alive."

"Will do, ma'am."

"Russell says you should call him, too."

Allaben poured himself another glass of water and walked to his study. There were no messages on the machine. And for good reason – it was switched off. He had not reset it before rushing out of the house the night before.

Behind his desk two oak filing cabinets sat side by side. He pulled open the drawer labeled F-J, fingered through the G's, and extracted a file folder. Taped to the inside of the file was a small silver key. With the key Allaben unlocked the top left-hand drawer of his desk, then withdrew from the drawer a hinged aluminum case the size and shape of a cigar box. He opened the case.

At its center lay a handgun – a Sig Sauer 9mm automatic. The gray barrel gleamed dully in the weak light. Pressed into the grainy K-Kote grip was the model number, P228. A beautiful gun – elegant, simple, nothing wasted. He released the magazine, slid it from the grip. It held a full clip. He didn't remember reloading after he had last used the gun, which had been in the spring. Folliard had invited him to D.C., asked him to bring along his gun in case they found some time for target practice. That had been Folliard's first attempt to get Allaben back on the horse. Typically, it had been tactless and kind all at once. Folliard loved to shoot. They had gone to a private firing range. It had been the first time since his wife's shooting that Allaben had fired the weapon. And so far it had been the last.

Gun in hand he trudged upstairs. His ankle was sore and now both hands ached. Rest, the doctors had said, and plenty of it. But it wasn't even five yet. Put things in order. Prepare. Then he would rest. In the back of the bedroom closet, hanging in a tangle of belts and braces, he found his shoulder holster. He deposited it next to the gun on the bed.

It was time to get back into the habit. He fitted the holster over his shoulder and tightened the straps – he'd lost a few pounds since the last time he had it on. Then he tucked the gun barrel into the leather sleeve of the holster. The heft of the gun threw the harness a little out of kilter. He made a few minor adjustments and everything was at last in order. He was therefore armed and ready when Pedro barked at the doorbell downstairs.

The gun and holster made a considerable impression on Frankie Boyd, who stood facing Allaben in the open doorway. In Frankie's sullen eyes there was evidence that the hardware had lent Allaben's credit a significant boost. They stared at each other in dumb surprise.

"Frankie?"

"My mom sent me over. Here."

He held out a manila envelope. Allaben took it. Frankie pivoted, set one foot on his skateboard, and launched himself down the walkway.

Allaben addressed his retreating back. "Tell your mother I'll call!"

Unheard or unheeded, the cry received no response. The boy was already half a block away.

Allaben closed the door, his attention now concentrated on the envelope. It had been folded lengthwise, and it was stained with mud. He held the envelope to his nose – it smelled of smoke. Only then did he remember what he had forgotten.

Which first – call Kate Boyd or look through contents of the envelope? Had she looked through it? He returned to his study and dug up her number, then tapped it out on his desk phone. The line was busy. He sat for a moment, vacantly eyeing the envelope. It had been a near thing. Five feet closer to the kitchen when it blew up, another minute on his back in dazed helplessness, Kate silent on the flickering lawn. The banal difference between life and death. Only a whisker's breadth, true, but to the living a miss is as good as a mile. He had spared Miranda these observations.

The mantel clock struck six. He pressed the redial button. Still busy. All right, he would try later. He padded to the kitchen, envelope in hand. Through the doorway to the garden came a drift of cool air, the first hint of evening. He pulled the vodka bottle from the freezer and a lemon from the refrigerator.

Rain water had pooled at the center of the patio table. It shivered when Allaben set down the glass. He wiped down a lawn chair, but enough moisture remained to dampen his back and seat when he sat down. He took a long, deep swallow. Then he opened the envelope.

The most substantial of its contents was the summer issue of "Klan Watch." Allaben leafed through the 8-page newsletter, skimming through the articles, letters, and listings that filled its pages. At page 5, he came to a stop. Here was a compilation of items about militias and hate groups that had recently been in the news. Someone had highlighted a paragraph two-thirds down the page. The paragraph referred to the arrest in Allegany County, Maryland, of two young men affiliated with a militia group known as the Potomac Resistance League. The men had defaced graves in an old Jewish cemetery near Harper's Ferry.

In the margin next to the story, someone had neatly drawn a coiled snake.

There was also a pile of newspaper clippings – a feature story from the Baltimore Sun, a series of articles from the Washington Post, plus a score of news items printed in the Frederick and Hagerstown papers. All were devoted to one of two topics, the militia movement or Mason Greer. Allaben was taken aback. Mason Greer? Several of the articles had been marked up with a highlighter or underscored in ink. No doubt about it, Curtis Gwynn had taken an extraordinary interest in the career of Mason Greer and the doings of the Potomac Resistance League.

And there was more. At the bottom of the manila envelope was another, smaller envelope, a white rectangle that had probably once held a greeting card. The flap was tucked but not sealed. Allaben drew from the envelope a sheet of wallet-size photographs, head-and-shoulder school shots. He recognized the student at once. Staring back at him in duplicate was the Parker boy, as solemn and alert as an owl.

The sheet had originally consisted of six photos, arranged

in two columns of three, just like the ones in the packages that Miranda brought home from school every year when she was little, each year complaining that they were even lousier than the ones of the year before. Allaben wondered if the Parker boy cared as little for his photos as Miranda did hers. He wondered, too, what had become of the sixth of them, the one that had been neatly snipped from a corner.

He turned the sheet over. On the back of each was neatly printed, in blue ball point, "Lancer '91."

Question upon question. He leaned back and searched the purplish face of the evening. What would Gwynn be doing with a photograph of young Donnie Parker? And what was it doing in the same envelope as the other things? And why the coiled snake in the margin, the snake that looked a lot like the one tattooed on Gwynn's forearm and on the shoulder of the guy in parking lot? The mottled sky yawned with indifference. Allaben would have to find the answers himself. He polished off the vodka in one long gulp. Then he went into the house to try Kate Boyd again. Now he owed her twice.

24

In the rear-view mirror Allaben watched a big black SUV come barreling up behind him. It flashed its lights and pulled out to pass. As it swept by, Allaben glanced at its driver, a burly, crew-cut item with a cell phone pressed to his ear. Pasted to the sedan's backside was a blue bumper sticker that shouted "VOTE MASON GREER." It was the sixth such sticker Allaben had seen this morning, and he had only covered half the distance from Frederick to Shepherdstown.

Something had changed. What it was precisely Allaben couldn't say. But between yesterday and today there was a difference greater than could be explained by a calendar. He studied the scenery through the car windows. If there was a clue in the trees, in the sky, in the morning shadows, he couldn't make it out. In the sultry air that rushed through the window were all the signs of another scorcher, a carbon copy of the day before. In half an hour he'd need the air conditioning to keep the heat at bay.

Shepherdstown lay complacently in the hot morning sun, like a confection ready for the oven. He slowed as he passed Lin Irwin's gallery. The green Jeep was parked at the curb before the storefront, but he could see no one behind the prints that hung in the shadowy window. Presumably, her husband would be alone, at least until lunchtime. More than enough time to conduct their business without interruption.

It was only when he topped the crest of the hill and the big white house came into view did Allaben realize what had been troubling him about Roger Irwin. Everything about him was picture perfect – house out of Architectural Digest, good looks, riding boots, bandanna, beautiful wife. Even his breeding, the old-money manner, was like something acquired from a catalog of "only the finest." At first glance he seemed nothing more than the sum of his tastes. But Allaben knew there was more to him than there seemed. He had done his homework, studied the files Folliard had sent. Irwin had started with nothing. Born the son of a factory hand, he'd had good grades in school, won a scholarship to engineering school, did one year of ROTC – from which he'd resigned for health reasons – and got his master's degree from Cal Tech. He'd then joined an engineering firm, got married and divorced in less than a year, supervised a big-ticket project in Manila, and set up his own consulting firm living on Navy contracts. He'd married Lin Posio and retired a year and a half ago. They had no children.

So much for the official record. Unofficially, according to Folliard, Irwin had for some years before he retired been in the pay of Naval Intelligence.

Allaben drew up in front of the garage and turned off the engine. No one in sight. He peeked into the garage. One bay was empty – that would be the Jeep's. The white Jaguar filled one of the other two slots. His own face came reflected into focus in the square pane of glass set into the door. A number of vices might be read into that face, but envy was not among them.

A bead of sweat bled from beneath his hat brim and trickled

down his temple. A good day for the pool, a good day to admire your wife in the pool, a good day to join her in the pool, as one thing may lead to another. Or wasn't it like that for them?

The doorbell was answered by a petite black woman in wire-rim glasses. Mr. Allaben was expected; he could find Mr. Irwin in the horse barn around the back. Allaben followed a brick pathway that circled the side of the house and passed through a gate set into the bristling green hedge. The barn was of weathered gray boards that looked like they'd been stripped from the rickety frame of an old relative. A small tractor sat squarely in the middle of the doorway.

The passage from dazzling sun to deep shadow left him momentarily blind. The air was still and fragrant – hay, leather, sawdust, horse flesh. Dim light seeped through the windows. To his left was the saddle room. Across the way was the feed area and an open stairway that led to a hayloft.

A long, cantankerous snort came from the back of the barn. Allaben walked past two empty stalls, past a wheelbarrow, past a third stall occupied by a stolid, sloe-eyed mare. At the fourth he came upon Irwin, who was crouched beside the haunch of a huge chestnut gelding. Irwin was on one knee, massaging the animal's foreleg. The horse did not seem to care for the ministrations. With its back hooves it performed a little jig. Irwin pulled at the lead. The horse snorted again, this time as much in challenge to a new human presence as in protest to Irwin's nursing.

"Easy, Cupecoy. Easy," he soothed. "Unless I miss my guess, it's just Mr. Allaben paying us a call."

Irwin rose from his crouch and faced Allaben over the horse. A wry, shallow smile curved in parallel to the animal's back.

"I'd offer my hand," he said, "only it's covered in liniment."

He gave the horse's shoulder a comradely slap and ducked under the tether. He pulled a towel from a peg and began to work at his hands. The horse twisted, gazed solemnly at Allaben, its fine head posed beside its master's. Irwin's smile appeared once more.

"Taking the measure of me, Inspector?"

"Professional habit," said Allaben.

"Why don't we compare notes, then, one agent to another?"

So he'd been briefed, probably by Folliard. His voice was colorless. There was nothing in the delivery to suggest whether he meant to be ironic, whether the corn was raw or boiled. Allaben had the odd sensation that he was reading from a script. The next line was obvious.

"Felix."

"Felix it is. And Roger, of course."

The horse whinnied, as if scornful of these human pleasantries.

"Do you know horses, Felix?"

Allaben shook his head. He'd never understood the attraction, despite Ozzie's arguments on their behalf.

"They're very shrewd animals, wonderful judges of character," Irwin went on. He paused, then added carelessly, "Whereas we humans are often and easily fooled."

"Maybe so," Allaben returned, "but it's we who ride them, not the other way around."

Irwin chuckled. "You're nobody's fool, Inspector. And for that reason alone I owe you an apology. I should have been more forthcoming before. But now Sam Folliard's put me in the picture."

"You both could have saved me some time."

"Long habit, you see. Never break one's cover unless it's absolutely necessary. We're trained to be circumspect, which in my case merely reinforces predisposition. I guess you're not so easily satisfied. You'll go to some lengths, take the trouble to look over your shoulder when you hear someone behind you – while I'm content with mirrors. Plain laziness, I confess."

"I don't trust mirrors," said Allaben.

"I didn't say I trust them, only that I'm content with them." His forehead wrinkled in a sardonic frown. "There's iced coffee in the house," he said. "We can talk there."

They sat facing each other over the big desk. Before each rose a cloudy glass brimming with iced coffee. Irwin rested his arms against the desk, pressed his fingertips together, gazed steadily at his guest.

Allaben took a long pull from his glass.

"Who signed you up?" he asked.

"We'd been out here about a year." Irwin was cool and deliberate. "Lin was set up in her gallery. She didn't need my help any more, and I wanted something to do. So I put out some feelers to people in Washington, let it be known I was available. Pretty soon I got a call from Folliard. It turned out he was acquainted with an old friend of mine. I went to Washington to see Sam. We talked. Then he made his pitch. I liked the sound of it. As simple as that."

"It's him you report to?"

"Not directly. One of his subalterns."

"Is your wife on the payroll?"

"No. And she's not at all interested in my extracurricular activities."

"So she doesn't know what you're up to."

"No."

"Anyone outside of Washington?"

"If you mean anyone local, the answer is no. That's the way it's got to be," Irwin went on. "My assignment is to keep tabs on a regional anti-government network. It goes by several names. The outfit here is called the Potomac Resistance League, PRL. A bunch of lunatics – survivalists, white supremacists, kindred spirits. I'm mostly interested in their bankers, though. The agency is taking this stuff very seriously these days. And no wonder."

"What's your relationship?"

"I know something about explosives. And I profess to be sympathetic, of course."

"Sympathetic to what?"

"To their aims – to resist, violently if necessary, the confiscation of American liberties by an overreaching central government, and to expose the state's ruthless conspiracy to stamp out individual freedom."

"And their means?"

"Justified by the ends, to their thinking. And it's not all bluster, either. They've assembled quite an arsenal. M16s, RPGs, radio equipment, C4. They keep it locked up in one of the outbuildings."

"Where's it coming from?"

"Friends in the military."

"I mean the money, the wherewithal."

A dim crash sounded from a couple of rooms away. Irwin cocked an ear in its direction.

"That would be Priscilla," he said. "She's dropped a plate." He listened intently. "Often one is followed by another. Nervous fingers. She knows I've heard it, you see." Neither man spoke. The house was eerily silent. Satisfied, Irwin returned to the matter at hand.

"Money," he resumed. "Some of it comes from sponsors like myself. Some of it is cash skimmed from businesses, some raised at spaghetti suppers. And some, maybe quite a lot of it, comes from beneath very shady rocks. Crime in the cause of liberty is no crime, that sort of thinking. Fraud, embezzlement, money laundering, work for hire, you name it."

"Might murder and arson be added to the list?"

Irwin paused to consider. "I take it you mean the death of Curtis Gwynn."

"He was collecting information about this Potomac Resistance League."

Irwin shrugged.

"You don't seem surprised," said Allaben.

"They enlisted him," Irwin explained. "Through the Fish & Game Club, one of their recruiting grounds. Ex-cop, loner, half-crazy. He fit the profile."

"How did you come by that information?"

"I can't tell you that."

"You have a source inside?"

"Not at liberty to say."

"A name would be useful to me."

"Tell me what you want to know. Maybe I have the answer. If I don't, I'll try to get it for you."

Allaben hesitated, caution going nose to nose with expedience. He did not altogether trust Irwin, but neither did he have much alternative. In order to get he would have to give. But give carefully.

"Do you know Mason Greer?" he asked at last.

Irwin did not seem in the least surprised by this turn. "I know *of* him. I've met him at the Fish & Game Club, of course, but I can't say I *know* him. Who knows a politician, for God's sake?"

He sipped coffee and waited impassively for the next question, which Allaben suspected he knew in advance of its asking.

"Could there be some connection between Greer and the PRL?"

"His brother-in-law is tied to the militia in a big way. But I'd be very surprised to learn that there's anything on paper to link Greer to them. He's a lot more careful than Don Parker. He has to be. What has Mason Greer got to do with Gwynn?"

"Apparently Gwynn took an interest in him."

"Did he?" Irwin blinked deliberately, as if shutting away that tidbit for safekeeping.

Allaben pulled a piece of paper from his pocket and handed it to Irwin.

"Does that mean anything to you," he asked.

Irwin looked at the paper, then at Allaben.

"A snake? Why do you ask?"

Allaben told him why. Irwin let a few seconds pass before replying.

"It does mean something. It's an emblem of the PRL."

"Do all members wear it?"

"No. Only those who've earned one, usually for some special service – in defense of liberty or resistance to tyranny. It's awarded like a medal."

"How many?"

"I don't know the exact number. A couple of dozen, I guess."

"Do you have one?"

Irwin smirked. "You better hope not."

"Do you have a list?" Allaben asked.

"Of recipients of that tattoo?"

"No – of members of the Fish & Game Club who are also in the PRL."

Irwin allowed him a quarter of a smile. "Good for you," he said. "Yes, I do, as a matter of fact."

"Can I have a copy?"

Allaben wondered if the doubts that played in Irwin's eyes weren't very close in nature to those he had himself entertained only a moment before.

"I'll give you a copy," Irwin said, "if you'll give me your word that no one else will see it."

"Done."

"And, furthermore, that you'll inform me immediately of any developments in your investigation that might in any way bear upon my operation. If someone's to be the death of me, I'd rather it weren't you."

Allaben nodded his agreement to the terms, whereupon Irwin stood, as if to signal that the interview was now concluded. So far as Allaben was concerned it was far from concluded. He was about to insist that it wasn't, even if in doing so he torpedoed the ship they'd both just agreed to board, when Irwin turned on his heel and stepped to the wall nearest the desk. There he stood face to face with a framed map, a fine tracery of black on ivory, a little foxed at one corner.

He paused, listening intently for heaven knew what – Priscilla's footsteps, a stair squeak, a car pull into the driveway. Allaben could hear nothing but the steady hum of air conditioning. Neither, apparently, did Irwin. He tugged at a side of the frame. It swung open to reveal a safe built into the wall behind it. In quick order he dialed the combination, removed a plain business envelope, closed the door of the safe, spun the dial for good measure, and returned the frame to its proper position. Allaben got to his feet. It seemed the thing to do. The two men stood facing each other across the desk, like clock figurines waiting for the hour to strike. Irwin's left hand held the envelope. His right he extended to Allaben. It would be a gentleman's agreement. Agreement was fine by Allaben. He only hoped, as he took first the hand and then the envelope, that each knew what the other meant by gentleman.

25

Mallory was slouched against a patrol car, arms crossed and hat tipped back, when Allaben pulled up at his battlefield office in Sharpsburg. The midday sun beat down like a mallet, pulverizing the air into glittering shards of light. Allaben felt himself begin to droop the moment he stepped from the cool cocoon of his truck.

"What in blazes are you doing out here?" he asked.

"Pure obstinacy," said Mallory. "I don't believe in giving in to the weather. Makes you soft."

"Call me a creampuff if you like," said Allaben has he headed for the door of the squat stone building, "but let's get out of the sun."

Mallory leaned through the open window of the patrol car and withdrew a sheaf of papers, then followed Allaben through the doorway. They settled in the annex, where the purring of the fan was now producing something besides noise. Otherwise, the room was just as Allaben had last seen it on Tuesday.

Mallory tossed the papers on the metal desk. "Some things for you to look at," he explained. "Phone records for Gwynn's place, May through last week. The only calls of interest, as far as I can see, are several to Pam Parker – work and cellphone – and a few to Mason Greer. There's the one to your number, too, like you said. Pam we know about, but Mason's a surprise."

"Gwynn was interested in Greer. I found a couple of newspaper clippings in Gwynn's apartment."

"When was that?"

"The night of the fire. They were in an envelope stuck inside a book. The envelope must have come out of my pocket when I took that gainer from the window. The woman in the house next door picked it up, I guess. Her boy brought it over to me last night. I'd forgotten about it."

"How you feeling?" Mallory gave Allaben's shoulder a little prod. "That hurt, for example?"

"Yes, it does. Thanks very much," Allaben admitted ruefully. The truth was, he hurt all over, despite the heavy-duty painkillers he'd swallowed.

"I'll live," he went on, "as long as you keep your distance." He paused again. "Listen, Wick, I haven't told you about something that happened the night before last. I had a run-in with some good ol' boys in the parking lot after the Keys game."

He gave Mallory a 25-words-or-less description of what had happened.

The sheriff gave him a blank stare. "Christ, Felix, why didn't you tell me? Did you recognize them? Could you ID them?"

"Never seen them before. One, the guy in charge, had a tattoo I've seen a couple of times lately – a coiled snake ready to strike. Know anything about it?"

Mallory paused to consider. "I do not," he answered, shaking his head. "I will check into it, though. You say this was two nights ago?"

Allaben nodded. "If it was planned, I'd like to know how they knew I'd be there. Maybe they've been following me. I don't think they expected to see Carolyn. But they sure as hell knew all about me."

"Do you want me to post a cruiser in front of your house?"

"Thanks, Wick, but I can take care of myself. I wouldn't mind seeing them again, though, on a level playing field."

"Nobody takes a cheap shot at a friend of mine. That ain't allowed. Everybody in the county knows that, which is why I can't make heads or tails of this business."

"I don't think these guys were locals."

"Why not?"

"The guy who was running the show knew what he was doing. Wouldn't take a chance like that."

Mallory pondered for a moment. "A snake, you say?"

Allaben considered, then decided to confide in his friend. "Yes. Gray with red trim. The same one Curtis Gwynn had tattooed on his arm."

Mallory considered this piece of information.

"I don't know what to make of it, either. You sure you don't want some protection?"

"I don't want protection, Wick. I want some answers."

"Anything else in the envelope?" Mallory asked.

"A newsletter about Klan and militia activities. There was a story in it about militia groups, one of them in this region. And wallet photos – school pictures, by the look of them – one missing from a sheet of six."

"Who?"

"The Parker kid. Donnie Junior."

Mallory squinted in puzzlement, then shook his head.

"Jeez, Felix. I'm zero for four today. Nope," he said, "I can't make that one out."

"I'm not doing much better," Allaben allowed, happy for the chance to share at least some of Mallory's confusion. Because the rest of it, the link, if there was one, between Greer and the militia he'd have to keep to himself, at least for the time being.

"You say these clippings were about Mason?"

"One from the Hagerstown paper, friendly. Two, not so friendly, from the Frederick Post."

"Stuart London?"

Allaben nodded.

"He's got it in for Mason," Mallory said. "Ever since what Mason said on TV. London printed an article lambasting him for supporting prayer in schools. Mason was on one of those talk shows and got asked about it by a caller. He just plain lost his cool, which doesn't happen very often. Said he wasn't going to stand for a lecture from godless homosexuals and their fellow travelers. It caused quite a stink."

Allaben flipped slowly through the pages of printout. Date, time of day, number called, duration of call.

"Greer never mentioned Gwynn?" he asked.

"The name never came up once that I can recall."

Mallory pressed a finger against the margin at the top of the third page. "Here's the first of the calls to Mason," he said. "It's to the office in Hagerstown. Two more the next day. Then a call to his home number. I'd like to know how he got that."

"Maybe he got it from Pamela Parker."

"Pam wouldn't give him Mason's home number. At least I don't think she would."

"Maybe she didn't give it to him. He could have gone through her contacts list or address book."

"Of course, we don't know whether Gwynn ever talked to him," Mallory cautioned.

"No. But I'm going to find out."

Mallory offered Allaben a quizzical look.

"Are you thinking Mason's got something to do with Gwynn's death?"

"Why shouldn't I think it?"

"You'd know why if you knew Mason. There's some things in this life that are impossible even though you can't give a reason." He paused to concentrate, as if mindful that clarification were in order. "I never knew of a murder that didn't have some need behind it. And Mason's not a needy man."

Allaben returned to the printout.

"Have you identified any of the other numbers?"

"The directory's on the last page. Lots of listings. Take it with you to study at home. You'll see that the last one's to the B&B near the battlefield."

"And we know that he made no long-distance calls."

"Not on that Saturday night, at least from his cell. There aren't any phones in the rooms."

"So we've got him leaving Frederick in time to arrive at the battlefield by 9:00. Spent the day in uniform with scores of other re-enactors. He was at the Mansfield Tavern from about 7:00 to 10:00. The manager at the B&B says he turned up there a little after ten and went straight up to his room. And that was the last time he was seen alive."

"Second to last," Allaben corrected.

"I stopped by the tavern this morning," said Mallory. "Had a talk with Lamb, the owner. Nothing new. His story backs up everybody else's, including Lilly's. You got that list from D.T., right?"

"Yes. Everyone in the tavern that night. Maybe I'll visit Mansfield's again, too."

"Well, give my regards to Simon if you do. A true friend to lawmen."

"Was Simon there?"

"As big as life."

"He said something to me when I was in there Monday," Allaben mused.

"I'll bet he did – something mystical."

"Everything about this case is too damned vague," said Allaben, staring at the corner of the desk where Snyder's note had been stuck. "There's no place to plant your feet, nothing solid."

"How about some lunch, get some solid food?" Mallory interrupted. "We can talk with our mouths full."

Allaben glanced at his watch. "Can't," he said. "I'm due at the hospital for a follow-up."

"Well, Felix," said Mallory as he picked himself up to leave, "I'm following your lead. Want me to talk to Mason?"

Allaben didn't. Why have to wonder whether old friendships would put a brake on Mallory's investigation? He watched the sheriff's palm print evaporate from the desktop. He'd tackle Mason Greer and the Parkers himself.

"No," he said, "not yet, anyway. I've got to think it out. Have you got anywhere with Snyder's death?"

"There's nothing down that road, Felix. Poole's alibi checks out for Sunday, and I haven't found anything by way of motive for him wanting to see Snyder dead."

"And the Baltimore contingent?"

"Four out of five are off the list. They've all got alibis – solid ones."

"What about the fifth?"

"Maitland. Evan Maitland. Haven't caught up with him yet. The latest trace was a call from Oregon."

Allaben remembered Maitland very well. Of the five whom Gwynn had accused of taking money from drug dealers, he alone had not denied the charges. But neither had he turned state's evidence. He'd served his time and then dropped out of sight.

"Did you talk with his wife?"

"'Course we did. And it's ex-wife, by the way. She says she hasn't heard from him in years."

"Well, don't give up on him, okay?"

"Are you trying to tell me how to do my job?"

"Sorry, Wick. It's been one of those days."

Mallory straightened his belt, trimmed his hat. "I'll see you at the barbecue tomorrow?"

Allaben nodded. "Yeah. I got an email from Mrs. Greer's assistant yesterday."

"Good," pronounced Mallory. "Because it's likely to be interesting." And with a careless salute he took his leave.

Allaben folded up the pages of printout and tucked them in his pocket. His leg itched through the salve and dressing. "It could have been worse." So the doctor – a solemn kid with an Eastern Shore accent – had assured him. "The bones aren't brittle yet." Snyder's bones probably hadn't been brittle, either. A lot of good that had done him. Not so long ago, Snyder had warmed the chair Mallory had just vacated and penned Allaben a cryptic "See me." Wishful thinking, as it had turned out. All Allaben had seen of Snyder was a twisted silhouette chalked on stone. Like everything about this case. Vague.

26

A burly, dark-suited man stood at the entrance to the drive leading to the home of Arthur Howe, Esquire, formerly a partner in the law firm of Howe, Evans, and Greer, LLC. The man put up a hand to signal Allaben to stop, then stepped to the side of the truck as Allaben rolled down the window. Something bulged in his jacket pocket. He was sweating profusely.

"It's by invitation only," he announced.

Allaben produced his invitation. The man stared with grim concentration at it and its holder in turn, as if trying to reconcile the irreconcilable. He backed up two paces, allowing himself a more sweeping view of vehicle and driver, shrugged noncommittally, and waved Allaben on.

"There's valets at the house," he said in parting.

In the mirror Allaben watched the man pull a radio from a jacket pocket and tuck his chin to the mouthpiece.

The driveway formed a semicircle set into a broad, sloping lawn. At the top of the hill sat a massive brick house, neo-Georgian in design, with limestone pilasters set into the facade and chimneys jutting like conning towers from the roof. Allaben pulled up before a portico and was immediately relieved of his keys by a liveried valet, who hopped into the truck and whisked it away.

Two men stood in waiting at the doorway. One was a stony-faced fellow in a suit identical to the number worn by the gatekeeper below – professional muscle, like his colleague. The other, a young man with a clipboard, was better dressed – white slacks, blue blazer, rep tie – and more cordial in demeanor. Shoeshine and a smile. Just out of college, by the look of him.

The smile broadened as Allaben approached, and was verging on a beam when a muted summons issued from a radio hidden beneath the bouncer's jacket. The bouncer whispered in the greeter's ear, then slid through the doorway into the house. Geniality undimmed, the greeter stepped forward in welcome. Allaben introduced himself.

"Oh yes, Mr. Allaben. Thank you for coming, Inspector. I'm Brad Richards. I work for Mr. Greer. He's eager to meet you. Now if you'll just follow me, I'll lead you through the house."

The foyer smelled of furniture polish and flowers. A bouquet of gladiolas erupted from a vase on a side table. Richards led Allaben from the foyer through a hallway hung with prints of hunting scenes. Along the way they passed an elaborate stairway and several doors, all shut except the last. Through this Allaben glanced into a spacious library. Two men stood framed before a window, their backs to him. One pointed at something outside and delivered a comment that drew a snort from the other. Then both turned in unison toward the doorway, as if in expectation. One of them, a large, stout, man in a pearl-colored suit, Allaben thought he had seen recently. Where? The other, the comedian, was Don Parker. A grin spread over his face.

"Perfect timing, Inspector," he said. "It's in with the good and out with the bad."

At the end of the hallway French doors led to the backyard patio. These opened suddenly, and a jostle of legs, arms, and torsos came hurrying toward Allaben. In the lead was Richards' partner in the greeting party. Directly behind him was a portly, grim-faced young man. It was Stuart London, and Stuart London was plainly being shown the way out.

"You're a witness, Felix!" he exclaimed as he came abreast of Allaben.

His escorts muscled him along another couple of feet before he managed a temporary halt to the grunting, ungainly procession.

"Crashing the party, Stuart?" Allaben smiled.

"Greer's not got the guts to do it himself!" London shouted. "He's got to have these goons do the dirty work."

"You're trespassing, Mr. London," said one of the rear guard. "You've got no rights on this property."

"I've got a right to civil treatment," London returned. He was dark-eyed, flushed, and tousled. His summer flannels were twisted, and his shirt collar had sprung. Only his defiance saved him from looking ridiculous.

"The bum's rush is no better than he deserves," came a voice – not one that Allaben knew – from the library. Then Don Parker chimed in.

"It's not the bum's rush, Lester. It's the dance of the sugar plum fairy."

"Will you lead, Donald? Or shall I?" London snapped.

A sort of mean confusion reddened Parker's face. He stepped toward London. The bittersweet odor of burned sugar exuded from him. Rum and something, and lots of it.

Allaben put himself between London and Parker. To the

former he said, "Go home, Stuart. I'm not in the mood for a brawl."

London winked at Allaben, and then, without further fuss, allowed himself to be escorted down the hall.

Parker dismissed his retreating antagonist with a wave. "C'mon," he said to Allaben, "let's get you a drink. Then I'll introduce you to the state's next attorney general."

The doors opened onto a vast flagstone patio, into a corner of which a kidney-shaped pool had been sunk. Beyond the patio a manicured lawn fell away toward a beech-lined fairway. Two large tents had been pitched on the lawn beside the patio. In their shade sat long tables, covered in blue cloth. A metal barbecue trough was sputtering and smoking off to the side. Across the patio a bandstand had been assembled. A woman stood at the front of it, mike in hand, crooning some standard that Allaben recognized but couldn't name. Guitar, drums, and keyboard formed a trio behind her. Wick Mallory stood nearby, an audience of one.

There were some fifty or so people milling about in twos and threes and fours, the men in slacks and shirtsleeves, the women in day dresses. A few of the faces Allaben recognized, but most were unknown to him. A bar had been set up under the nearest tent. Parker pitched and rolled in its direction, like a ship skidding in heavy weather.

Allaben trailed in his wake, taking in and being taken in by the other guests. Pamela Parker suddenly emerged from behind a screen of pastel-shirted backs, slipped to her husband's side, and whispered something to him as he sidled up to the bar. To Allaben's nodded greeting she replied with a tight, mean smile. She raised a full glass of wine, and promptly drained its contents. Another two or three of those, Allaben thought, and the fur would surely fly, never mind the occasion. She looked like she wouldn't mind a scene.

Parker seemed already to have forgotten him, and that was all right with Allaben. He asked for a vodka and tonic, then stood nursing it in the shade of the tent while he looked over the crowd. His stomach tightened; he hadn't eaten since breakfast.

It looked like he'd have to make the rounds himself. As much as he hated making small talk to people he didn't know, he couldn't just stand there alone with a drink. Mallory still hadn't taken notice of him. The sheriff stood rooted to a spot directly before the crooner, rocking slightly on his heels. When the last note trailed off and she took her bow, Mallory led the applause. The singer pointed to Mallory in acknowledgment. He seemed to take this as an encouragement, for he ambled to the lip of the stage and mouthed something. She grinned, then pivoted to the guy at the keyboard. Nods went back and forth. Mallory would get his request.

Allaben handed his glass back to the barman. Fortification in hand, he would do his duty.

"Mr. Allaben?"

He turned and found a woman smiling before him. She was petite, slender, fair in complexion but raven-haired. In her dark eyes there was a sort of jaded challenge that hinted of long practice in the social graces. She took the refill from the barman and put it in Allaben's left hand, then grasped his right in both of hers.

"I'm Emma Greer. Thank you for coming, Inspector. I feared you might not. You see, I've heard about your recent misadventure."

Somehow or other, without Allaben being quite aware of how she had managed it, her hand was on his arm and they were walking side by side across the patio. It was, he thought, the velvet glove to the iron fist that Stuart London had received. Guests nodded on right and left as they passed, like courtiers bowing to lords bound for an audience with the king.

"What is it, exactly, that you're investigating, Inspector?"

"I'm not honestly sure, Mrs. Greer."

"And are you an honest man, Inspector?"

"Yes," he answered plainly.

She offered a wan smile. "To my husband's mind," she said, "there is no greater riddle than an honest man. I'm curious to see what he makes of you."

Their path took them past the barbecue pit, where the chefs were busily painting sauce on steaming ribs and sizzling chickens, to a group of three men standing in tight conference at the edge of the pool. One of the men, the tallest, was listening intently to the other two as they addressed him in turn. When the tall one caught sight of the two petitioners approaching, his face unfolded into a broad smile. Allaben did not need to be told that this was Mason Greer. The man was the spitting image of his sister, and of his nephew too, for that matter, the kid who had stared at him at the Burnside Bridge overlook.

"Now, honey, who's this here you've brung me?" he boomed. The good-old-boy was laid on so thick it had to be meant for irony. Greer's candy blue eyes widened in support of the extravagance.

"It's no one if it isn't Inspector Felix Allaben," she drawled. Gone from her voice was the weary timbre of only a moment before. Sarcasm now filled its place. Allaben felt he was being drawn into a farcical conspiracy. What part was expected of him?

Greer sent his wife a sly look that was equal parts rebuke and concession, and then began to pump Allaben's hand.

"You're doing me an honor, Mr. Allaben. Wick Mallory can't

say enough about you, and that's endorsement enough for me. It's high time I made your acquaintance. I said as much to Emma just the other day, didn't I, honey? Weren't those my very words?"

She had turned to study Allaben's face. Greer watched the back of her head, waiting for her dutiful nod before resuming. "I'm always happy to shake the hand of a lawman."

He offered his hand, and Allaben took it. Greer's grip was strong. So was Allaben's.

"Thanks for inviting me," he said.

"I hope you're a Republican," Greer smiled.

"I'm not a party man," Allaben replied.

"It's not party men I'm interested in, Mr. Allaben. It's steady hands. The people feel the drift in this country and mistake it for gravity. Nothing you can do about gravity. It's the way of nature and no denying it. But the drift I'm talking about is moral drift. Graft, cronyism, special interests. You've got a car skidding off the road and no one willing to take the wheel. No one's making the tough choices. Purging the pork. Chopping the fat. Well, see here, Mr. Allaben. Put me behind the wheel and, I promise you, she'll straighten out. And when she does, our kids and grandkids won't be behind the eight ball, footing the bill for all these damn government hand-outs."

"We'll need to talk, Mr. Greer," Allaben said.

"Of course we will. I'll have Brad check my schedule."

"I don't mean politics."

Greer looked at him coolly, the smile still in place.

"You mean that unfortunate business at Antietam, then. The sheriff's kept me abreast of it. Told me of your harrowing adventure of the other night, too. Believe me, Inspector, I'm as eager as you are to see this business put to rest for good. It's practically in my backyard. Though I don't see how I can help you."

"How about tomorrow?"

"Sorry, can't do it. I'm booked all day. I've got a speech in Baltimore, another fundraiser, a TV spot to tape." As he spoke, Greer spotted someone approaching them, making his presence known, but keeping his distance. He raised his eyebrows and nodded once in that direction. Allaben never turned his head. He was keeping his eye on his target.

"I'm sorry to press you, Mr. Greer. I know you're busy. An hour of your time and we're through." He had every intention of booking himself into that schedule.

"We could go inside right now. I never knew an hour's worth of business couldn't be done in ten minutes if the right men are doing it."

"Not here. I'm your guest."

Greer's smile widened into a grin. "Wick was right about you, Mr. Allaben," he said. "You're not to be put off. I'll be at the Fish & Game Club Tuesday. There's a shoot that night. Come watch. We'll talk afterward."

With that he turned to acknowledge the recipient of his nod. It was the hefty guy again, the one in the pearl-colored suit who had been in the library with Parker. With a wink at Allaben, Greer headed toward him. The audience was through.

Allaben felt a little sick. Something in his gut wasn't right – a roiling sensation just below the diaphragm. It might have been hunger or it might have been the opposite of hunger. The heady smell of the barbecue allowed no middle ground, no straddling the fence. It made you nauseous or ravenous, one or the other. But this was one of those times when it was hard to tell.

He shielded his eyes. The sun beating down on him didn't help any. For an instant he allowed himself to wonder if some funny stuff had been slipped into this drink. But only for an instant. He steered back onto the path of common sense. What lay down the other path? He didn't care to know. Look at what Gwynn had gained by it.

"Are you all right, Mr. Allaben?" asked Emma Greer. "Why don't you get some food into you? See if those ribs don't make you feel better. The sauce is Mason's doing, a Greer family specialty."

Allaben took this to be his exit cue. It was time for another guest to receive her attention. Her gaze was already fixed on something behind Allaben – something disagreeable, to judge by the frown that wrinkled her eyes.

"Damn him to hell!" she muttered. "He's sloshed already."

Allaben did not need to turn to see whom she meant. A bray came from just behind his right shoulder, and with it the sweet reek of rum.

"Well, isn't this cozy. I'm glad to see you've met Emma, Mr. Allaben. You know what they say, 'Behind every great man …' and Emma's the living proof. You've met my wife, too, haven't you? Sure you did. I bet she ate you up. The strong, silent type. 'Course, I'm not a great man. Good enough to collect the money – no problem on that score – but odd man out when it comes to making of sky and earth and water. It's like my dear wife says, I'm always on the outside looking in. She says, 'You couldn't find your hand in your pocket, Don.' Implies I'm a little dim, a little kid playing with big kids. Little, little, little. Well, little does she know the things Don has found in his pocket."

He stopped suddenly, blinked, lifted his hand, saw it was

empty. A look of befuddlement passed over his face.

"You've had enough, Don," Emma Greer ordered.

Parker considered the judgment. "Right you are." His voice gathered with resentment, the ballast he would need to plow through the swells, a forlorn dinghy in a heavy sea. "I *have* had enough. Enough and then some. Only so much a man can take." He turned to face Allaben. "Only so much poking into other people's business, too."

Though he had not raised his voice, Parker's challenge sounded unnaturally loud. A web of silence seemed to have been spun around them. What had happened to the music? Allaben did not allow himself to glance around. No reason to, as he was sure of what he would find – the knots of people nearby curiously eyeing this little rhubarb in the making, others just beginning to feel the ripples.

Anger knotted at the back of Allaben's neck. He concentrated on undoing it. He couldn't believe that Parker would try something stupid, not here, but anger wouldn't help if he did. Nor would the half-finished drink in his hand. Without turning from Parker he held out the glass to Emma Greer. She took it. He let his shoulders relax, shifted his weight to the balls of his feet. He was ready.

So was Wick Mallory. Suddenly at hand and standing just behind Parker, like a genie summoned from a lamp. His right hand came down with a thud on Parker's shoulder. From a distance it might easily have been seen as bluff camaraderie, a warm-up smack to a teammate's shoulder pads. But Parker wasn't wearing pads. And even through half a bottle he could still see the warning in Mallory's eyes.

"What are you getting up to, Don?" Mallory asked. His voice was hard as flint.

Parker said nothing. A tepid smile crept up his face, stopping at the dead end of his eyes.

"If you've got business of a private nature, Don, it ought to be pursued elsewhere."

Mallory's grip tightened. Allaben knew his strength. It must have hurt. Bluster drained from behind the pink scrim of Parker's eyes.

Parker craned his head, scanned the crowd. His shoulder was still in Mallory's grip. "If you don't let me go, Wick, I can't repair to the refuge of the bar," he said. "I've got to fuel up or I've got no chance at all of catching Pamela. Looks like she's about to lap me."

Pamela Parker stood fifty feet away, her backside snuggled against the front of a sinewy man in a pale Hawaiian shirt and faded jeans. Allaben recognized him immediately, even without his uniform number – Rod Hurley. They swayed languidly to the music. Parker shook his head sadly, then offered a sheepish smile. Mallory lifted his hand from Parker's shoulder, slowly, like a crossing gate once the train's gone by.

Parker reset his neck in his collar, jerked at the lapels of his jacket, and started off toward the bar. His second step landed squarely on Allaben's toe.

27

It still hurt twenty minutes later.

Allaben sat with Mallory on a bench, their backs to a cedar dining table. The table was the one farthest from the barbecue pit in the line of tables that stretched from the grills to the verge of the bandstand. They had the table to themselves. Behind them were their leavings – one plate littered with the carcass of half a chicken, another with a dozen well-gnawed ribs.

Excepting the throb of his foot, Allaben felt appreciably better. He *had* been hungry. And now the better for half a chicken and a heaping portion of potato salad, he no longer felt like murdering Donald Parker. He was even prepared, in the spirit of charity, to grant the bastard the benefit of the doubt. Parker probably hadn't *meant* to step on his toe. And he was grateful to Mallory, too, for stepping between him and Parker's retreating back.

"Let it go, Felix," Wick had advised. "He's not worth another sore hand."

The sheriff directed Allaben's attention to Pamela Parker, who now stood staring at her brother from just outside the ring of well-wishers who encircled him.

"She's a fine-looking woman, don't you think?"

"Rod Hurley seems to agree with you. Why do you suppose

he's here? A contributor, maybe?"

"I don't know. Celebrity. Maybe he's here to supply some star power."

"Former star power. And already rounding first, I see."

They weren't the only ones staring at Pamela at the moment. The fellow in the pearl-colored suit, having just concluded his chat with Greer, had her in his sights as well. Was that his assignment – to shadow her, keep her from embarrassing her host when the booze was starting to loosen her lips?

"Are you still pining for her?" Allaben joked.

"I wouldn't be the only one," Mallory replied. "She never lacked for suitors. I could never figure out what she saw in Don Parker."

"She doesn't seem to see much in him anymore."

"Parker's a lush. Mean but gutless. Pamela settled for a big pillow with slicked-back hair. God knows why. She could have had anybody."

"Maybe she didn't see it that way."

"She was beautiful. Still is."

"But not the faithful helpmeet." Allaben excused himself of hypocrisy with the reflection that he was speaking in the line of duty.

Mallory emptied his beer and grabbed another bottle from a cooler behind him. His dance over, Rod Hurley was nearing there as well, looking thirsty. Handing him the bottle he'd snatched for himself, Mallory greeted the former star. "Hey, Rod, enjoying yourself at our little gathering?"

"Thanks, man," he replied, twisting off the cap and raising the bottle. "You bet."

"So, how long you expect to be down here striking out the

kiddies?"

"Till I get tired of the crab cakes here, I suppose." But he wasn't looking anywhere near his questioner when he answered. With a little nod he added, "Love them crab cakes," then took his leave.

"Let's get back to faithfulness," Mallory said, turning back to him. "I'll tell you something about faithful," he said. "First place, I happen to know that Don took the lead in that department. Doesn't excuse her, I know – two wrongs don't make a right – but you need to see the big picture. Second, if a woman won't go to bed with you, it's not because she loves her husband, and it's not because she's got a boyfriend. Some other reason, maybe, but it's not faithfulness. Truth is, we're not made to be faithful, Felix. Man or woman."

Allaben sometimes wondered if Rebecca, in one of her manic binges, had flung marital fidelity aside as yet another bourgeois confinement. He'd never asked her, though he'd more than once wanted to.

The two men sat in silence for a few moments. The sun had begun its slow glide from the sky's summit. Mallory turned his attention to the girl on the stage. She was crooning "Will you still love me tomorrow?"

"Quit ogling her, Wick," said Allaben, "and talk to me about Mason Greer."

Mallory was not to be so easily distracted from the object of his attentions. "She's singing to me," he returned out of the side of his mouth. "And her name's Lena."

In truth, Lena did seem to be concentrating her effort on Wick. Allaben wondered if she was interested in him because he was a handsome lug or because he was a sheriff, or both. Some women are weak for cops. Curtis Gwynn had taken full advantage, and more often than not, ignoring Allaben's protest, had then provided detailed accounts of his conquests.

Had he treated Don Parker to the same? Allaben wondered. It's one thing to know that someone is putting the blocks to your wife, another thing altogether to hear a play-by-play from the mechanic in question. He'd have to check his alibi again, and Pamela's, too, while he was at it.

The music stopped. His knee suddenly was wet and cool. Why? Allaben emerged from his ruminations to find himself scrutinized by Mallory. A beer bottle was lodged between his thigh and Mallory's.

"Jealousy," he said.

Mallory smiled laconically. "You're inscrutable, Felix. I like that about you."

He volunteered his beer bottle in salute. Allaben tapped it with his own.

"I was thinking about Don Parker and Gwynn."

"Parker's got an alibi."

"I know he does. He's also got a motive, which is more than can be said for anyone else right now."

"God, you're a stubborn cuss, Inspector. Makes me glad we're on the same side."

"I'm glad to hear it. Now maybe you'll give me a rundown on all of these movers and shakers. Who's that, for example?"

He pointed to the man in the pearl-colored suit talking with Emma Greer, the same man whom he'd seen just seen trailing Pamela Parker, and whom he'd noticed twice before: standing in the library with Donald Parker and, prior to that – as he now recalled – playing with his food at Carolyn's, wearing an ivory colored, fringed cowboy jacket.

"His name's Dawson. I don't know him too well, but I hear he's a high-roller. Trucking, I think. Has a hand in things. The rest is pretty much the same old crowd. Business mostly, county leaders, some local society thrown in. Oh, and that lanky guy that's approaching them – that's Dale Froehling, the guy who lost his state senate seat to an ex-hippy in a skirt when the ticket got split in the last election. Can you believe it? Mason was sure pissed."

"Yeah, I know who Froehling is."

"He's running again. I'll guarantee you that Dawson won't let that happen a second time."

"I think this Dawson's been keeping an eye on your Pamela. What do you know about that?"

Mallory knew nothing. "But that wouldn't be such a chore, now would it, partner?"

"Who's the big guy in the seersucker?" Allaben nodded toward the knot of people surrounding Mason Greer. The tall man who stood at his elbow had occupied that position for the last half hour, basking, it seemed, in the glow of Greer's celebrity.

"That's Mason's old law partner, Jameson Howe. Bigger Jim, to his friends. His father was tall, too," Mallory explained.

"Is he involved in the campaign?"

"Everyone here's involved in the campaign. Mason has made Jim Howe a lot of money, a lot more than Jim could have made on his own. He's got the connections and the manners, but not a lot upstairs. That's just between you and me, buddy. So it's only fair that Jim should make a few calls and shake a few hands, throw a party even, come fundraising time."

"I hear Greer's got millions in the campaign chest."

"Mason? Sure he does. But he'll go through that and more, much more, before polling day."

"What about you, Wick? What's your stake in this?"

"I've known Mason since we were kids. He's always been there for me."

"I know. You and Don Parker and Mason Greer, and God knows who else. But I know it's not out of school spirit that you're playing this game."

"Mason will make a difference in this state. He already has. And he'll make a difference to me. No bones about it, Felix. It's like I said, I don't want to retire a county sheriff. I'm not knocking it – I've done well by this job – but I've had my fill of D.W.I. and domestic disputes. I want to be top cop, not county cop. Mason's going to change things."

"First he's got to win the election."

"He'll win."

"With the money he's got, he ought to."

"People listen to him, Felix. They like what they hear."

"I don't."

"You're not people."

Allaben snorted. He had nothing to say to that, and Mallory knew it. They sat silently for a moment, satisfied with each other. The party was winding down. Two teenagers discreetly cleared the table behind them. At the barbecue pit a solitary chef manned the grill, and he was hurting for customers. Allaben looked for Greer, found him at the far side of the bandstand, studying index cards. That could mean only one thing. He tapped Mallory's knee.

"I'm getting while the getting's good."

"Mason's going to speak in a minute."

"Damn! I hate to miss it."

"Just a pep talk. Not a speech or anything."

"I don't need any pep," Allaben said. He emptied the bottle and stood.

"You should at least shake his hand," Mallory said. "Say thank you and good-bye."

"I never knew you to be so keen on etiquette, Wick."

"I never knew *you* to be so … unkeen."

"I've got unfinished business with Mason Greer."

"What business?"

"A couple of questions to ask him."

Mallory stood, too. He brushed his hair with his hand. The golden crop shimmered.

"I've got a question on my mind, too, Felix. I want to know if Lena is busy tonight. Soon as she finishes this set, I'm going to find out."

He grinned, slapped Allaben's shoulder, then swaggered toward the bandstand.

Allaben had got as far as the French doors leading back into the house when he felt a tap on his shoulder. He turned to find himself face to face with the hefty one in the pearl-colored suit, now sporting a shrewd but not uninviting grin, and reaching out a fleshy, rather large right hand.

"Don't believe we've met. Name's Lester Dawson. I'm with the Greer campaign."

"Felix Allaben." He took Dawson's hand.

"Pleased to meet you, Felix. I hear you're the fellow's going to get to the bottom of these battlefield deaths. It's good to know we've got a steady man looking into them. Terrible thing, those deaths. On hallowed ground, no less. Tragic stuff."

"Well, the place does have a reputation to keep up."

The remark drew a doubtful squint from Dawson, who either missed the sarcasm or preferred to pretend that he did.

"We're glad you're here, though I was under the impression that this was Wick Mallory's stomping ground."

"Federal land, so federal case."

"There you go. True enough. Besides, I'm sure Mallory could use some help. Good law officer – don't get me wrong – but not used to murder investigations. I heard a rumor, by the way – something to the effect that you think the ranger's death might not have been an accident. Anything to that?"

"Sorry, but I'm not at liberty ..."

"Sure. Understood." He paused, then changed gears. "Mason asked me to see if we can't offer you any assistance. You know, Mr. Allaben, these national historic battlefields of ours are very important to him. Takes a personal interest in them. Mason wants our national heritage preserved and protected, whatever the cost. And with September 17th approaching, you know ..."

Allaben wondered where Mason Greer, champion of states' rights and foe to big government, thought the money for that protection and preservation was going to come from. But this was not the time to challenge the Greer agenda. Let's turn the tables, he thought.

"What is your part in the Greer campaign, Mr. Dawson?"

"Oh, I do my bit, help him with introductions to folks I know."

"Fund-raising?"

"Sure, some fund-raising. A little of this and a little of that."

"Why do I get the feeling you're selling yourself short?"

Dawson allowed a sly smile. "Because you're a smart fellow who appreciates modesty. And I'll go further, Mr. Allaben. In my experience, smart fellows like you know which side of the bread the butter's on."

"That would be Mason Greer's side."

"Damn right. Mason's a mighty good friend to have, Inspector. He never forgets a friend. And he thinks the world of lawmen. Just ask Wick Mallory."

"Don't have to ask. Wick's already told me."

Dawson shifted his ample frame from one foot to the other. One of the black-suited security detail came walking down the hallway. He nodded at Dawson, who resumed when the man had passed.

"I understand you're going to talk to Mason about those battlefield deaths."

"Some routine questions."

"I'm sure he wants to help you. I'd like to help you, too."

"How can you help me, Mr. Dawson?"

"Call me Lester."

"How can you help me, Lester?"

Dawson frowned. "Don't know, off the top of my head. But if something comes up, all you got to do is pick up the phone. Brad's got my numbers."

An amplified voice came from the patio.

"Sounds like Bigger Jim's starting the introduction," Dawson observed. "I better get back to the party."

He held out his hand again and gave Allaben a good-natured

grin. "You take care of yourself now."

Allaben thought about that good-natured grin as he made his way through the house and was ushered through the front door. He thought about it some more as he stood on the veranda, waiting for the valet to deliver his truck. Why, he asked himself, if it was so good-natured, did that grin seem to whisper, "But watch your back"?

28

It was a five-minute drive from his Hagerstown hotel to Mason Greer's undistinguished campaign headquarters, a drive Lester Dawson had already made a number of times that summer.

He parked his Range Rover in one of the "Reserved" spots in the lot behind the office building, then walked through the back door. It was freezing inside. Greer, he thought, must be keeping the A/C blasting to make sure his overworked staffers kept slugging back the strong, hot coffee and hitting the phones.

He marched through the busy war room, where Emma Greer waved a hello, and continued straight to the elevator. He took it one flight up, walked down a corridor, and knocked on the door of Greer's office. Maryland's next attorney general was waiting for him. He was sitting behind his massive desk, coffee mug in hand. Dawson settled into the chair closest to the desk. He placed his Stetson upon it. It was a gray model today. Greer put his mug down on a large leather coaster emblazoned with the motto, which Dawson could read even upside down, "Don't Tread on Me."

"Nice hat, Lester," Greer observed.

"Took her off to show you this isn't just a hat rack, Mason," Dawson answered, leaning forward and tapping his ample cranium.

"It's what's inside that noggin that I prize, Lester. That was one bang-up fundraiser at Howe's place yesterday, wasn't it?" Greer picked up the mug and swilled back what remained in it.

"Another bonanza, Mason. Just keep your hands out of the till and off small children and you're a shoo-in."

"No promises, but I shall do my best. Meanwhile, I saw you having a chinwag in Howe's sun room with that Fed, what's-his-name, Allaben. How'd that go?"

"Nothing lost, nothing gained. We were just getting acquainted. What can you tell me about the Gwynn case? And the ranger? Any progress there?"

"I've got the sheriff working on it, side-by-side with the Fed."

"Wick Mallory?"

"None other. You know Wick. When he finds out something, you'll be the second person to know. Right now, I think they're floundering."

"Any guesses, Mason? Anything I should know?"

Mason Greer stood up and stepped past his guest in the direction of his coffee maker, his new prized possession. He inserted a pod of Italian roast and set the machine in motion. "Sleek gizmo here, Lester. Try one?"

"Thanks, but the tank's full. Now the other guy – the ranger – are the two deaths related, you think? Or did he just plain fall off the tower?"

It was a question that troubled Dawson. He resisted the temptation to twirl his hat, as he often did when he wanted help with his thinking. Instead, he gently rubbed the the brim between his fingers, kept silent, and waited.

Greer, with refill now in hand, answered, "The name's Hal Snyder. And I have no clue. Probably fell, seems he was a hooch hound. Sounds like he got soused and dropped overboard. That's what the sheriff thinks. As to Gwynn, Wick thinks it might have been a family affair. The worst part, Lester, it's my family."

"*Your* family? What about your family?"

"My damn sister and her idiot husband. Always up to something. She drinks like a pirate and changes bed partners like I change socks. Pamela knew Gwynn, and Don knew that she knew him, if you take my meaning."

"So is Allaben looking at you? Bound to, I guess. And you could do without the publicity."

"He's in my face, yeah. In fact, when I talked to him yesterday, I invited him to the club for a sit-down."

"You did? Look, Mason, I, I need to know everything. We've got something going down that can't be interfered with. I don't want any feds nosing around that club and its grounds, not now."

"I'll sit him down and then send him off."

"You do that. And tell me, by the way, that Gwynn guy – why the hell was he ever let in? That's on you. I sure wish you'd run it by me."

Greer had returned to his desk with his refill. "Mistakes were made, Lester. I'll give you that. But you know I don't decide who joins. I never even met the man. Now let's move on, shall we? You came running over here with something to tell me. So tell."

Lester Dawson told. But he did so as he'd promised Dale Froehling he would. He disclosed nothing specific about the plans, nothing that could be used against Greer. And he promised Greer that whatever was going to happen, there would be no one getting hurt. He assured him, as well, that no local men would be involved.

"All right, Lester, thanks for the heads-up. We'll leave it like that if you think best."

"I do. You just see about bringing this investigation to a close."

"I'll do what I can, Lester. Light a fire under my sheriff, see what I can unearth from Pamela and Don. And I will ward off Allaben, or try to – he may be the hard-to-ward-off type."

29

Allaben stood across Market Street from the Sojourner Shop, sizing up the face it presented to the world. A butter-yellow awning cast in shadow the upper reaches of the storefront of repointed brick. Above the awning the morning sun glinted on the windows. A discriminating, knowing face, well satisfied with itself – as well it should be. Nestled between a coffee bar and a pottery store, the Sojourner occupied a prime piece of gentrified Frederick real estate. The Visitor Information Center was directly across the street and the city's trendiest inn just around the corner. The shop's owners had chosen their site well.

Although he lived just five blocks away and had walked past the bookstore scores of times, this visit would be Allaben's first. The last time he had crossed this threshold was some twenty years ago, when on the other side of that doorway was a drugstore. He remembered the occasion well. Home from college and full of himself, he had sauntered to the counter and coolly asked Mr. Kay for a package of Trojans. The same Mr. Kay to whom Allaben's mother had taken Felix for elixirs when he suffered from whooping cough. Mr. Kay had frowned, and Felix the eighteen-year-old had gloated. But if Mr. Kay had disapproved, it was not of copulation, as Felix then thought, but of time, which had turned a customer of cherry-flavored cough syrup into a hormone-charged fornicator.

A sign was posted on the door, far too small and far too distant for Allaben to read. But the sign was of less interest to him than the fact that through that door Curtis Gwynn had passed a week ago Friday, when he had left behind his place of employment for what turned out to be the very last time.

An odd place for a man of Gwynn's prickliness to secure a livelihood, unless perhaps his employers kept him at arm's length from the customers. Allaben would see. He crossed the street.

The sign, hand-lettered and taped to the lacquered door, read "Help Wanted."

"The feeling is mutual," thought Allaben as he turned the handle and opened the door. A chime sounded deep inside. From behind a partition at the rear of the store came a woman's voice.

"Be right with you! There's coffee on the table."

Allaben looked around. Little remained of the drugstore that he remembered. The floor still stepped up about two-thirds of the way back, but the half-step that had once eased the way for arthritic Mr. Kay was gone. In its place a ramp had been constructed, covered in the same forest green carpet as the store. The pressed-tin ceiling was the same, it was true, and the cabinets looked familiar. But everything else – from the chrome-and-leather chairs to the computers on the desks – was as fresh as the steaming pot of coffee on the glass coffee table beside him.

He had no sooner parked himself in the middle of a sofa before the table when he was on his feet again. A woman had appeared from behind the partition, a petite woman dressed in a sleeveless, powder-blue blouse and a white skirt. She walked down the ramp to greet him.

"Welcome to Sojourner's. Did you have some coffee?"

Allaben removed his hat.

"Thanks," he said, "but I've already had my fill."

She smiled. "All right, then. What can I do for you this morning?"

"Are you Mrs. Terry?"

"Yes," she said, still smiling, "I'm Peg Terry."

That would make her one of the owners. The other was her husband, Thomas. Allaben had reviewed the files over breakfast. Background collected by the Frederick police and the notes of Mallory's interview with the couple last Monday, the day after Gwynn's death. It had obviously been a cursory affair, and Mallory had not thought it worth the trouble to investigate them further. To his mind they had nothing to do with Gwynn's death. But just for the record, each vouched for the other. They'd gone to bed at 10:00 Saturday night, got up at 7:00 on Sunday, and then gone to an 8:00 mass. There was nothing to show whether Mallory had bothered to check their stories. Probably not, simply because it was too easy to check. And who but the innocent would claim worship as their alibi?

Peg Terry certainly looked innocent enough. She was pretty, too. A little round perhaps, but in all the right places. Black eyes, black hair, fair skin. Friendly. She was the sort of woman it would be nice just to be around; and if the quarters were a little close, then so much the better for Mr. Curtis Gwynn.

Allaben returned her smile and introduced himself. Her smile faded.

"You're here about Curtis."

He nodded. "Can we talk for a few minutes? I won't keep you very long."

She sat down opposite him in one of the leather-and-chrome side chairs. Allaben placed his hat on the sofa and then took a seat beside it. He waited as she composed herself, chin up, hands clasped in her lap.

"I hoped to talk with your husband, too."

"Tom is having his pool therapy. I drive him over after church, then come here to open the store."

Allaben waited.

"My husband is disabled, Inspector," she explained.

Of course. The ramp had been built for a wheelchair.

"I'm sorry, Mrs. Terry."

"Tom is very strong. Physically and mentally. I'm so proud of him. He's made such a lot of progress."

"An accident?"

"Racing a stock car. Three years ago."

"You've had this business for two years?"

"Yes. Tom was in rehab for a year. He had to have something to do."

"And before that?"

"The accident? Tom was a pilot. I knew the travel business, and Tom had some properties in the area. He sold two of them and we bought this place with the money."

A thought occurred to Allaben, but he decided to keep it in reserve.

"How's business?"

"Good. Real good. We're doing fine."

"How many people do you have working here?"

"It's just us right now. We took Curtis on a year ago February. He walked in one day all worked up over a sign we had in the window. A word was spelled wrong. I spelled Edgar Poe's middle name wrong. An *e* instead of an *a* in Allan. Which to hear him tell it was unforgivable. Nothing would do but we had to fix it right then and there. Little things were big things to him."

She smiled, then asked, "Did you know Curtis?"

Allaben nodded.

"Then you know what I mean."

He nodded again. Indeed he did know what she meant. But he also knew that if little things were big things to Gwynn, big things were even bigger. Allaben went on to ask some routine questions, listening in her answers for what she did not say as much as what she did.

Gwynn worked four days a week, closing up the store on Tuesdays and Wednesdays, and opening it on Thursdays and Fridays. Tom didn't like his wife in the store alone any more than could be helped. Occasionally Gwynn would fill in for Tom on a Saturday or Sunday, but generally he kept his weekends free for battlefield activities. He did in the store whatever needed to be done. He was reliable, trustworthy, enthusiastic – almost to a fault. There was the time, for example, when he had practically dragged a curious but timid family to America's oldest ginkgo tree, a fifteen-minute brisk walk from the store. Yes, he could be stubborn and argumentative, especially if historical fact was at issue, but in every other respect he had been a model employee. Never missed a day, always on time, perfectly dependable.

And what of last Friday? Had he mentioned to them his plans for the weekend?

"No more than usual. He said he was going to Sharpsburg for a firing demonstration and another one, too, I think he said. He left here at five, when he usually clocked out."

"Did he seem gloomy, upset about something?"

"He wasn't quite himself. A little distracted maybe. I didn't give it much thought then."

"He said nothing about meeting anyone?"

"Not that I recall."

"And you expected him back on Tuesday."

"Certainly."

"Did he get any calls on Thursday or Friday?"

"Not here. I never knew him to make a private call or to get one, except once or twice for a doctor or dentist appointment if he forgot his cell."

"Visitors?"

She shook her head. "He never talked about his private life. He was kind of secretive about himself."

"But you knew he'd been a police officer."

"Oh, sure. He told us about that, of course. And his schooling."

"Did he talk politics?"

"Only to say he despised all politicians. He said that a lot."

"Anyone in particular?"

"Said he never knew one walked higher than a snake."

"Clubs, organizations, friends?"

Again she shook her head. "I know it sounds strange, but he hardly talked about anything except the weather and history. He had a lot to say about history. Loved the Civil War, everything about it. That's why he took the job, because it would give him time to read and write. He spent a lot of time in libraries, looking things up."

"Did you know he had a tattoo?"

"No, I didn't."

"You never saw a tattoo? A coiled snake?"

She shook her head no.

Allaben thought. Maybe it was a recent acquisition? Could the medical examiner tell? He made a note to call Laroux.

"Did Curtis ever mention Mason Greer?"

"The man who's running for attorney general?"

To his nod, she returned another shake of her head.

"What about the Potomac Resistance League or PRL?"

"Sorry, Mr. Allaben, but I can't help you with that, either. Curtis was a passionate man, you could tell, but he kept himself private."

"Like he was hiding something?"

"No. Like he had a plan he didn't want anyone to know about. That's the best I can describe it."

"Did he talk about family?"

"I don't know that he had any."

"Did he drive to work?"

"Oh, no. He always walked. He picked up the paper on the way."

"Would he go out for lunch?"

"Usually he brought something. Ate it in back." She nodded toward the rear of the store. "There's a little kitchen back there, and a bathroom. Everything's set up for Tom."

"Did you ever see him socially?" He let her interpret the *you*.

"You mean go out together? No, we never did. Tom and I don't do much of that anymore."

Allaben looked about the store for a moment. He glanced at the reproductions of *Harper's Weekly* Civil War drawings, and then at the black-and-white photos of London and Paris, of Prague and of New York, before turning his attention once more to Peg Terry. She waited patiently for the questions to resume.

He had one last question to ask.

"When your husband sold his properties, Mrs. Terry, was it through an agent?"

"Yes."

Allaben said nothing, but studied her with frank curiosity. She withstood a few seconds of this scrutiny with apparent equanimity. A few more were all it took for gravity to draw down the corners of her mouth and to turn equanimity into resignation. She looked straight into his eyes.

"Yes," she repeated. "That awful Parker woman sold them for Tom."

The Washington County Sheriff's Department put Allaben on hold. He studied a photo of Miranda while he waited for Mallory. Rebecca had had it framed as a birthday present three years ago, and it had been on his desk ever since. A twelve-year-old Miranda looked back at him. A serious, intelligent girl, just at that age when, in fits and starts, childhood was slipping off her, shed like an outgrown skin. To his mind she was the spitting image of her mother. Or rather, she had been. For in the last three years she had come more and more to look like him, so much so that friends remarked on the resemblance. Allaben himself couldn't see it, and he had no recent photos at hand. Rebecca had been the household's photographer. No matter: the best evidence was Miranda herself. If all went well, he'd soon have her back. If Russell and Douglas could be persuaded do give her up.

"Felix! How's my barbecue buddy?" Mallory seemed to be in a good mood.

"Did I miss anything?"

"You missed a soul-stirring speech."

"Then I guess the answer is no."

"I hear he collected near a hundred grand."

"Big spenders."

"It's an investment. That's the way to look at it."

"That's the way *you* look at it."

A long sigh issued from Mallory's end of the line.

"Let's not get into that, Felix. I'm not often as satisfied as I am right now. Had a night sweet as a handful of lilacs with a songbird who shall remain nameless. The citizens of Washington County are calm. It's a nice peaceful Sunday. Why don't you take the rest of the day off?"

"I visited the Sojourner Shop this morning."

"The what?"

"The place where Gwynn worked. I had a talk with Peg Terry."

"Don't tell me you're looking at them."

"Why not?"

"They were in church, for Christ's sake! And sure as hell the husband didn't shoot him."

"He might have hired someone."

"Felix! Would you listen to yourself? This isn't like you at all. You're grasping at straws."

"I'm just thinking out loud."

"Well, think a little quieter."

Mallory was right. It was far-fetched. Allaben thought of the wheelchair ramp, and of Peg Terry's hands lying quietly in her lap even as she recounted the shameless way that Pamela Parker had flirted with her Tom and, not content with that, tried to take advantage of him. No. Allaben couldn't make it work. She might have had cause to wreak vengeance on Mrs. Parker, but not on Curtis Gwynn.

Mallory was right about this peaceful Sunday, too, he thought. Some R&R would be useful – distraction from this fruitless wrangling with the facts.

The Keys game started at 4:00. Hurley would be on the mound. Allaben pulled out his phone and called Delvecchio, who promised him two seats behind the dugout. That accomplished, he stood for a minute staring at his phone again, as if in search for encouragement. Who was he kidding? He'd asked Del for *two* seats. He tapped "favorites" and scrolled down to the entry for Carolyn. She hadn't bothered to add a last name.

30

There were no windows in the big kitchen at Carolyn's restaurant. The track lighting glinted on steel and brushed aluminum, but it did not give the time of day. Morning, noon, or night – it was impossible to tell. It happened to be 7:00 in the evening, and Carolyn and Allaben had the place to themselves. Behind their voices the only sounds were the hum of the refrigerator and the rattle of air conditioning. Allaben thought it a little eerie, but it was obviously not so to Carolyn. She was more interested in continuing the dissection of Rod Hurley's latest performance, and pressed his case even as she bustled about the kitchen, collecting the knives, pots, and saucepans she would need to prepare the private dinner she'd promised.

"You aren't being entirely fair," she protested. "How about that one inning when the bases were loaded? He struck out those two guys and then got the last one to hit a grounder to the second baseman. Plus, he helped his own cause with that single."

There was something to her argument, Allaben admitted, although the next day's papers would be more likely to focus on the extent to which Hurley was pounded by Single-A minor leaguers. And he was pounded. When he wasn't walking batters or hitting them with errant fastballs, he was being touched up for four runs and seven hits in five innings and change.

Every one of those hits had brought a groan from Carolyn, who had followed the game with the same concentration she now applied to opening a bottle of pinot noir. A dimple formed at the intersection of her forehead and her nose. She looked up suddenly and caught Allaben watching her. Allaben thought himself unreadable. He was wrong. A sly smile lifted the corners of her mouth.

"So he has one good inning. Maybe a dozen good pitches. A hint of some movement on the fastball, a flash of the Cy Young winner. Did you see the look on his face when Del took him out of the game?"

"Nope. I did notice Del's face, though. As red as Jean-Paul's when I question the menu."

"Del knows that the brass will side with Hurley if it comes down to 'It's him or me.'"

Carolyn said, "I'm sorry Del couldn't come tonight." She looked at Allaben expectantly.

He knew that she meant what she said but that she'd be happy to hear him reply, all the same, 'Me, too. But I'm not sorry it's just the two of us.' Which happened to be exactly what he was thinking at the moment.

She poured wine for Allaben, then lifted her glass in a toast.

"What will it be?" Allaben wanted to know.

"What do we have in common?" asked Carolyn.

"The past."

"Then let's drink to the future," Carolyn declared, "that we may have that in common, too."

She took a sip of the wine and then got down to business, handing Allaben an apron – as he was designated the *sous chef* –

and then tying hers over her jeans and tee shirt.

"Pasta with shiitake mushrooms, onion, garlic, some Asiago cheese, and a green salad. Sound okay?"

Within a half an hour, the two were seated at the chef's table. Carolyn had set it with two candles, which protested bravely against the dimmed light. She gave him a minute to sample the fare.

"So what do you think? Is it edible?"

Allaben pronounced the dish without doubt the finest anyone in Frederick was eating at that moment. "Poor Del doesn't know what he's missing," he added.

The conversation ranged from the woes of managing in a league in which the "Ten-Pin Topple" contestant on the dugout roof draws as many cheers as the guy with the game-winning hit, to the trials of running a successful restaurant. At length the talk turned to Allaben's case.

"Or is it still off-limits?" Carolyn asked.

Allaben gave her a succinct accounting of the investigation to date – progress and lack of same.

"So you're stuck," she said.

"Like a pony in a bog. The more I thrash about, the deeper I sink."

"It's only been a week."

"A week's a long time for a case like this."

"I suppose it's a good thing," Carolyn observed, "that he was a loner – Gwynn, I mean. No family. That's what I hear, anyway."

"I think it helped get him killed. Whoever did it knew that no one would make a stink. No protests, no vigils, no Mom on TV begging for help in finding her son's killer."

"What about those goons at the ball park, that guy with the

snake tattoo?"

"All I know is that the tattoo probably has a bearing on the case. Gwynn had the same one."

"Really? A snake?"

"Yes. Exactly the same."

"Have you tracked down the 'artist' who did it?"

"No. It looks like professional work, but it wasn't done in Frederick."

"You'll figure it out, Felix," she told him. "I know you will."

"What makes you so sure?"

"Because you're good at what you do, whatever it is. You were always … smart. Quick. You always got the answer first."

"Are you giving me a pep talk?"

Carolyn smiled. "I'm patting your back so you'll pat mine – quid pro quo. You'd better go on and on about all of my outstanding qualities."

Allaben's phone vibrated in his pocket. That would be Miranda, checking to see if her father was still alive. Now or later? Now, he decided. Later might be inconvenient.

He pulled out the phone, mouthed "Miranda" to Carolyn, then got up and walked off with the phone pressed against his ear.

When he returned to the table a few minutes later, everything but the candles had been cleared away. The wine glasses had been replaced by two snifters of cognac. Carolyn cupped her snifter and gently swirled the brandy.

"You know, Felix," she said, "you can talk to her in front of me."

"She says she wants to make a shrine to her mother – photos, a bottle of her perfume, jewelry, her gardening shears. The thing is, she says it like she's planning a party."

Carolyn raised her eyes from her glass. "Maybe it shouldn't just be you and her."

"And a ghost? Is that what you mean?"

"No, Felix, that's not what I mean. I mean we're grown-ups. You and me. I could help you."

"With Miranda?"

"Why not?"

The candles had burned down nearly to the base; in a minute or two they would gutter. Carolyn's bare arm lay on the starched white tablecloth. Allaben reached; he cupped his hand over the smooth back of hers. She gave him a lazy smile.

"Come home with me."

31

If Stuart London was suffering any ill effects from the treatment he'd received at Saturday's barbecue, Allaben saw no evidence of it this morning. London's eye was bright, his complexion rosy, his self-possession fully intact.

"It's good to see you again," he said in greeting to Allaben. "You know I don't usually leave parties in so dramatic a fashion."

London was dressed in pressed linen trousers, pale blue shirt, and bow tie. A navy blazer hung behind the door. His office stood out as an oasis of color among the warren of drab cubicles and glass-walled offices that constituted the metro department of the Frederick Post. House plants crowded the window sill behind the polished desk, and black-and-white photos, matted and framed, hung on the walls. Two upholstered armchairs sat upon a carpet.

Allaben placed his hat on the corner of London's desk and settled into one of the armchairs. From this vantage, he noticed that one of the photos was of London and Carolyn huddled nose to nose over a table in the latter's restaurant. Allaben looked more closely. On the matte beneath the photo was an inscription that read, "All news begins as gossip. Love, Carolyn."

London nodded at the photo, then raised an eyebrow in Allaben's direction. "I'm her favorite newshound. And she's my favorite source. Nice to be someone's favorite anything, don't you think?" He punctuated this remark with a meaningful wink.

Allaben responded with a polite smile. He could see this line of conversation turning into something out of a high-school movie – or, even worse, a parody of one – if he didn't nip it in the bud. He decided to change the subject.

"Regards from Russell. He and Douglas have been hosting my daughter this summer."

London nodded in acknowledgement.

"And regards from Don Parker," Allaben added.

"I can't stand that lush."

"I'm not very fond of him, either."

"You know what they say, Felix. Careful who you lie down with. That's true in more ways than one."

"'Whom.'"

"What?"

"'Whom' you lie down with, not 'who.' You call yourself a wordsmith?"

London grinned at Allaben. "Okay, Felix, you've done your duty by way of small talk. What can I do for you?"

"I'd like to ask you a few questions about Mason Greer."

"What's in it for me?"

"Are you interested in the murder of Curtis Gwynn?"

"Should I be?" A pause, then, "Do you think Mason Greer's involved somehow?"

"You have to understand," Allaben said, "that I'm operating on a hunch here. And I've got to have your word that this is off the record, at least for the time being and maybe for good."

London hesitated, then nodded agreement. "So talk to me,

Inspector."

"I suppose you know, Stuart, as someone who's taken an interest in the career of Mason Greer, that his sister Pamela has a reputation of her own, and that Curtis Gwynn had been the latest notch in the lady's resume."

Another nod from London, and a ho-hum expression to chase it. Allaben would have to do better than this.

"But if you are also aware," Allaben went on, "that Gwynn was keeping a file of sorts on her older brother, that Gwynn had been calling him at his office and at home, then we're switching seats."

London picked up a pencil and began absent-mindedly to tap the desk with it.

Allaben went on. "And as uninterested as I'd like to be with any of the Greer family, these are facts that I can't ignore. If there's even an inkling of a connection between Gwynn and Mason Greer, I have to look into it, see if it leads anywhere."

London pointed the pencil at a row of three chest-high metal filing cabinets that filled the bottom half of the wall behind Allaben.

"It's all in there – newspaper and magazine articles, photos, press releases, and some of my 'valentines' to him, as well. Greer is what one might call a piece of work. He's no friend to new ideas of any kind – and new, for him, means post-Crusades. His idea of a minority is an interest in a start-up company. Here, take the file with you, if you like. Read it for yourself."

He got up and walked to the file cabinets, unlocked and opened a drawer, withdrew a fat manila folder.

"It's all public record," he continued. "I've got some other stuff – rumors, hearsay, anonymous letters, that sort of thing. Dirt, in short, but all of it uncorroborated. He has a lot of enemies, myself included, but until today I'd never heard that Curtis Gwynn was on the list."

Allaben thumbed through the file that London set before him.

"I don't know for a fact that he was an enemy, at least not one of the sort you mean. Greer denies ever having spoken to him."

London reclaimed his seat. "I don't suppose that Gwynn recorded the calls," he asked.

"If he did, there's no sign of a recorder," Allaben replied, noting to himself that he hadn't been looking for one when he'd searched Gwynn's apartment. Maybe someone had beat him to it?

London pursed his lips and scratched delicately at his chin.

"Greer is a first-rate politician, which is to say that he doesn't leave evidence. It wouldn't be like him to get caught, especially by an amateur."

"Caught at what?" Allaben asked.

"Well, there you are," said London. "You'll have to help me if I'm to help you. You say he's not a suspect."

"He's got an unshakable alibi. He was out of town."

"I wouldn't put anything past him, not if the stakes were high enough."

"And what are high stakes to him?"

"His career, first and foremost. You can read through this file if you like." He tapped the manila folder. "But I can tell you right here and now what you'll find – a steady, almost obsessive climb to power. Greer's got where he is today through sheer determination, through guts, and, most importantly, through an absolute sense of destiny. His internal compass needle has always been aimed straight at the top. And God help those who get between him and where he's meant to be."

"What about money?" Allaben asked.

"Wealth has come with power, but it's not money that drives him. Mind you, he knows how money is made, what deals to sign on to and which ones to let pass. He has shaken all the right hands. But money is only a means to him, just as the moving and shaking business is. Soon he'll be one of the most powerful men in the state."

"He'll win the election?"

"He'll win it going away. And then there'll be hell to pay for those of us who haven't seen the light, who don't subscribe to the mandate he'll claim. That's why you'd better be careful. Me, too. Frankly, it's a scary prospect. He's got all the makings of a first-class demagogue."

"What could stop him?"

"Scandal. Something personal. Something that shows him up for a two-faced hypocrite and puts the lie to his self-righteous bullying. But I'm not hopeful on that score. Believe me, I've pried under the rocks and opened the closet doors. He doesn't drink, he doesn't gamble, he doesn't cheat on his wife. He doesn't like boys, either, which is always a possibility with these prophets who thunder against us fags. Wife and kids are spotless. You know about his sister and brother-in-law, but he can't be held responsible for them."

"As a matter of fact," said Allaben, "I'm going to pay them a call when I leave here."

"Well, it's a dirty job, but someone's got to do it."

"Don Parker made it pretty plain on Saturday that he's not a member of your fan club."

"Don Parker's an ass, but he's only as dangerous as his brother-in-law permits him to be. It's the distaff side of that family you have to look out for. I'd steer clear of the lady's bed, even if I did play on your team. Bad things seem to happen to those who share it."

Allaben considered. If Pamela Parker were to be believed, she had done the jilting, at least in the case of Curtis Gwynn. Granted, it was a big "if." Perhaps he would put the question to Don Parker. Had he demanded that his wife dump Gwynn, as she insisted? And if he had, why?

"That other file, Stuart," Allaben said, "the juicy one. Any chance I could peek at it?"

"Love to, Felix, but no can do. Even *I* have standards."

Allaben nodded. "Fair enough," he said. "Then maybe you'll look through it, let me know if you find anything in there that might be of interest to me. I'd especially like to hear if there's any mention of an emblem – a coiled snake poised to strike. Gray with a red border."

London looked at him curiously.

"Okay," he said. "As long as I protect my sources. And with the understanding that it's quid pro quo. I'm a great believer in mutual back-scratching."

32

The Parkers lived in Brookside Meadows, a new development of winding streets and modest split levels and center-hall colonials. All of the thoroughfares were named for birds. Allaben turned right onto Royal Tern and left onto Swallow Lane, which rose gradually toward the crest of a hill. He found the Parker house near its peak.

Allaben pulled into the sloping driveway and parked by the closed garage, where the blacktop leveled.

Parker answered the front door's bell. He was in his shirt-sleeves, his tie was loosened, and his breath smelled of whiskey.

"I was just taking some lamb chops from the freezer," he said. It was a statement of fact, not an invitation. He left just enough room between himself and the door frame to let Allaben pass. "Kitchen's down the hall and to the left," he added.

Allaben walked ahead, not at all happy to have Parker at his back.

Pamela Parker sat at a counter separating the kitchen from the dining area. Her back was to Allaben as he entered, and she did not bother to turn until her husband announced, "We've got company, Pamela."

This news did not seem to strike her as of much interest. A wine glass sat on the counter before her and, beside it, a half-empty bottle of wine. Parker rounded the counter and fetched a tumbler of whiskey from its sink-side dock. Then he parked himself on a stool opposite his wife.

"I'd offer you a drink, Allaben," he said, "but you're probably on duty. Besides, I don't like you."

Allaben glanced around the room. The dining table was set for two.

"Maybe he's not on duty," Pamela finally put in. "Maybe this is a social call."

"No way, honey-bunch," her husband answered. "It's the long arm of the law for sure, come to bother and annoy us just as we're about to have dinner."

Allaben nodded at the defrosting meat. "It looks like you're one plate short. Where's your son?"

Mrs. Parker glared at him. "I've told you I don't want him involved in this."

"I've got a few questions to put to the two of you," said Allaben. "And then I'll be on my way. But they're not the kind of questions you'd want him to overhear."

She softened a little. "Donnie's out with friends. I don't expect him for dinner."

Allaben turned to her husband. "You don't seem so protective."

"He's my son, too," he replied airily. "Only I'm not so worried as Pamela is about what he might hear."

"You would be if you weren't such an ass," his wife shot back.

Allaben was prepared to let them go at it. He might learn something interesting if they let loose at each other. But Mrs. Parker seemed to be thinking the same thing. She pulled herself up, refilled her glass, and smiled icily. The bottle was now three-quarters empty, a wounded soldier steadily losing blood.

"Let's get on with this, Inspector. I'm showing a house this evening."

"Just ask what you've come to ask," Parker added, "so we can send you merrily on your way."

Allaben turned to Pamela. "Who asked you to stop seeing Curtis Gwynn?"

"I told you ..." Pamela began.

"I did," her husband interrupted. "I put an end to it, Allaben. It was between me and my wife."

Allaben kept at Mrs. Parker. "You're sure it wasn't your brother?"

"I think I can tell the difference between my husband and my brother," she drawled, "even after quite a few of these." She drained the wine in one long swallow.

"What in the world would Mason have to do with this?" Parker burst out angrily. "Don't you think we can manage our personal business ourselves? Mason has no say in what my wife and I do. We make our own decisions, just like any other couple. *We* decided that Mr. Gwynn had overstayed his welcome. And that's all there is to it. Our business alone. Mason had no part in this thing. I doubt that he even knew the guy."

"There were phone calls from Gwynn to Mason Greer's office and his home. I can understand why Gwynn might have called here a few times, but why would he have called your brother-in-law?"

"Too bad you can't ask Gwynn," Parker replied with a smug smile.

"I don't think I'd like his answers any more than I like yours."

"You're totally lost, Allaben. If you knew your business, you'd know better than to waste an important man's time, and Mason Greer is an important man."

"Is he important enough to have earned a badge of honor – a snake tattoo?"

Parker looked at him guardedly.

"A snake? I don't know what the hell you're talking about."

"What about you, Don?" Allaben continued. "Have you made the grade?"

Parker scowled at Allaben, then at his wife, who ignored both of them in favor of the wine bottle. She filled her glass. The soldier was now officially dead.

Parker picked up his own drink. "I think you ought to get the hell out of my house."

Allaben thought so, too. There had been something in Parker's sullen bravado that had been very satisfying. He'd taken him by surprise. But he was more certain than ever that, of the two, it was Mrs. Parker he should continue to press. Only not in the company of her husband. She used him as cover, just as she used the wine.

He turned to go. Parker walked him out, still holding his drink, then followed him to the driveway. The late summer sun threw Allaben's shadow against his truck. It would be hot inside. Allaben opened the door. Parker leaned against the front fender.

"Allaben," he said, "I know all about you." He paused for effect, like an actor about to deliver a speech. A car was rumbling up the street, a car in need of a new muffler. Otherwise it was quite still. Allaben studied the sky like a farmer waiting for rain.

"You used to be police," Parker continued, "but you're not police anymore. Now you've got some plastic badge makes you think you're Washington's answer to Dick Tracy. You think you know what you're doing, but you don't. If you're not real careful, you might get caught looking the wrong way. Or you may not be ready. But you know all about that, don't you, Dick? Just look at what happened to Mrs. Tracy."

Allaben said, "Put the glass down."

"Why should I do that?"

"So it doesn't fall and break when I hit you."

Parker grinned. He'd had a lot to drink.

"Okay, Dick," he said. He bent over slowly and placed the glass on the asphalt. As he straightened up he sent a roundhouse punch toward Allaben's head. Allaben stepped inside it, and in the next instant they were standing nose to nose, Parker's arm wrapped around Allaben's neck. Allaben needed room, and Parker wasn't going to give him any, so he slammed the top of his forehead into the bridge of Parker's nose. Stunned, Parker backed away. He kept backing away until he bumped into the garage door. A drizzle of blood began to seep from his nose.

Parker licked his upper lip, tasted the blood.

Allaben stepped calmly up to him.

A look of confusion wrinkled Parker's face. "You're going to hit me again? I'm bleeding, for Christ's sake. You win, okay?"

Allaben didn't answer, so Parker hunched over and covered up, hiding his face behind his arms. But Allaben wasn't interested in Parker's face. Instead he aimed a quick, hard kick at Parker's right shin, just below the knee. From Parker came a hoarse scream. He toppled over, clutched his knee, and drew himself up into ball. Each breath brought a suck of agony.

Allaben stood over him.

Then he heard the front door slam shut. And there was Pamela, tumbling out onto the front stoop. She swayed unsteadily for a moment, then reached for the railing with one hand while she tried, without much success, to keep the wine glass vertical in the other.

Parker gawked at his wife. "Pamela!" he shouted. "What the hell?" He started for her, but it was too late. She stumbled on the first step, failed to regain her balance, then collapsed and twisted to the ground. She lay face-up on the slate walk that curved to the driveway. Her drink had crash-landed as well, and the glass had splattered onto the paving tiles. Wine was beginning to drool toward the asphalt.

Parker kneeled beside her. She pushed him away.

"You dumb bastard!" she screeched. "Can't you see anything before it hits you?"

Parker glared at Allaben. "You going to stand there or are you going to help me?"

Allaben helped get Pamela first to a sitting position and then to her feet. She looked at her husband and Allaben in turn, treating each to a cocktail of alcohol and contempt. But she did not resist when Parker put his arm around her waist and started her back to the house.

Allaben retreated to the driveway once more.

The rumble behind him suddenly quit. He turned. An old Buick had pulled into the driveway. A teenage boy gawked from behind the wheel. The door on the passenger side opened, and another boy stepped out. He stood behind the open door, gravely studying the scene before him. His gaze first rested upon his parents, supporting each other at the entryway to the house, then on Allaben.

Allaben had seen that gaze before. It was the same stare as had been leveled upon him near the bridge at Antietam Creek.

33

"You kicked him?" Folliard's voice was dry, bemused.

"I kicked him." Allaben's was matter-of-fact.

He switched the phone to his right hand to leave his left free to manage the coffee cup. He took a sip. It was still hot. The newspaper was spread out on the kitchen table before him. He'd been reading the sports pages when Folliard called. It was not yet eight-thirty, so Sam must have gone into his office early. Pedro hadn't been fed yet. The dog sat by his empty bowl, gazing solemnly at his master.

"Why didn't you just take your ball and go home?" Folliard asked.

"The bastard went too far."

"You've been trained not to respond to provocation."

True. He had heard – and taken – much worse as a street cop. But twice now he'd let Parker get to him. "So I'm out of training," he said.

"Are you okay?"

"I'm fine."

Not true. He had slept badly and awakened tired and out of sorts. It peeved him to think of how easily he had lost his temper at Parker's goading. Parker of all people – a flabby jackass with a big mouth. To make matters worse, he had a new hurt to add to his aches and pains, a sharp twinge in the left side of his lower back. He must have pulled a muscle in the scuffle.

"What the hell did he say, anyway, to make you blow up like that?"

"He was going on about something – I wasn't paying much attention. Then he made a remark about Rebecca."

"So you kicked him."

"He wasn't worth risking my hand. It hurts enough already. So I went for the three points."

"Was it at least worth the visit?"

"I'd feel better if his kid hadn't seen it all."

"That's not what I mean," Folliard began. A note of impatience had crept into his voice.

"I know, Sam, I know," Allaben said. There was a pause. He had a suspicion about what was coming.

"Because, Felix, certain parties are making noises …"

"Certain parties who want me to put up or shut up," Allaben finished.

"Not *want* so much as *insist*."

Allaben resisted the urge to blurt, "I'm trying." He knew that nothing he could say was surer to irk Folliard. He would accentuate the positive instead.

"Pamela Parker is mixed up in this – I'm just not sure how. Her husband's got something to do with this militia. But he doesn't call the shots, he just makes the arrangements. I think he's incidental to Gwynn's murder."

"You think she might have shot him?"

"It's possible. She knows how to handle a gun. She claims she was only interested in him for the sex, but maybe there was more to it than that."

"Is there someone we don't know about yet?"

"It's all here, Sam. I don't have to go farther, just deeper. I'm sure I've talked to Gwynn's killer. Whoever pulled the trigger had to know that Gwynn and Irwin were going to meet at the Creek by Burnside Bridge. Which means that the killer either was at the Mansfield Tavern the night before or learned that night about the meeting from someone who was. The Parkers were there. They left late, went home, drank some more, talked to nobody else. That's their story. Roger Irwin left about 10:00, went home to his wife. He told her about the next morning's meeting. Husband and wife are each other's alibi, for both couples. D.T. heard about the meeting, too."

"D.T.?"

"The sheriff's deputy. All of these people overheard the argument and knew of the Sunday morning meeting. Also the bar's owner and the barmaid and an old guy, a regular, warming a seat there. The only other people in the place were other re-enactors and some locals, and they were off in a corner minding their own business."

"You've cleared Irwin?"

"Whoever shot Gwynn made sure that Irwin would be late."

"By flattening the tire on his car."

"That's the way I see it. The shooter wanted Gwynn alone. A few minutes would do."

"So where does that leave you?" Folliard pressed.

"Like I said, Sam, it's right below me – the mother lode. I've just got to dig deeper."

"Are you going to be digging deeper into Mason Greer?"

Allaben paused. “Is he one of the ‘certain parties’?”

“In all probability this is Maryland’s next attorney general we’re talking about, Felix, the kind of guy who gets a cabinet post in Washington some day, maybe even more than that. And here you are bothering people in a serious way – during a campaign, no less – and not getting anywhere. Or at least that’s the way it looks.”

“And what do you say to that? Is that how it looks to you, Sam?”

It was Folliard’s turn to pause. “I say that it’s a sticky, thankless job and I picked the best man to do it.”

“Then let me get to work,” Allaben said.

“You do that,” Folliard replied. “But make it quick. Because you haven’t much longer to prove me right.”

34

Allaben fed Pedro, then warmed up a second cup of coffee and mapped out the day.

Dig deeper. That's what he had told Folliard, and that's what he would do. Starting at the battlefield, where he had first entered the picture. He strapped on his holster, slid in and secured the gun, and put on a jacket. Pedro beat him to the door. Allaben considered. Why not? He could use the company.

In a few minutes man and dog were in the truck and underway. Pedro rode shotgun, snout thrust out the window. Allaben listened to the news on the radio – nothing about Gwynn's death or Snyder's or the arson. Nothing about an assault in Brookside Meadows, either. Felix Allaben did not rate a mention. Mason Greer did, however. The latest poll showed him with an 18-point lead over his opponent. Stuart London and Folliard were right – this election was stacking up as a shoo-in. Greer wouldn't want anything to taint his victory.

In sports news, Delvecchio's club had won again; in fact they had something of a post-season winning streak going. Was that good or bad for Del? A reasonable person would expect that management would recognize his skills and reward him by moving him up a notch or two in the organization. On the other hand, the

Orioles had seemed content in the past to keep Del right where he was, raising and nurturing their youngest farmhands. Maybe he was doing too good a job at it.

And finally, the weather. Hot and humid, chance of a thunderstorm in the afternoon or evening. High in the mid 80s. Current temperature in downtown Frederick: 76. WFRE news time: 10:06.

Half an hour later they were on the other side of Boonsboro, passing the cannon, markers, and monuments testifying to the fact that in this vicinity, in September of 1862, two great armies, one of blue and one of gray, had met and mauled each other. The result had been the greatest one-day bloodletting of any battle in American history – Americans butchering Americans on American soil, to the tune of 23,000 young men dead, wounded, or missing in about twelve hours.

Man and dog crossed the Antietam at what in 1862 had been called Middle Bridge. Allaben turned left before entering Sharpsburg and moments later pulled into the small parking lot that overlooked Burnside Bridge.

Antietam Creek glimmered in the morning's light as it slipped under the three arches of the stone bridge. A young couple stood upon the bridge, gazing downstream, in the direction of Snavely's Ford. Antietam. The word meant "swiftly moving water" in some Native American tongue. Who would know which tongue? Theodore Poole, of rifled guns and smoothbores, might. Poole knew Hal Snyder, too – maybe knew more about Hal than he had let on. Allaben made a note to talk to him again. Maybe Poole would know what Hal had meant by "See me."

Allaben set off on a worn, grassy path leading to the head of the trail that follows the creek. Pedro quickly took the point, keeping a good twenty feet ahead of his master. Allaben paused for few seconds when they gained the trail head to look out across the creek. A few more yards and he'd reach the spot where Gwynn had stood when the bullet had crashed into his head. The thick woods that covered the steep western bank would provide an excellent lair from which to await the arrival of Gwynn.

Man and dog continued along the Snavely Ford Trail, traveling in a southerly direction along the creek. Allaben observed that the flow was irregular, alternating from swift to unhurried in its journey to join the Potomac. He observed also that it was deep, almost chest-high in some places, and even deeper in others. If the creek were as deep in 1862, it would have been a formidable task for infantry to cross it. It was easy to see why Burnside would order General Rodman far downstream to get his division from the water's east side to its west.

Pedro suddenly loped off in pursuit of a squirrel. He came to a halt at the foot of a towering elm.

"Pedro!" Allaben called.

The dog barked again but didn't budge from his post. A lot of fuss for a squirrel, Allaben thought. In the deep shade of the trail, he could see nothing of Pedro's quarry. But the dog could, and so greeted his master's approach with a growl of warning. Allaben mistook the dog's purpose.

"I don't want your squirrel," he said. "Come on, Pedro, let's get going."

He was a few feet from the dog, who stubbornly held his ground, when a figure dropped from the tree, landing beside Allaben in a three-point crouch. In the time it took Allaben to reach his gun, the figure sprang up to stand before him. It was Donald Parker Junior. Donnie.

There was nothing in the boy's face to suggest that he found anything out of the ordinary in this form of meeting. He reached for Pedro, who seemed to be of the same mind.

"Nice dog," he remarked. "Labs are my favorite."

Allaben's heart-rate had by now returned to normal. His hand slowly dropped from the shoulder holster. "What are you doing here?" he asked.

The boy explained that he'd been making deliveries in town, had spotted Allaben, followed him to the battlefield, and taken the trail from the other direction. He'd climbed the tree and waited for them.

"I wanted to see what you'd do," he said. A rueful smile appeared on his face. "Especially after last night."

Allaben gazed steadily at the boy. It was the first time he'd seen him shift out of neutral. The smile made him look older and more like his mother. There was more of regret in it than of irony.

"I'm sorry you had to see it," said Allaben.

"I'm sure he deserved it."

"He's your father, Donnie. Like all of us, he's got his good days and his bad ones."

The boy's expression turned sardonic.

"He's a jerk. Her, too. She's been a boozer for as long as I can remember. And when she's drunk you wouldn't believe the stuff she says. Totally out of control. And lately it's been getting worse. I hate them both. Nine more months and I'm out of there for good." He picked up a stone and skimmed it across the creek: one, two, three, four, five skips.

Pedro had grown bored and resumed the ramble downstream. Allaben nodded in that direction, and the boy signaled agreement. They walked together in silence for about fifty yards before the boy pulled up.

"This is it – Snavely's Ford, where Rodman crossed. He had to march his division twice as far downstream as McClellan's engineers said he would have to. You know what General Rodman's middle name was? It was Peace. Isaac Peace Rodman. He was a Quaker from Rhode Island. And this was his last fight – he was shot in the chest, up there," Donnie explained, pointing to high ground ahead of them and to their right. "He died two weeks later, on September 30. That's my birthday."

"I guess you've studied the battle."

"I've read about it. And I've been here a lot."

"Do the rangers know you?"

"I don't know. Maybe."

"Hal Snyder?"

"Who?"

"The ranger who fell from the tower."

The boy shrugged. "I might have talked to him once or twice. Why ask about him?"

"I'm curious."

"I guess it's your job to ask questions." He smiled the same rueful smile as before. "I hardly knew the guy. He was tall. What else do you want to know?"

"Ever come here after the park closes?"

"Sure. Lots of times. It's easy."

"I know," said Allaben. "I did it, too, when I was your age. We'd wait until the sun went down, then slip under the chain gate and walk Bloody Lane, end to end, imagining that we were there the night after the battle. Imagining all sorts of things."

"Bloody Lane gives me the creeps, especially at night," the boy said. "Thousands died there – kids my age, a lot of them. Who cares what uniform they were wearing?"

Donnie paused for a moment. Then he asked, "Do you believe in ghosts?"

"No," Allaben replied, "not as things you can see or hear or feel. But as images or ideas that affect the way you think about the battle, and about life and death, for that matter – yes, I guess I do. I sure did believe in them when I was your age. At the top of the tower with a six-pack, especially when the moon was full."

The boy's response was immediate and curt. "I don't drink."

"I didn't say that you did."

But Donnie wasn't satisfied with the concession.

"No way I'm going to end up like them," he insisted.

Whom he meant by "them" went without saying. But there were other matters that still needed tending. Allaben waited a moment before asking another question.

"When were you here last?"

The boy seemed grateful for the change of subject.

"The day after that guy was found dead by the creek," he said. "I saw you."

Allaben nodded. "I wondered if you remembered. You didn't seem to take much notice."

"I noticed," the boy replied. He started to go on, then stopped. Allaben could guess what the boy had been about to say: "I notice a lot more than I let on." And he could guess as well the reason the boy hadn't said it: "A lot of good it's done me."

Anger rose in Allaben's chest. Had this boy's parents any idea of what they had done to him? Certainly not his father – Don Parker was too absorbed in himself. And his mother? Pamela Parker had tried, was still trying, to protect her son from the mess she made of her life – a mess that now involved a murder.

"What were you doing here that day?" Allaben asked.

"The same as today."

"You heard about the shooting?"

"It was on the news."

"You told the sheriff that you got here about 8:00."

"Yeah. I had to be at work at 9:00."

"And before last Monday – when was the last time before that?"

"The sheriff asked me the same thing. It was in June, around the end of school."

"You're sure of that?"

"I'm sure. And I didn't shoot him, if that's what you're getting at."

It was, of course, exactly what Allaben was getting at. He liked the kid, and he was inclined to believe him. But he couldn't let the boy off the hook because he felt sorry for him. They walked in silence for several minutes more until they reached the overlook parking area. Several other cars had joined Allaben's and the boy's, and a handful of people could be seen on or in the vicinity of Burnside Bridge below. Pedro raced to the side of Allaben's truck. No way this dog would be left behind. The boy glanced at his watch.

"I've got to get back to work," he said. "Sorry I surprised you back there."

"I'm glad we had a chance to talk," Allaben replied. He pulled a card from his pocket and handed it to the boy. "If you think of anything, give me a call. Anytime. And it doesn't have to be about the case."

The boy received the card gravely, nodded, then started for his car – an old green Toyota parked at the opposite end of the lot. He stopped after he'd taken a few steps.

"I knew about my mother and that guy who's dead," the boy volunteered quietly, "but I didn't know him. I had seen him at the gun club a few times, too. We never spoke."

Allaben decided to take a chance. "That doesn't mean you didn't hate him, though. It would be understandable, even natural, that you'd hate him, maybe even hate him enough to try to throw a scare into him."

"What?"

"Well, for example, by taking a run at him in Frederick a couple of weeks ago. In one of your father's Toyotas. A white one."

The boy gave him a long look. Finally he said, "You can't prove it."

"I don't care about proving it. I just want to know one way or the other."

"You're guessing, aren't you?"

"Yes, I'm guessing. The question is, Am I guessing right?"

"Let's say you're on the right track. I didn't hate him, though. He was just another one of my mother's 'friends.'"

"It seems he took more interest in you than you did in him."

"Me?"

"He had pictures of you in his apartment, Donnie. A sheet of school photos. Any idea why he might've wanted them?"

The boy shrugged. "I suppose he got them from my mother."

"Probably. But why?"

He shrugged again. Plainly he had no idea. "Is it important?" he asked.

Allaben more and more had the feeling that it was.

35

The building and grounds of the Fish & Game Club could not be seen from the narrow winding county road that Allaben traveled. It was only a small wooden sign that gave notice of its presence to passing motorists, and the sign itself was tucked nearly out of sight behind a thick stand of evergreens shadowing the road.

Allaben could not slow in time to make the turn. He made a sharp U-turn on the empty road. At the signpost he turned onto a narrow lane that sunk from the road at a steep incline, crossed a shallow brook, then swung back to the right, where it leveled off and followed the stream for a quarter of a mile. Another turn, this one to the left, brought him to a dead end in the form of a half-acre parking area. The lot was enclosed on three sides by a snake-rail fence. On the far side, a gravel path led through an opening in the fence to a lodge of rough-hewn timbers. To the left of the lodge stood a cluster of sheds.

Although the sun was no more than 15 minutes beneath the horizon, it was dark enough for the photo-sensitive lights at the corners of the lot to have bloomed into life. Allaben spotted Mallory's cruiser parked near the path. Near to it, he saw Mason Greer's shiny black Lincoln. There was room between it and a hastily parked white Range Rover with Kentucky plates. It had a playing-card size emblem of Confederate flag glued to the lower corner of its rear window on the driver's side. Allaben pulled in and cut the engine. In the vapory light, Greer's car gleamed a phosphorescent green.

A muffled bang sounded from beyond the lodge, echoed almost immediately by another bang. Allaben stepped from his truck, locked it, then took stock of his surroundings. The air was warm and still. Crickets had set up a dry, rhythmic chirp. Another bang sounded, and then, close behind it, another. A yelp, some clapping, and a few playful hoots.

A security camera surveyed the entrance to the lodge. But if his approach was monitored, it did not raise an alarm. No one appeared at the glass doors to bar the way. He opened a door and walked in. He found himself in a large anteroom lit by wall sconces. A trophy case stood against one wall, and an array of antlered deer heads decorated the other. Straight ahead of him was another set of glass doors that led to the shooting range. To his left was a hallway covered in gray industrial carpet. To his right, through an open entryway, was the great room. It was fitted out with sturdy coffee tables, club chairs and couches. A massive stone fireplace filled the better part of the far wall. Here and there a table lamp had been turned on. Their light seemed to barely reach the high, beamed ceiling.

In a corner near the fireplace was a small bar. Tables and chairs were arranged nearby. Behind the bar a man was wiping a glass. Two men in polo shirts sat at one of the tables and another, wearing what looked like the same Hawaiian shirt he'd worn to the barbeque, sat on a bar stool. Delvecchio wasn't kidding about this guy and his guns. But neither Rod Hurley nor any of the others paid Allaben any mind. Nor did they seem to pay any notice to the intermittent blasts that sounded outside. Allaben decided to have a look at the rooms that opened off the hallway.

The first door was locked. The second, according to the sign fixed to it, housed the club's membership office. The door was open and the lights were on. Allaben peeked in. A middle-aged man sat at a desk, studying a computer screen. Allaben tapped on the doorway.

"Mr. Moore?" he asked.

The man peered at his visitor from above the frame of reading glasses perched precariously at the tip of his nose. He had an expensive haircut and a deep, leathery tan.

"Come on in and have a seat," he said. "I won't be a moment."

Allaben took the chair that was offered him. Shotguns boomed outside, and a muffled cheer went up.

"Must be some rare shooting going on tonight," Moore commented without turning from the monitor. "And here I am, stuck with a members' mailing and a temperamental computer."

Allaben smiled politely and waited. The office was small and simply furnished. Besides the desk and chairs there was only a file cabinet parked in a corner. A key was fitted into the lock of the top drawer, which was a few inches open. No windows, and nothing on the walls but a calendar and a clock. The minute hand advanced twice before Moore finished pecking at the keyboard before him.

"There," he said, "that's done. Now, what can I do for you, Mister …"

"Allaben."

"Allaben?" He tilted his head back and closed his eyes. "Allaben." He swirled the name as if he were testing its vintage.

"Gene Delvecchio gave me your name," Allaben explained. "He says you're the man to see regarding membership."

Moore glanced at the clock, then at Allaben. The import was clear – it was an odd time, an inconvenient time, to be discussing membership.

"It's late, I know," Allaben acknowledged. "I've arranged to meet with Mason Greer after the shoot. Since I'm here, I thought I'd just stop by your office on the chance that you'd be here, too."

The mention of Mason Greer's name seemed to cast Allaben's presence in a different light for Calvin Moore. He put his fingertips together.

"Well, Mr. Allaben, in order to become one of us, you have to be sponsored by a member in good standing. I'm sure that you will appreciate our reasons for insisting on this policy. We're not exactly a country club, but we do like to think of ourselves as a fraternity of sorts, a group of like-minded individuals who like to shoot and to hunt, who tie their own flies."

"I'm not here to apply for membership," Allaben interrupted.

"Then why?"

"To ask you about one or two of your members."

"Our records are confidential." Moore's tone turned guarded.

Allaben showed him his credentials.

Moore pursed his lips and frowned. He shrugged. "All right, Mr. Allaben. After all, we have nothing to hide. I'm just doing my duty, trying to protect the privacy of our members."

"If I were a member, I'd expect nothing less," Allaben said.

From a desk drawer Moore drew a cloth-covered ledger. "We haven't entrusted our list to the computer," he explained. "Some on the governing board feel things should be done as they always have. Besides, there's no guarantee that it would be any more secure on a hard drive than on paper."

Allaben nodded at the ledger. “Do you know all these folks?”

“By sight, yes, probably all of the current ones. Some I know much better than others, naturally.”

“Did you know Curtis Gwynn?”

“Not very well. Poor man.”

“Is he missed?”

“By some more than others, I expect.” To judge by the tone of his voice, Moore was one of the others. He opened the ledger, leafed through the pages, tapped a finger at the entry in question. “Here he is.”

“Who was the sponsor?”

“It was our retired Navy officer, Roger Irwin.”

Allaben was momentarily stunned. Irwin? That cagey spook had dealt him another joker. Of course – it would be Irwin. It had to be. But who was it, then, who had brought Irwin in? The answer to that came almost immediately. Irwin’s sponsor must have been the source that he had spoken of the other day. It was the name he wouldn’t give up.

Moore broke in to Allaben’s rumination. “Do you know Roger Irwin?”

“Yes, I know him. But I wasn’t aware that he’d sponsored Curtis Gwynn. Do you see much of Irwin around here?”

“Some. He comes by now and again. But I can’t say I’ve spoken with him to any extent. Drops in, shoots … shoots quite well, actually, though he’s not participating in the tournament tonight. Mason is, however. You can see for yourself.”

He stood. Calvin Moore had had his fill of Felix Allaben. He’d be more than happy to hand him off to the nearest taker. Allaben stood, too, and then followed Moore out of the office and down the hallway to the doors that led to the shooting range.

The doors opened onto a shallow yard bounded on the far side by a tall cedar hedge. A wooden gate was set into its center. Allaben pushed it open. Before him was the shooting range, a fan-shaped arena that stretched flat and even for seventy-five yards before rising to a curtain of woods. Deep forest stood close up to each side. Two banks of field lights, mounted atop tall wooden masts, were all that held back the night. Outside the perimeter it was already black.

Low bleachers stood between Allaben and the shooters, and there was a lull in the shooting as he approached. All the same, there was no mistaking the nature of the event in progress. The bitter smell of gunpowder gave it away.

He paused as he came abreast of the bleachers. The spectator nearest him, an old fellow in a cardigan, leaned over and announced, "It's between Greer and Parker now." The two competitors stood at opposite ends of the clay semicircle that connected the shooting stations. Greer was only thirty feet from Allaben, while Parker's station put him another hundred feet distant. Both men wore canvas hunting vests; both stood at ease, guns loaded. A good-natured heckler in the bleachers offered some advice to Parker, who retorted with a grin and a rejoinder. There was a smattering of laughter. Then it was still – so quiet that Allaben could hear the crickets sing.

That's when he noticed Wick Mallory standing just a few paces past the cardigan. He eased over to the sheriff.

"Wick."

"Hey, buddy."

Allaben made out Lester Dawson, perched in the bleachers, maybe fifty feet away. Dawson, who'd been the first to do the spotting, was nodding discreetly in his direction. Allaben returned the salute. Now he knew who belonged to the Range Rover.

"Lester Dawson's over there," he observed to Mallory.

"Who? Oh, yeah, Dawson."

"What's he doing here? "

"How should I know? I guess he goes where he wants. Don't ask my permission."

A man in a dark blazer rose from the first plank of the bleachers and took a few steps forward. He faced Parker and Greer in turn.

"Final stage," he declared. "Mr. Greer will shoot first."

Greer assumed the firing position, the shotgun poised but not yet pressed against his shoulder. The barrel glinted dully in the cocoon of high-wattage light.

"Pull!"

A deep twang sounded. The disk flew from the trap, skimming to Greer's left across the shooting range. He fired. The disk, only clipped at the rim, wobbled out of sight. Greer immediately swiveled, his cheek still tucked against the gun stock, and waited in readiness for the second bird. Again, the release sounded and again the disk flew from the trap, this time bearing to his right. Greer followed its flight, took aim, and at the last moment squeezed the trigger. The disk burst into fragments and disappeared in the night sky. Greer stood back. Smoke curled from the muzzle of his gun.

Applause rattled from the bleachers, but Greer did not acknowledge it. His brother-in-law had yet to shoot. He discharged the spent shells and rested his gun against the rifle stand.

Parker took up his position and prepared to shoot. Two clean hits and the match was his. He looked settled and composed. Allaben watched him closely. How much had he drunk today? Enough, apparently, to keep himself steady – he'd managed to make it to the final round, after all. But was enough to get him to this point too much to go all the way?

A voice bellowed from the bleachers: "You've got him right where you want him, Don!"

Parker smiled broadly. He raised his gun.

"Pull!"

The saucer shot from the trap. Parker was immediately in trouble. He had started his lead too quickly and now had to pause to get the target in his sights. It was enough to throw off his aim. He fired. The disk flew off unscathed.

The match was as good as over, but Parker never missed a beat. He swiveled, aimed, pulled the trigger again. The second bird disintegrated in a puff of shards and dust. Parker held the shooting pose just for a second, then relaxed. A steady clapping broke out in the stands. He waved his hand in acknowledgement.

Winner and runner-up met at the top of the semicircle. They shook hands, then turned to wave at the spectators. It was only then that Greer saw Allaben. The easy smile of victory tightened.

Fifteen minutes later, Greer sat with Allaben at a corner table in the great room. An invisible wall had risen around them. None of the chattering crowd milling about, drinks in hand, came closer than ten feet. There seemed a tacit understanding that Greer and guest were not to be disturbed.

On the table before them were two glasses of whiskey and a

gleaming maple humidor. Greer lifted the lid and turned it toward Allaben, who declined the offer. Greer selected a chocolate brown cigar for himself. He ran it slowly under his nose, smiled appreciatively, then drew open a shallow drawer set into the base of the box. From the drawer he drew a cutter. He nodded at the humidor.

"A beautiful piece, isn't it? Hand-made. I've got one just like it in my study at home."

Allaben lifted his glass. "Congratulations on your victory."

"Too bad for Don," Greer said. "He usually makes that shot."

Allaben nodded in the direction of the bar, where Parker, tumbler in hand, now occupied the spot that Rod Hurley had held earlier.

"Looks like he's making it now," he observed.

Greer scowled. "Don's been under a lot of pressure, Mr. Allaben. Why don't you let me worry about him? He's my brother-in-law. And he's harmless. You've found that out for yourself. News travels fast around here."

Allaben glanced in Parker's direction, just in time to see him shift his gaze away. "I think your brother-in-law would like to know what we're talking about."

"Come to that, Mr. Allaben, I'd like to know. You didn't haul yourself all the way out here to counsel me about Don Parker." Greer lit the cigar, blew a stream of smoke away from Allaben, then squared around to face him again. He allowed himself a boxer's grin, sure he'd have to take a few but confident that at the end of the fight he'd be the only one standing.

Allaben came straight to the point. "Curtis Gwynn had something on you, didn't he?"

Greer was unfazed. He calmly fashioned a reply. "It strikes me as provocative, even a sort of harassment, that you should press me about Curtis Gwynn. I barely knew him, and can't imagine what you mean by this absurd allegation that he 'had' something on me. You forget who you're talking to, Mr. Allaben."

"What did you talk to Gwynn about when he phoned you?"

"Phoned me? I've never spoken with the man."

"He called you twice, and the records show that the calls lasted for several minutes each time."

"I don't remember any calls. Perhaps he talked with one of my staff."

"He called you at home, too. Do you have a staff there, as well?"

"From time to time I do. And my housekeeper. Do you think I just pick up the phone when it rings?"

"Gwynn took an interest in your career. Had a collection of articles. Did you know that?"

"Look, Mr. Allaben, I told you I never talked to him. I don't know anything about him."

"Your sister never talked to you about him?"

"Never. I knew about these flings of hers, of course. She knows that I disapprove strongly. Her behavior is disgusting, an insult to everything I stand for. We don't get along and we don't see each other much. But I suppose you already know that. Now, what else do you want to know?"

Allaben turned over another card. "Gwynn also had in his possession information concerning a militia group called the Potomac Resistance League. Their badge of honor is a coiled snake. Ever hear of them?"

"Nope."

"Nope? Sorry, but I'm afraid that 'nope' won't do. I have it on good authority that they meet right here at your club. I hoped you could shed some light on their activities, maybe even describe your relationship with them."

Greer sat back casually, then stared fixedly into his questioner's eyes. "I have no relation with such a group. And to hell with this 'good authority' of yours. A man in my position is used to rumor-mongering."

"I think that there's more to it than rumor, Mr. Greer."

Greer sucked at the cigar. The end glowed like a warning light.

"And I don't give a good goddamn what you believe," he said, "any more than I do the perverse ravings of that newspaper friend of yours. Yes, I know that you two are buddies. It's just the sort of rubbish that London would publish if he could, but he has no more evidence, no more substantiation, than you."

"What about your brother-in-law? I've heard that he's an officer of some sort in that weekend army. Any truth in that?"

Mason Greer glanced toward the bar, and seemed satisfied by what he saw there. He returned his gaze to Allaben.

"You heard? My old auntie hears things, too. You'll have to do better than that if you're going to keep my attention. Tell me what you've seen, what evidence you've collected, what you can prove. Otherwise, stop making a nuisance of yourself."

"Curtis Gwynn also had some school photos of your nephew. That surprised me. Does it surprise you?"

Greer looked at Allaben without looking at him. Allaben fought the urge to turn in search of the object of Greer's faraway gaze and concentrated instead on his hard blue eyes, which in another instant had reclaimed the here and now. The lazy smile returned.

"It's as much a mystery to me, Mr. Allaben, as it appears to be to you. You disappoint me, truly you do. I expected more from you than this fishing expedition. If you don't mind – and even if you do – I'll take my leave now. I have some hands to shake before I call it a day. You're not going to provoke me like you did my brother-in-law."

With that, Greer emptied his glass and stood. Instantly, as if summoned by magical incantation, half a dozen men were huddled around him. Allaben found himself on the outside looking in. He noticed that Parker was not among the glad-handers and hangers-on who crowded around the man of the hour. Nor could he be seen at the bar. There was nothing left for Allaben to do but leave.

As Allaben made his way back through the parking area to his truck, he noticed that the fencing that corralled the lot did not actually form a true cul de sac. Set into the fencing was a gate of metal pipe bars that blocked a gravel road leading into the woods. Allaben looked around – there was no one in sight. He climbed over the fence and dropped onto the gravel.

He walked on the grass fringe of the road. After he'd traveled fifty yards through the woods, he came to a clearing perhaps a half-acre in size. Along one side of the clearing stood an elongated rectangular structure made from metal sheeting. Two loading docks were set into its longer side. He stood for a moment to take stock of what he saw. A truck was backed up against the further bay. Thanks to the light leaking from the open bay, Allaben could see that the truck, a moving van, was being loaded. Or maybe unloaded, he couldn't tell. He could, however, catch snippets of conversation, curses and directions mostly, from the small group of men laboring at the job.

Allaben cautiously approached the bay nearest him. The gate was raised only about a foot. He pulled out his cell, slid his arm under the gate, and blindly snapped some photographs. He'd send them to Washington tomorrow. Suddenly, the sound of a cell phone came from the further loading dock. He stopped and listened – dead quiet at first, then some low, mumbled orders. Had he been detected? Had he triggered a motion sensor?

He retreated into the brush and made his way back to the parking area, first slowly, and then at a brisk pace, despite the branches and brambles that slapped and tugged at him. His heart was pounding as he reached his truck.

Allaben started out of the parking lot with the truck's headlights off. The sky was hazy and moonless, and he could see no further than a few yards into the thick, shadowy woods beside him. With regular glances into his rear-view mirror, he snaked along the rutted dirt road, clattered over the bridge, and, with headlights turned on, regained the smooth asphalt of the county road that had brought him here. There wasn't a car in sight, behind him or ahead. It had cooled off a little, and he opened his windows all the way.

He collected himself. Yes, he'd ridden a little adrenaline rush, but now he was out of harm's way. He thought about the shooting match and his conversation with Mason Greer. He'd have to come back at Greer sooner rather than later, but when he did, he'd have to come armed with more than hunches. Greer could not be bluffed.

Parker, too, would have to be pressed. Parker who had surprised him with that last shot, the one that had blown the clay pigeon to smithereens. Had he choked with the first shot and then, when it no longer mattered and the pressure was off, made a meaningless bull's eye with the second? Or had he deliberately missed the first shot – let Mason Greer win – and then hit the second for punctuation, a sign to any who might suspect that, yes, he could easily have blown apart both if he'd so wished?

"Or am I reading too much into this?" Allaben wondered.

He hadn't the leisure to consider the problem further. An ominous coughing noise was coming from beneath him. The truck sputtered and slowed. He looked at the fuel gauge – empty. But that was impossible – he'd filled the tank on the way out. He pushed the accelerator to the floor. The truck shuddered forward another hundred feet under its own power, then coasted to a stop. He managed to pull to the side of the road, although not completely off it. There was only a yard of shoulder between the road surface and a deep ditch that ran beside it. He turned off the engine and the lights, released the hood latch, removed his flashlight from the glove compartment, and got out of the truck.

The night was black as pitch. He switched on the flashlight and kneeled on the gravel in front of the truck. The beam showed nothing beneath the truck, nothing broken and nothing leaking. He opened the hood and shone the flashlight on the engine. It was clean, quiet, cool. The gas line had been cut. It had to have been. He was no mechanic, but what other explanation could there be? He had only come a mile from the Fish & Game Club. He could walk back there. But why go back to where the sabotage must have been performed? No, he wouldn't give them – or whoever it was – the satisfaction. He had his cell with him. He'd call upon the Washington County Sheriff's Department to help him out of this one.

He walked to the driver's side door, then stopped. A car was coming. He heard it before he saw it, coming from the direction of the Fish & Game Club. A fan of light rose over the hill a half a mile behind him. Then the car topped the crest and the headlights came into view. Even at that distance they seemed terribly bright. He heard the engine whine. The car was moving fast, too fast.

Allaben switched on the flashlight and waved it in an arc. The driver had to have spotted his truck – unless he was blind drunk – but why take chances? The car might stop or it might not. Allaben didn't much care either way, as long as it didn't plow into his truck.

The car hurtled down the road without slowing at all. The headlights dimmed, then came up high again. It occurred to Allaben that he had better think the worst – those lights were bearing down upon him like a predator's eyes. No good to be in front of the truck – *it* could kill him, too, if it was struck hard enough. In five strides he was past the rear bumper. He dove toward the ditch as the car roared past, inches from the side of the truck. He rolled down the bank and landed in three inches of water. He lay on his back, breathing fast. The flashlight had fallen on the shoulder. It cast a net of light above him. He sat up and listened. The car was already far gone.

36

Lester Dawson was just weaving his way out of the misty Catoctin Mountains, not far from where he knew Camp David to be cloistered, when his private phone, the one he kept in the Range Rover, sang out with "Garry Owen", its newest ring tone.

Without a word of greeting, an angry Mason Greer launched into him.

"What the hell was that about last night, Lester? Have you lost your mind?"

"Hold your horses, Mason. What are you talking about?"

"That funny business on the road – with Allaben, of course. Was that your work?"

"Never mind whose work it was. The point is that …"

"The point is that scaring Allaben won't get rid of him, damn you!"

"Listen to me," Dawson soothed, "you're getting worked up over nothing."

"No, you listen to me," Greer returned. "That cop is pestering me, my family, and who knows who else. My sheriff has no leads. His deputy is clueless. I'm in the dark. Damn it, what the hell are you keeping from me?"

Lester Dawson's work depended in large part upon his keeping his head and managing information, which in turn meant anticipating and manipulating reactions to that information. He had to focus on the big picture, not let less significant things sidetrack him. Sure, Greer was anxious, but Dawson had reckoned on that.

"I can't stay on the phone for long, Mason. The roads are slick and I'm in a hurry. You just stick to your campaign and leave the rest to me."

"That's what I'm starting to fear – losing control of things to you. What do you know that I don't, Lester? That these law officers don't?"

"I know they won't uncover any murderers at the gun club. And I know there's nothing else there for anyone to find. Not anymore. Everything's been taken care of."

"Everything's been removed?"

"For now."

"So, what do I do, Lester?"

He'd prepared for this, too. "First, Mason, you settle down. Then you invite Allaben to your office. You sit behind your big honking desk and look calm and collected. Maybe you're looking at one of your TV spots when he arrives. You're unworried, you smile. You invite his opinion. That's what you do. You're Maryland's next attorney general with your sights set even higher."

"Yeah, but what do I say to him, besides 'What do you think of my promos?' "

"You tell him it pains you that he was so badly treated after leaving you at the gun club. Tell him you're relieved that he didn't get hurt. Say it like you mean it. And tell him that you'll ferret out who was behind it. Show anger, concern, commiseration. If he starts in again with the third degree about the PRL, you man up, look him straight in the eye, like you're about to come clean about something. Make him think it's he who made you own up. You tell him that, yes, there's a group of guys with a common purpose who gather at the Fish & Game Club. They shoot, talk guns, drink. And they talk politics."

"Are you sure about this, Lester?"

"Absolutely. You assure him you're not one of them. Tell him that you don't know most of those guys too well, but your impression is that they're upstanding citizens, local businessmen, American patriots. Something along those lines. You don't necessarily approve of their ways, but you sympathize with their concerns, as do the good people of Maryland."

Greer started to protest again, but Dawson pushed patiently and steadily on.

"Mason," he said, "you tell him all this, you invite him to keep on looking our way, and you know what? He won't look anymore. He won't because he'll know he'd be barking up the wrong tree while the possum's getting away."

"I hope you're right." Greer sounded half-persuaded.

"I know I'm right. You're a shrewd politician. I've seen you in action. Hell, just stick to the truth. No need to misinform or fabricate. Don't say any more than you have to. Just get your story straight. Now I got to go," Dawson said in conclusion. "We'll talk again later on."

The mist had already dispersed as he passed under I-70 and

turned left off state route 66 and into the northern outskirts of Boonsboro. He pulled into a homely gas station, as unpresuming as the hamlet itself. It gave him a sense of satisfaction, of all's right with the world, to know that the kid filling his tank and washing his windows front and back had no idea whose car this was and what its owner was up to.

Back on the road and starting in the direction of Frederick, Lester Dawson decided he would put Mason Greer and Felix Allaben out of his mind for awhile. Once Boonsboro's early morning traffic and its single traffic light were behind him, he dialed a number in Martinsburg to clarify a last-minute change in timing.

On the verge of some real excitement, some real action, his juices were flowing. He felt no jitters. He was ready.

37

Allaben sat at his kitchen table, a steaming cup of coffee before him. Pedro lay asleep beneath the table. It was 8:45. Mallory had promised to have the truck returned by 9:00, and Mallory was usually good to his word, so when the phone rang, Allaben assumed it would be the Sheriff of Washington County announcing that the reunion of driver and vehicle was only moments away.

"Did I wake you up?" It was Carolyn.

"No."

"I did, didn't I?"

"No."

"Well I should have. You need your rest after last night."

How could she possibly know about last night? "Do you have someone tailing me?" he asked.

"Better than that – I have Stuart London and his police scanner."

"I'm fine, Carolyn. Thanks for asking. Nothing damaged but my dignity."

"You should have a bodyguard, Felix. I'd volunteer, but you need someone a lot bigger and meaner than me. There are some folks out there who don't like you as much as I do. Or haven't you noticed?"

"I've noticed," he said. "Believe me, I've noticed. A life is, after all, a terrible thing to have blown up, burnt, or run over, especially when it's your own. But today is Allaben Makes Progress Day. Mark it on your calendar. To begin with, I get my truck back, and in running order, too, thanks to the Washington County Sheriff's Department. Then I'll pay a call or two. You don't get answers worth a damn unless you've got the right questions. Today, although he's a little worse for wear, Felix Allaben has the right questions."

"I've got a question, too."

"An easy one, I hope. It's too early for riddles."

"That reminds me. Stuart told me that he has something for you, some information, I guess. He said you might want to talk to the sheriff about it."

"He wouldn't tell you what 'it' is?"

"No. And not for lack of trying on my part, I might add. I couldn't get anything out of him. He was playing the big tease."

"Good for him. So what's the question?"

"The question?"

"You were going to ask me a question."

"So I was."

"Well?"

"I've forgotten."

Allaben thought for a second, and noticed while he was thinking that Pedro had roused himself, which meant, more often than not, that the dog had heard something that his master had not. So Allaben was not surprised when, just as he was about to deliver his next line, a loud knock sounded at the front door.

❧

D.T. stood on the other side of the screen door. Just behind him was a young man in a T-shirt and dungarees. He wore a yellow baseball hat with "Hoyt's Auto" stitched across it in black.

"Morning, Inspector," said D.T. "We've brought you your truck. Gary here fixed it up good."

Gary stepped forward and presented Allaben with a dog-eared credit-card receipt and a ball point pen.

"Includes a full tank of gas," he drawled.

The paperwork completed to his satisfaction, he withdrew to the passenger seat of D.T.'s patrol car.

Allaben and D.T. walked together to the side of the truck, an inanimate assembly of steel, rubber, and plastic – or so went Allaben's thinking – altogether insensible of the close calls to which it had been witness. Which reminded him, had Hal Snyder been a witness, too? Perhaps an unwitting one, not conscious that he'd seen something – maybe important, maybe not – until well after the fact? After they'd talked at the crime scene, for example. Perhaps he'd remembered something, left a note for Allaben: "See me."

"D.T.," Allaben asked, "do you recall if there was anything odd about the way Hal Snyder was acting just before he died? His wife mentioned that something was bothering him."

"Yes, I know, sir."

"Yes, you know what – that he was acting funny, or that his wife noticed it?"

"His wife. She said as much to me."

"She did? When did you talk to her? At the funeral?"

"No, I wasn't at his funeral. It was the day after Gwynn's death. The sheriff said if we were going to investigate, we might as well do it right. Hal Snyder could have been there before Irwin showed up. A crazy notion – the sheriff said so himself – but he told me I should find out more about Snyder just to prove it was crazy. He told me to play it very innocent, so as not to upset the missus."

"Did you learn anything?" Allaben asked.

"I learned that he got to work darn early, earlier than the other rangers, and that he stayed later, too. I learned that he liked to cap off most days with a climb up the tower for a final look-see over the battlefield. I guess he also took a flask up there with him sometimes. As far as Curtis Gwynn was concerned, Mrs. Snyder never heard the name before, not from Hal, anyway."

The deputy removed his hat and wiped the sweat off his forehead, just above the crease made by the brim.

Allaben pressed on. "Who else did you talk to? The other rangers?"

"Mostly Poole. The one you met."

"Was it Poole who told you when Hal got to work each day?"

"He told me that Snyder beat him there most mornings. But it was Mrs. Snyder who told me how early he usually left for work. She said he was a real early riser, left the house by six o'clock."

"So you visited Mrs. Snyder, and she hinted that Hal was acting bothered."

"Didn't hint. Came right out and said it."

"But she didn't know by what."

"No. He was pretty snappish with her is what she said."

Allaben thought for a minute. D.T. shifted from one foot to the other. He allowed himself a yawn. He'd take his time driving back, and he'd have Gary to keep him company.

"And afterward," Allaben resumed, "you wrote all this down for the boss?"

"No sir. I simply told him what I learned as soon as I learned it."

"And that was the end of it? You didn't pursue it any further?"

"No need. Snyder went and got himself squashed. Can't talk to a dead man."

"Or listen to one," returned Allaben.

D.T.'s brow furrowed in puzzlement. "All due respect, Inspector, but that case is closed. Those kids saw him. He got drunk and fell off the tower, the poor slob. Simple as that."

Poor slob? Yes, anyway you looked at it.

Got drunk? For certain. The autopsy proved it.

Fell? Allaben didn't think so.

Allaben returned to the kitchen. He owed Wick Mallory a thank-you call.

"No problem, Felix. The least I could do."

"Was it the fuel line?"

"Cut clean through. You were set up. And you were damned lucky, too, by your account. Caught in the headlights like that. No deer could've done as well. Any idea who it might have been?"

"A couple. Don Parker, for one. He was at the club."

"I could talk to him."

"You'd be wasting your time. We've got nothing, and if it was him, he knows we've got nothing."

"But if it *wasn't* him, Felix, he might know who it was."

There was a dead-end silence. Then Mallory headed in a different direction.

"You saw Mason there, didn't you? How did that go? Did you learn anything?"

"He's holding something back. My instincts tell me that he's hiding some connection he had with Gwynn."

Mallory hesitated. "I'm at a loss here, Felix. I mean Mason's a tough customer. Everyone knows what a son-of-a-bitch he can be. He's ambitious as hell. About knowing Gwynn better than he's letting on, well, I don't know what to say. He's never mentioned the guy to me, not once. I'm fairly certain he hadn't been socializing with him either. But with what all that's been going on around here in the last couple of weeks, nothing would surprise me. Hate to say it, but it's true."

"Wick, has he ever spoken to you of an outfit called the Potomac Resistance League?"

"No, he never has. I've heard about them, though. White supremacists, anti-government, the whole package, I think. They're in West Virginia mostly, parts of Maryland, too, I hear. Never had any problem with them on my turf."

"They have a problem with me."

Allaben reminded Mallory of the parking lot episode. He could almost see the light bulb light over Mallory's head.

"Felix," the sheriff ventured, "maybe it was them that took a run at you last night."

"Maybe. And maybe it was Don Parker in the car. It amounts to the same thing."

"You mean Don's one of them?"

"I can't prove it."

"Maybe there's a good reason why you can't."

"Wick, these guys are set up at that gun club, using it as cover. I'm sure that some members don't know what's going on. But I'm willing to bet that Don Parker's in the know. At least that. And probably Mason Greer, too."

38

Irwin kept Allaben waiting just long enough to make it seem deliberate. How long could it take for Priscilla, who had answered the phone, to walk to Irwin's study and tell him that Mr. Allaben was on the line? She had asked Allaben to leave a message, as Mr. Irwin had said he was not to be disturbed, unless it was his wife. Allaben had insisted, politely, and sent a reluctant Priscilla off with the advisory that this was police business. It wasn't strictly true, but Irwin would get the message.

When at last he picked up the phone, Irwin could not quite keep his annoyance from souring his buttery voice.

"I was with my maps, Allaben. What's so all-fired important that it couldn't wait for an hour?"

"You might have told me that you sponsored Gwynn for the Fish & Game Club."

Silence at the other end. Then, "Hold on." Allaben heard a click.

When Irwin came back on, he asked, "How did you find that out?"

"Is that a scrambler I just heard?"

"Yes, it's a scrambler. I don't take chances. Now tell me how you found out."

"I went out there last night. I talked with Calvin Moore."

"I'd have thought he'd be more discrete."

"I mentioned Mason Greer's name."

"Was he there?"

"For a trap shooting competition. I talked to him, too."

"I trust you didn't mention my name."

"Trust? That's a funny word, coming from you."

"I've got a lot at stake at that club and with those people, Allaben. We've been through all of this once already. They're a dangerous crowd. You can't be too careful. I can't have anyone – even you – mucking things up."

"Like Curtis Gwynn? Was he the bull in the china shop? You sponsored him because you knew the PRL recruiters would see him as ripe for picking. There's no way Moore and his crowd would have allowed him in. How does it work? One of the PRL people has the power to overrule the membership committee?"

"Something like that," Irwin conceded.

"Who?"

Silence again. "Not Mason Greer, if that's what you're thinking – or hoping – but someone close to him. Name's Lester Dawson."

"Dawson." It was Allaben's turn to think. An idea came to him. "Did Dawson sponsor you?"

"Yes. I let on that I have money and I'm willing to put my money where my mouth is. That's where the gun club comes in. The PRL contingent uses it for banking."

"And for recruiting."

"From time to time. They keep and test weapons there, too, on the rifle range. Some heavy duty stuff. It's a handy resource all the way around."

"Handy for double agents, too – you and your mole, Curtis Gwynn. They must have licked their chops at the sight of him."

"He was perfect." An air of pride crept into Irwin's voice.

"Yes, but someone must have tumbled to him, and now he's perfectly dead. What happened? Did you lose control of him? And now you're worried that your cover's blown, too? You should have told me all of this before."

"I'm not the telling type, Allaben. I'm only telling you this now so that you won't go barging in there again. I have no reason to think that I'm in danger, yet."

"Does Folliard know about this?"

"Yes."

"All of it?"

"Yes."

Allaben didn't know whether to believe him or not. "Who killed Gwynn?"

"I don't know."

"Is that why I'm here? Did you ask Folliard for help?"

"No. My orders are to cooperate, not to volunteer."

"You mean, don't answer a question that's not been asked."

"If you like."

"I don't like. We don't have to be buddies, Irwin, but if I were you, I'd want me on your side. Especially now. You're safer telling me than having me find out myself."

Allaben listened to Irwin think.

"You haven't asked any questions regarding our means of communication, Gwynn's and mine," Irwin suggested.

"No, I haven't. Thank you. Well, then, how did you two keep up? He would need to brief you. You would need to give him his instructions. You didn't move in the same circles. Except for the club your lives didn't overlap."

"The club would serve for the run-of-the-mill exchanges," Irwin offered. "We could talk there if we were careful."

"But the meetings were only every other week." Allaben was beginning to see the light.

"That's right," Irwin prompted. "And the next regular meeting would be tonight."

"So if Gwynn uncovered something really hot, say late last week, he'd either have to wait until tonight … or find some other way."

"We never use phones," Irwin offered as encouragement. "Rules of the game these days."

In his mind's eye Allaben saw Curtis Gwynn's face, saw it in the photo that accompanied the story of his death. Gwynn would find some other way. The question wasn't whether, but how? Then the answer came to him fully illuminated. It was so obvious, explained so much, it made him laugh.

"Inspector?"

"Sure he'd find some other way," Allaben said. "Like stage an argument in the bar in order to arrange a rendezvous by Antietam Creek, a stream he knew to be more shallow and less wide than it was in 1862 when Burnside had to ford it."

39

Mason Greer's campaign headquarters were housed in a drab, three-story brick building in downtown Hagerstown. Allaben found it easily enough. The banners festooning the plate-glass windows made it nearly impossible to miss. As he maneuvered his truck into one of the metered parking spaces nearby, he noticed a brawny man in a Stetson leave the building. Allaben watched him unlock the door to a Range Rover across the street and slide into the driver's seat. No mistaking him. It was Lester Dawson. Allaben had half a mind to pull out and follow him, just to see what Mr. Dawson's next port of call might be. But he had been summoned by Mason Greer – by his assistant Brad Richards, in point of fact – for a private meeting at 6:00. It was now 5:50. An opportunity like this might never again present itself, and Allaben was curious – very curious – to learn the reason why Greer wanted to see him again so soon after showing him the door.

Richards greeted Allaben and ushered him past cartons full of flyers, posters, and bumper stickers, then past a dozen volunteers murmuring into headsets, to a small elevator tucked into a wall in the back. They rose to the second floor. Richards led Allaben down a short hallway to a door at the end. He knocked twice, opened the door, and nodded Allaben in.

"He's expecting you, sir. It's the doorway on the right."

With that, Richards excused himself, pulling the door closed behind him. Allaben listened to him walk back to the elevator. He waited until he heard the elevator door slide shut.

The doorway on the right led through a corridor to a big, rectangular office. There were windows on two sides, but slatted blinds kept out the late afternoon sun. A dim floor lamp cast a meek spray of yellow in a far corner. Otherwise, the room was quite dark. Deliberately dark, so that Mason Greer could view to best advantage the succession of images that beamed soundlessly from the TV before him. The electronic light flickered over his face. Allaben could not see the screen, but he could tell that whatever it was that Greer watched gave him satisfaction.

Allaben advanced into the room, and Greer held up a palm to acknowledge his presence. Then the screen went dark. Greer pressed a button on the remote and the TV sputtered off. He pressed another button, this one on his desk, and track lighting bathed the room with pinkish light.

Greer swiveled his desk chair to face Allaben, who had taken up residence in the plum-colored armchair opposite.

"Drink? Coffee?"

Allaben declined.

"All right, then, let's get down to business." He wagged a thumb at the television. "That was the rough cut for my next ad. Powerful stuff. No sound yet, but powerful stuff. I'm going to be the next attorney general, Mr. Allaben, and there is nothing in the world that can stop me. Nothing and no one. So I thought we should clear the air, you and I. Because I respect you, Allaben. I said to you last Saturday that there is no piece of business – none at all – that two reasonable men can't settle if they're of a mind to settle it. I'm of a mind to, and I hope you are, too."

"Now you're a stubborn cuss," he went on, "and you've got it into your head that I played a part in the shooting of Curtis Gwynn. You're wrong, but I'm probably not going to sway you, whatever I say. You're going to believe what you believe and you're not going to give it up."

Greer paused, as if to give Allaben one last chance to prove him wrong. Allaben said nothing. He waited.

"I admire that," Greer continued, "even though I think it's wrongheaded in this case, and I fear you've set yourself on a path that leads nowhere but full circle. But that's your business. It's only when it intrudes on mine that I feel obliged to voice an objection. I've thought about the talk we had last night at the club. And I've been informed of what happened – or almost happened – to you after you left. I spoke with Sheriff Mallory this morning. It won't do to have you draw erroneous conclusions from either of those things. It won't help you and it won't help me. That's why I asked you here this evening, so that we can talk privately and candidly about this matter, see if we can't get past it once and for all."

Again he paused, and again Allaben sat impassively. Greer smiled. It seemed he knew his man.

"So why don't we start again, just as if we're back at square one, just as if we never had that talk at the club last night?"

"Question you?" Allaben asked.

"Fire away." Greer checked his watch. "I'm betting this won't take longer than ten minutes."

Allaben thought for a moment. What was this all about? What was in it for his host? And why the sudden turnaround? The answers couldn't possibly be as simple as those advanced by Greer. Or could they? In any event, here was a chance that Allaben couldn't afford to squander. He could worry over the whys and the wherefores later. Better concentrate on motive, the only chink in Greer's armor. His alibi was air-tight; it had been checked and double-checked.

"Okay," Allaben began, "let's talk about the Potomac Resistance League, the PRL. Do you know of them?"

"I've heard of them."

"Are you a member?"

Greer snorted. "No. Certainly not."

"Do you know that your brother-in-law is a member?"

"I suspect he may be." Greer answered slowly, deliberately.

"And Curtis Gwynn. Do you know that he was a member?"

"No."

"He was collecting information about you and the PRL."

"Do you mean he was spying on me?"

"Why would he be spying on you?"

"I can't imagine. But I'll tell you this, Mr. Allaben. He might have dug until doomsday, but he'd never find anything that put me in the ranks of the PRL."

"Did you know Gwynn?"

"I knew he was consorting with my sister."

"How did you know that?"

"It wasn't the first time she'd shamed herself. Wick must have told you that he was not a stranger to Pamela's charms."

"Sure, back in high school."

"Post graduate, too, as you might say. As recently as this spring." Greer studied Allaben's face. "You didn't know?"

Allaben shook his head.

"Well, then, I guess I'm telling tales out of school. Wick's always carried a torch for her." He dismissed the matter with a wave of his hand. "Not important, Inspector, and certainly not relevant to your case."

"Did her husband know?"

"About Wick? I don't think so."

"How do *you* know?"

"Not from Wick, if that's what you're asking."

"You keep an eye on your sister?"

"Wouldn't you? I don't welcome scandal, Inspector. Not in my position. I'm in a fight for high office, as you know."

"You welcome the sheriff of Washington County, who you now tell me was sleeping with your married sister, but you don't welcome scandal?"

"I can trust Wick Mallory. I've always trusted him."

"How did their romance end?"

Greer shrugged. "I never learned. Just fizzled out, I suppose."

"Was it you who scotched the affair with Gwynn?"

"It's a husband's duty. Don scotched it."

"Did you have to remind him of his duty?"

"We talked, yes."

"What else did you talk about? Did he keep you abreast of the activities of the PRL? Is he your liaison? Isn't it risky to be mixed up with a hate group?"

"I wouldn't call it a hate group."

"What would you call people who advocate white supremacy and anti-government violence?"

"Who are you talking about?"

"Those pals of yours at the Fish & Game Club, the ones who

sit on the same leather couches and use the same locker room as you do. The ones who blame the immigrants, say they spoil the gene pool. The ones who sport Confederate flags as pins or decals for their cars. That's who I'm talking about."

Greer sighed. "They *are* my friends. Local businessmen. Solid citizens each and every one. They're fed up with things, Allaben, tired of big government and meddling liberals. If they want to do something about the awful state this country is in, who will deny them? Not me. They have every right to use their influence and their money as they see fit."

"To burn houses to the ground? To vandalize cemeteries? To carry loaded guns into stadiums filled with families?"

"No. To make political contributions."

"Contributions to your campaign?"

"Yes, and to lots of others. Maybe you haven't noticed, but the silent majority isn't so silent anymore. And some of them are rich. If these good people want to add to my war chest, who am I to say no?"

"Aren't you worried about having your name associated with the PRL?"

"No, I'm not, Inspector. And I'll tell you why. In the first place there is no good reason why my name should be associated with them. We have friends in common, and that's as far as it goes. Like I say, Gwynn could root around all he liked. He'd never come up with anything but rumor and gossip, the kind of reckless allegations that Stuart London character trades in. But even if the association is made, what of it? I don't condone their means – in fact, I deplore them – but I do subscribe to their ends. Just like millions of other Americans. Many of whom will be going to the polls in November.

The way I see it, that association wouldn't hurt me at all. On the contrary. Mr. Gwynn could have shouted it to the skies for all I'd care. It might even have helped my campaign, not that it needs much helping."

Greer paused. An abstracted expression took possession of his face. He looked as if he were making sure he hadn't forgotten anything. Allaben decided to take a new tack. "Why did you lie to me last night?"

"Sheer orneriness," Greer replied smoothly. "You rubbed me the wrong way, Allaben. I'm sorry. I should have set you straight right from the get-go."

Allaben almost believed him. He'd have to think this through, see where it led, though he knew already that he wouldn't like the place it would take him.

Greer tapped the desktop with his fists. He was through if Allaben was through. Allaben was through. He stood. Greer checked his watch.

Allaben thought. He thought all the way from Hagerstown to Frederick, heedless of the sundown in his rear-view mirror. He thought as he walked Pedro and he thought as he wolfed down a takeout dinner. He thought about Mason Greer – why had Greer changed his tune? He thought about Curtis Gwynn and Roger Irwin and the Parkers – all three of the Parkers. He thought about Hal Snyder. He thought about tattoos and coiled snakes. Around and around he went, getting nowhere. It was just as Greer had said. He was back to where he'd started.

The afternoon paper sat on the corner of the desk, but he wasn't interested in the news. There was a pile of mail, too – mostly junk. He checked his phone and flipped on his notebook – nothing from Miranda. Pedro was in the garden and the house was still. Good for thinking. But his thinking had gone stale. He felt as dim as the gray light that slowly settled around him. If there was any more thinking to do, it had better be fresh.

He pulled open a desk drawer and dug out the envelope he'd found in Gwynn's apartment. It was rumpled and stained, just as it had been the day the boy had delivered it to him. He slid its contents from the manila envelope and laid them out before him – the newsletter and articles about Mason Greer and the PRL, and the smaller envelope that held the sheet of photos.

They must have meant something to Gwynn, all of these things. Otherwise, why bother to secrete them between the pages of a book?

For the first time since the night of the fire, Allaben reviewed his search of Gwynn's apartment. He remembered clearly now the position of the book on the shelf, the book itself, even the pages between which the envelope had been sandwiched – 190 and 191.

Allaben closed his eyes and congratulated himself with a smile. Could it be? 191! Yes, Gwynn had spoken to him, whispered in his ear. It could not have been an accident that he'd placed the envelope there. It had to be a reference to Special Orders No. 191, the instructions that General Robert E. Lee had dispatched to his commanders, the same instructions that somehow came into the hands of his adversary, General George McClellan. It had to be. Here was the key. It had been in Gwynn's hands; now it was in his own. The Special Orders were the key, and it was up to him to find the lock that the key was meant to open.

Not the connection between Greer and the PRL. He had exhausted that line of investigation. It was a dead end. Greer was right. Gwynn could not have hurt him by playing that card.

The photos, then? They were all that Allaben had left. He drew them from the envelope: five Donnie Parkers, a sixth gone missing. On the back of each, "Lancer '91."

Allaben glanced at the mantel clock. If he called the Parker house now, he'd probably get Pamela or Don, Sr. But he didn't want to talk to either of them.

Tomorrow morning, then. He'd call Donnie Junior at work.

40

The school lobby smelled of ammonia and floor wax. A green and white banner hung on a wall, welcoming the freshman class. Less than a week remained until school reopened, and by all appearances Middletown High – home of the Crimson Knights – would be ready for customers.

Allaben checked in at the security desk. He was expected – the principal had left word – and if he would just walk to the end of the hallway and turn right, he would find the way, clearly marked, to the library. There the librarian, Mrs. Montague, would be prepared to help him.

Allaben's heels clicked on the buffed tile floor. He peeked into an empty classroom: whiteboard, ranks of aluminum and plastic chairs. Turning right at the end of the hallway, he found himself at the threshold of a glassed-in breezeway that connected the main school building with the library.

Mrs. Montague was a spindly blonde, nearer forty than thirty, with a no-nonsense mouth and keen brown eyes. She shook Allaben's hand and led him past several banks of computers to a carpeted study area adjoining the library stacks. There she came to a halt.

"How can I help you, Mr. Allaben?"

"I'd like to see the yearbooks – the Lancer – for the years 1989, '90, and '91."

He might have asked for a Gutenberg bible to judge by the stare that the request earned him.

"You do have them, don't you?" he continued. "The principal told me they're kept with the school's archives."

Her eyes narrowed with suspicion. "What do you want them for?" she asked.

"Does it matter?"

"You answer first," she insisted. She'd had lots of practice with smart-alecks.

Allaben showed her his credentials. "Your turn," he said.

The suspicion immediately gave way to a "Well, I've got news for you" expression.

"It's just that you're the second person in two weeks to ask for an old yearbook."

Now it was Allaben's turn to stare. The librarian nodded solemnly.

"Another man came in not two weeks ago, sat here for half an hour with a stack of them."

"Ponytail?"

"That's him. He sat here and whistled. I could hear from my desk."

"He returned the yearbooks?"

"Oh yes. Of course he did. Do you know him?"

Yes. Allaben knew him. He nodded, but offered nothing more.

"So I guess it's not just a funny coincidence," she ventured.

No, it wasn't just a funny coincidence. There was nothing funny about it at all.

Allaben adopted an official tone. "Could I see the yearbooks, please?"

She paused only a second, long enough to assert her own brand of authority, then strode off through the stacks. In a matter of minutes, she was back with the books. She placed them on the table and then retreated to her office. From there she could keep an eye on him. Now she wished that she'd paid closer attention to the handsome young man with the ponytail who had smiled his way into the library and talked his way into temporary possession of the yearbooks.

The very same that now were before Allaben. He picked up the 1991 edition. The cover was deep red, pebbly, imitation leather. Embossed in the center was a raised emblem of burnished silver, a heraldic shield bearing the legend "Live to Learn." Above the shield, in gothic letters, "Lancer '91."

Donnie Junior had recognized the name the moment Allaben said it. "Sure, Mr. Allaben, it's the school yearbook."

Allaben opened the book. He learned on the first page that this was Volume 6, that it was presented by the class of '91, and that the principal was one Eugene Peters. He leafed slowly through the first dozen pages, stopping here and there to study a photo or to read a caption: a message from the principal, a dedication to a retiring teacher, the faculty and staff; then the freshman, sophomore, and junior classes. Allaben looked carefully at the last, and without the help of the key was able to pick out Wick Mallory – no mistaking the lantern jaw and caterpillar eyebrows – and in the front row Pamela Parker (Pamela Greer, then), happier than Allaben had ever seen her, but no less conscious of her physical advantages. She wore a snug white turtleneck that nicely shadowed the contours of her figure.

How many of the boys pictured here had she flirted with, giggled at, made fun of? Wick Mallory had carried the torch for her – kept carrying it, too, if Mason Greer was to be believed. Doubtless many of his classmates had set their sights on her as well. But Pamela's gaze would always be centered on the top of the heap, the big man on campus, the one voted most likely to succeed, a senior. But because the natural candidate would be her hotshot brother, the next best thing would have to do.

Allaben turned to the section devoted to seniors, some fifteen pages or so of mug shots arranged alphabetically, three to a page. Donald Parker was at the bottom right of one of these pages. The young man who smiled so winningly in the photo did not look so very different from the middle-aged lush whom Allaben had last seen two nights ago. Leaner and brighter of eye, of course, but remarkably the same in practically every other respect. Even the hair – it was fashioned in the same surfer's curl.

Class Treasurer, Drama Club, Varsity Football and Baseball, Junior Chamber of Commerce. Future Plans: College.

The one who got the girl, and all the baggage that came with her, the dowry that even then had begun to tatter and fray.

And the girl's older brother? Don Parker's best friend and brother-in-law to be? The young man who was going places, who even then was marked for bigger and better things?

Allaben flipped back through the pages. O'Brien … Neilson … Lapham … Klein … Iverson … Ickes … Hopkinson … Garvey … Frampton. He'd gone too far, somehow missed the page with Greer's photo and accomplishments. But on reversing his route through the alphabet, he failed to find it again. At the bottom of page 18 was Melissa Glenn; at the top of the next was Julie Jacobs. Where was Mason Greer?

When the answer to that question dawned on him, Allaben cursed himself. How could he have failed to see? For that matter, how could he have failed to predict? Mason Greer's picture was gone with the page it had been printed on.

Pages 19 and 20 were gone, and gone so neatly that Allaben had not at first noticed they were missing. Nothing remained of the sheet but a sliver tied into the binding. The page had been cut with a very sharp instrument, perhaps a razor. On closer examination, Allaben could see the score that the blade had pressed into the page beneath.

He glanced at Mrs. Montague, found himself the object of her scrutiny. She had not been so vigilant when this seat had been occupied by Curtis Gwynn. Had his whistling lulled her? Or had he merely waited for or engineered some distraction to claim her attention? A few seconds were all he would have needed, that and something sharp. Allaben shivered. Air conditioning or revulsion, or both? It was chilly – like a morgue, in fact – but no colder than the calculation that had been the cause of Gwynn's undoing. Sure, he could pour through the yearbook page by page, looking for incidentals. But that was just it. The missing page made all the rest of the pages incidental. The 2 + 2 was on the chalkboard. He didn't have to see the 4.

For the first time since he'd taken on the case, Allaben felt something like fear. He'd been menaced in a dark parking lot and he'd nearly been killed twice – first in the fire in Gwynn's apartment, then on a moonless country road. But neither time had he felt reason to hide, find a dark place where the bad guys would never find him. He'd been in the wrong place at the wrong time. He'd made a nuisance of himself and someone had tried to throw a scare into him. This was different. Now he suspected what Gwynn suspected, or even thought he knew. Allaben guessed that he had no more proof than Gwynn had, only the gut-sure knowledge that made sense of the whole thing, or most of it.

But he'd be smarter than Gwynn had been, not tip his hand so recklessly and go off half-cocked, as Gwynn probably had, filled with ardor for the justice of his cause. Even the years on the unforgiving streets of Baltimore had failed to beat the righteousness out of him. It had taken a bullet to do that.

He stood. Mrs. Montague stood, too. Allaben nodded. He was ready to go.

"Was it helpful? Did you find what you were looking for?" she inquired.

"No," he replied, knowing his answer to be both true and false at the same time.

He walked back down the spotless, cool hallway, where in a few week's time students would mill and jostle. If they were lucky, they would be spared at least some of life's nastiness. Innocence is a good thing, Allaben thought, and ought to be safeguarded, preserved for as long as possible. Truth would come calling soon enough.

He'd do it if he could, for any kid, just as he would for Miranda. Hold his nose and cut a deal, even if it only gained a day.

He walked out of the dark school into the shimmer of afternoon. The hot, sticky air felt good on his face.

41

Carolyn had put them at her table, where they could talk without fear of being overheard. Waiters and busboys passed by briskly as they made their way to and from the kitchen. Carolyn was working the room, favoring good-byes and tidbits of gossip upon the last of the lunchtime regulars. It was two-thirty. In another half an hour, gumshoe and reporter would have the place to themselves.

London had ordered a sampler of summer tarts. He picked at them with a fork as he gathered his thoughts. Allaben sipped from a glass of iced coffee, impatient for the reporter to begin. He had composed a brief of his own on his way back to town but was still not certain he should deliver it.

"Well, Stuart?"

London chose his words carefully. "You asked me if I had anything unsavory on Mason Greer."

"And you said that as far as his personal habits go, he's a model of virtue."

"He is. Squeaky clean family man. Nobody's ever caught him with his pants down – not literally, anyway."

"Has this got something to do with Wick Mallory? Carolyn said you wanted to talk to me about Wick."

"I'm coming to that. Just hold your horses."

A server materialized at London's elbow. She held a coffee pot. London asked if the coffee was regular or decaf. Informed that it was the latter, he gave permission to have his cup refilled. Allaben declined a second glass of iced coffee. The last thing he needed right now was another jolt to his nervous system. His mind was revved up high enough as it was.

London sensed it. He waited until the waitress was out of earshot and then resumed.

"Is Mallory a friend?"

"Let me worry about that."

"Mind, Felix, that this is nothing more than hearsay. Just a rumor."

"Understood."

"Okay, it goes like this. A couple of years ago Mallory pulls over a guy on Route 77. Middle of the night, middle of nowhere. A kid named Crowder. He's still a deputy – Mallory is – but on the way up. Crowder is high as a kite, and he's got half a case of beer in him. The other half is in the girl in the passenger seat. One other witness. It seems Mallory had someone with him in the cruiser. Not a cop. His name was Lester Dawson."

Allaben said nothing.

"Mean anything to you?" London asked.

"Maybe. Who's the girl?"

"Nobody. She moved to Arizona a year ago."

Allaben waited.

"Like I said," London went on, "Crowder is positively shit-faced, and he starts giving Mallory a hard time. Until finally he pops off once too often. Mallory yanks him out of the car and lays into him. I guess he just lost it. You know he's got a temper. And I hear this guy Dawson gets in a few, too, just for the hell of it. Anyway, it ends with Crowder beaten half to death and the girl arrested for drunk and disorderly.

"Now, ordinarily Mallory might have got away with it, no questions asked. Resisting arrest, et cetera. But the girl's screaming police brutality and reporters are starting to nose around. Wick Mallory needs a friend. He needs one like he's never needed one before because if no one goes to bat for him he's looking at a change of careers at best, maybe a taste of how the other half lives at worst.

"Here's where District Attorney Mason Greer comes in, the champion of the gallant officers who put their lives on the line every day, and the enemy of license, of bleeding hearts, and privilege. Give him credit – whatever his motive, it was a risk.

"He arranges a press conference and announces that blood tests have turned up traces of methamphetamine and marijuana in Crowder. He shows a packet of powder – suspicious-looking but never identified – allegedly found in Crowder's car, and he reminds all and sundry that the girl's blood-alcohol level was twice the legal limit when she was arrested. Guess what? Inside of days it was a nonstory. The girl shut up, charges against her were dropped, and she moved out of state. Crowder pled guilty to a reduced charge and got off on probation. And a year later Mallory is sheriff and Greer is talking about running for attorney general."

He paused for a sip of coffee but never took his eyes from Allaben's face. "So what do you think about that?"

Allaben thought that Mason Greer had done Mallory a favor – a big favor, saved his job for him. But Greer had profited by it, too. It couldn't have hurt an ambitious politician like Greer to have an equally ambitious county sheriff beholden to him. No telling what useful shreds of dirty laundry found their way from Hagerstown to a DA's desk, where they'd be bagged and put away for future use.

It made sense that Greer had done it. You have to go out on a limb sometimes in order to reach the prize. Greer had seen an opportunity and seized it. And he knew his man: Mallory had courted his kid sister for years. You learn a lot about a man when he fails to get what he wants.

"Anybody else know about this?"

London shook his head. "I doubt it. The whole thing was quickly forgotten. Crowder knew what was good for him, and the young lady moved to the desert. Who else would care?"

Allaben considered. He studied London's face. Carolyn trusted him. He trusted him, too.

"Stuart," he said. "I've got a theory. No proof, just some circumstantial evidence. I'd like you to hear it. It's not a tip, Stuart, not a news flash, not a leak. It's a theory. A theory that needs very careful safekeeping. Do you understand?"

London sighed, as if he knew that what was coming must surely disappoint him. With a nod, he signaled acceptance of terms. Then he planted his elbows on the table, bent forward, and put his fingertips to his temples. In this position he listened, eyes downcast, as Allaben told his story. Not once did he interrupt with comment or question or quip. In fact, he seemed indifferent to what Allaben had to tell him. To Allaben's eyes that was a good thing. Because of course London did hear – he heard everything – and what he heard must have prompted strong feelings. The fact that he did not visibly gloat said to Allaben that in choosing the reporter, he had not misplaced his trust.

When Allaben finished, both men sat in silence for a moment.

The rattle of metal came from the kitchen. Something had been dropped.

London pushed the dessert plate across the table. Allaben pushed it back. London would have to polish off the last of the tarts or face Jean-Paul's wrath.

The reporter sighed. "The story of my life. I always ask for more than is good for me." He leveled upon Allaben a morose smile. "So now I'm your insurance agent."

"And beneficiary. Someone else has to know, Stuart – someone who can make use of it if something happens to me."

"You've got a kid, Felix."

"Nobody knows that better than me. And not a word to Carolyn – okay?"

London shrugged acceptance.

"I can't do anything with this," he observed. "It's only a theory, as you've taken pains to remind me."

"I'm going to do something with it," Allaben replied.

"I still don't see how we go from a theory to a bullet through Gwynn's head."

"I think I do."

"I don't suppose you'd like to share your thinking with me."

"When I'm sure," said Allaben, "you'll get the exclusive. That's our pact."

"So what's next?" London asked. "Or is that classified, too?"

The kitchen door opened and Carolyn sailed out, the scent of ginger in her draft. She stopped by the table, looked first at London and then at Allaben. The latter shifted over to make room. She tucked in beside him.

"I'm going to have to shoo you fellows out," she declared, "so we can set up for dinner."

"Okay by me," London said. "I could use some fresh air." He stood slowly.

"You don't expect me to take that back into the kitchen, do you?" She nodded at the sole remaining tart.

"My eyes were bigger than my stomach – and no smart remarks, if you please."

"The only thing more deplorable to Jean-Paul than a tin palate is waste. And in that," she added, "we're of two minds."

"Blame your friend here," London said, "for putting me off my food."

Carolyn directed a look of inquiry at the man in question, but the man in question was giving away nothing. He was formulating an answer to London's interrogative: What next? He must move, and move quickly, to join the two guesses – who and why – into one certainty. It needn't be a certainty that could be proven in a court of law, but it must be one that he could act upon, one that would cause as little collateral damage as possible.

Less than a week to the autumn equinox: six-thirty, and evening had fully arrived. The string of clouds in the western sky was tinted with pink. Still sultry, though. Stubborn summer held the lease, and was not about to decamp. Not yet.

Allaben sat in the shade of his house. On the table beside him were a tumbler of iced vodka and a telephone. He was waiting for Folliard to return his call.

Pedro was rooting in the ivy at the far end of the garden. His tail wagged vigorously. He was after something, in a friendly sort of way. Maybe a mole. The garden needed tending. Allaben had neglected it for months. Rebecca had been the gardener in the family, never happier than with trowel or watering can in hand. Miranda, on the other hand, could care less. But kids don't care about gardens.

"You've got a kid." Stuart London's words. No need to say any more than that, the meaning was clear enough.

Are the stakes really that high? Allaben asked himself.

Yes, came the answer. Yet the answer didn't move him. He felt a sort of perverse indolence – slothful just when vigilance was most needed. Tired through and through.

Pedro had begun to dig. Shreds of green flew fore and aft.

"Pedro!" The damned animal would make a salad of the place. The dog saluted his elusive quarry with a good-natured yip and came bounding for his master, grinning with slobbery delight.

Allaben snorted. "Pedro, you crazy mutt!"

Rebecca wanted to name him Abner – a rare lapse in judgment and taste. What kind of a name for a dog was that? You have to be able to shout a dog's name, shout it and mean it. Abner! It doesn't work. Miranda had come up with Pedro. Because her best friend was from San Pedro.

Gwynn was from California, too. It seemed he had no family. His body still lay unclaimed in the county morgue. Snyder was in the ground, far deeper than Pedro could dig. Allaben winced at the image.

The ring of the phone gave him a start. He looked at his watch. Six-forty-five, right on the dot.

"Hello, Sam."

"Are you outside?"

"Out back, in the garden."

"I can always tell. Something different about the sound. Sorry," he went on, "I had someone in my office."

"I've been sitting here, thinking."

"Good. What have you got for me?"

"I've got a name."

"Oh?" There was genuine interest in Folliard's voice, a tone that Allaben had not heard before. He had the feeling that for the first time since he took on this case, his boss did not already know what he was about to tell him.

"Dawson. Lester Dawson. Ever hear it before?"

"No." Flat and direct. Allaben believed him.

"I saw him at Greer's barbecue. And yesterday, leaving Greer's headquarters in Hagerstown. He's active in the PRL, and is some kind of fixer for Greer. His name's on Irwin's list."

"So?"

Allaben gave Folliard a summary of the information he'd received from Stuart London, including the fact that someone had been riding shotgun with Wick Mallory.

"You want to guess the name?" he concluded.

"Lester Dawson. But where are you going with this, Felix?"

"I'm going to Curtis Gwynn."

Folliard grunted.

"He worked for you, Sam."

"I never heard Gwynn's name before last week."

"He worked for Irwin, and Irwin works for you."

"Don't go there, Felix."

"Are you sure you're not holding out on me, keeping something in reserve? The reason I ask, Sam, is that I'm ready to push the button, and I'd like to be sure before I do that I'm not going to risk my neck to find out something that you already know."

"Has Dawson got something to do with Gwynn's death?"

"Dawson didn't kill Gwynn. Dawson was out of town with Greer at the time."

"Then why bother me with Dawson?"

Allaben paused before answering. He was as satisfied as he could be that Folliard would not be in his way.

"It's not Dawson I'm after."

"Then who?"

"Someone who's been lying to me – one of the many, actually."

"Who?"

"Sorry, Sam."

"What do you mean, 'sorry'?" Folliard was exasperated.

"I'll take it alone from here."

"Goddamn it, Felix!" Folliard growled. "Why alone? Take it where?"

"To Sharpsburg. I'm going to take a walk near Bloody Lane."

42

An orangy peel of sun was just visible over the hills to the East. Allaben stood at the corner of the National Cemetery – the very spot where Snyder had stood the last time Allaben had seen him alive. It was from this point, or a point very close by, that Snyder had set out across the battlefield the morning of Gwynn's death. Allaben would retrace the ranger's steps.

He had learned from Poole that it was Snyder's custom to walk at least as far as the parking lot by Burnside Bridge, and on occasion to continue along Snavely Ford Trail. There would be plenty of privacy there, shrouded beneath the canopy of hardwoods and far from the prying eyes of busybodies, official or civilian. A fellow might pull a bottle from a hiding place and have a nip or two in peace, with none for company but the chirping birds and the gurgling nymphs of the creek.

A car slowed on the Boonsboro Pike fifty yards behind him, someone on the way to work in town. Otherwise, it was quiet as the grave. There wasn't a breath of air, and the battlefield lay still and serene before him. In a few hours tourists would be tramping over these grounds, but for now he had the site all to himself. It was less than a mile to that iconic bridge and the patch of grass beside the creek where Gwynn's body had been found. Snyder had guessed that twenty minutes had elapsed by the time he reached the scene. Allaben pulled a stopwatch from his pocket, pressed the button, and started out.

In minutes his canvas shoes were wet with dew. He walked deliberately, keeping a steady pace, in the direction of the bridge. Snyder hadn't hurried, even after hearing the shot. The sun, now clear of the hills, spilled warmth on Allaben's face. Soon it would be hot. Snyder must have been just about here – two minutes from the cemetery – when the shot sounded. What might he have seen?

Between Allaben and the bridge, half a mile away, a narrow drive sliced through the battlefield, intersecting with a spur that led to the parking lot above the bridge. That intersection was now in sight. Allaben checked his watch. If a car had left the lot that Sunday morning, it must have been in view from this point. There was no other way out. And once such a hypothetical car reached the intersection, it must turn north, the direction of the Boonsboro Pike, or south. That way led to both the Harper Ferry's Road and a back way into town.

Allaben pressed on. A dog yapped in the distance. The sun sparkled on patches of deep, wet grass. He paused for a moment at the intersection, then took to the center of the paved road leading to the bridge. He passed the Sherrick Farmhouse on his left, then the Otto Farmhouse on his right. A few minutes more and he would gain the crest of the slope that descended to the creek. By this time, twelve days ago, Gwynn had been five minutes dead.

Gwynn, the know-it-all Civil War nut. Gwynn, the fearless, by-the-book cop. Gwynn, the re-enactor who played a Yankee casualty at Bloody Lane. For all of his bluster, Gwynn was a man who took the high ground, never looked the other way. Allaben had witnessed it first hand, back in Baltimore, when he'd been called in after Gwynn had fingered a couple of dirty cops.

He remembered the first conversation with Gwynn. It was set in the grimy, windowless interview room in the Internal Affairs offices. Allaben had gained a reputation in the Detectives Bureau as a listener, the cop to whom, when everyone else had failed, even the most stubborn suspect finally spilled his guts. Try as he might, though, he had got nothing from Gwynn, nothing to suggest that he wasn't on the up and up, nothing that smelled fishy. And in getting nothing he had come to admire Gwynn's obstinate integrity, even as he deplored his foolhardy righteousness.

It was just like Curtis Gwynn to get himself killed and to take his secrets with him. Which begged the question: Would he still be alive if Irwin had shown up on time?

The creek lay straight ahead. Allaben marched on, the sun now full on his face. His neck and back were damp. At a bend in the road he stopped to check the stopwatch. The roadway here turned south and ran along the ridge parallel with the creek. The stream was hidden from view by a stand of trees between the roadway and the steep bank that descended to the water's edge. Snyder had been at this point when Irwin passed him in the Jeep. A wave from Irwin. Snyder recognized him as a re-enactor, didn't try to stop him, probably just wondered what he was doing there at that hour.

From time to time Allaben caught a glimpse of the gray-green stream that flowed below, but he did not stop until he reached the parking lot above the bridge. The lot was empty. On the morning in question, Irwin's Jeep had been parked near the head of the wooden stairway. No one in it. Which way had Irwin gone? Not likely the back way on Snavely Ford Trail. Probably down to the bridge and the creek, then. God knew why.

Allaben walked to the stairs and started down, just as Snyder had. He stopped just short of the bridge, just as Snyder had. From here the ranger had seen a man a hundred yards downstream crouching over a body dressed in Union blue. The body was Gwynn's. The man crouching over him was Irwin. Gwynn was dead. The next day, so was Snyder. Allaben pulled out the watch. The ranger's story checked.

He headed back to the Visitor's Center. It was time to talk to another ranger. About hats.

43

Allaben did not expect to find the Mansfield Tavern open for business. It was, after all, only 8:30 in the morning, a trifle early in the day for a seat on a barstool. He pulled into the parking lot anyway. There was a convenience store next door; he could buy a cup of coffee if, as he supposed, the door to the tavern was barred.

His was the third car in the lot. Numbers one and two were nosed up against the links of blackened railroad ties nearest the convenience store. Both cars were empty, though one had been left to idle. Allaben's shoes crunched over the gravel. Someone was mowing a lawn further up Main Street. A delivery truck rumbled by. Its driver offered Allaben a small-town wave, then downshifted as he started up the hill and out of town.

Allaben advanced up the cement walkway that led to the tavern. To his surprise, he found the door to the foyer open. The inside door required a gentle shove. He stepped in and looked around. There was no one in sight. He made his way past the statue of the general, the juke box, the trophies mounted on the wall, and the shuffleboard game. Everything was just as it had been before, including the odor of sweat, stale beer, and mildew. The light was dim, the bulbs and shades covered in dust.

A rattle sounded from behind the bar.

"Anybody home?" Allaben ventured.

He was answered by the heavy thunk of glass against wood. A big bald head rose above the bar.

"Jesus H. Christ, mister!"

"Sorry."

The man scowled at Allaben through rimless spectacles. His eyebrows formed a hedgerow that separated pale forehead from ruddy cheeks.

"Sorry? You almost cost me a quart of Schnapps."

He wiped the bottle with a tattered dishrag, then carefully placed it in the rank of bottles on the shelf behind him. His disposition had not softened when he turned his attention once more to Allaben.

"Who are you?" he demanded.

Allaben presented his shield and explained his purpose for being there.

The man sighed gloomily. "I wish to hell that fellow never darkened my door." He removed his spectacles and then subjected them to a thoroughgoing polish with the same dishrag with which he had ministered to the Schnapps bottle.

"You're the owner?" Allaben asked. "MacKenzie Lamb?"

"Call me Mac. Everyone else does."

"All right, Mac. I guess you remember that night?"

"I should hope so, mister. I been asked enough questions about it."

"I'd just like to hear about the argument."

"Which one? The fellow was a regular firestarter. First it was the Admiral, then Don Parker."

"The Admiral?"

"What's-his-name, the Navy man thinks so much of himself."

"Roger Irwin."

"The Admiral is what we call him around here."

Allaben heard a scrape behind him. He turned. Simon the barfly stood in the doorway.

"Morning, Mac," he called.

"Ain't open 'til nine, Simon, as if you didn't know."

Undeterred, Simon threaded his way through the tables.

"Maybe a coffee?" he asked upon reaching the bar, "seeing as how you've got a customer already."

"He's not a customer, he's a federal agent."

"Don't tell me he's a federal agent," Simon grumbled. "I know a goddamn lawman when I see one. And this one I seen before."

Allaben met the old man's stare evenly.

"How's your memory today, Simon?"

"My memory's good, but it ain't free."

Allaben turned to Lamb, who sighed as he stooped to retrieve a bottle of beer from the cooler beneath the bar. He set the bottle on a paper coaster before Simon.

"Five dollars."

Allaben fished a ten-dollar bill from his pocket and laid it on the bar.

"I was asking about a week ago Saturday night."

"That loudmouth that got himself shot." Simon took a long pull from the bottle.

"Do you remember what they argued about?"

"Sure I remember. It was fool quarreling with fool. First Mister Ponytail had a go with the Admiral. Something to do with fording the Antietam during the battle. I don't know why they get so hot and bothered over something that happened so goddamn long ago. Sure as hell they hadn't any more sense then than they do now."

"And how did Parker get involved in it?" Allaben asked.

Simon fortified himself with another long swallow, then continued. "Parker up and says if it's up to him he'd subdivide the damned place and put up houses. Good for business. Anyone could tell he's just being ornery, but Mr. Ponytail, he's a hornet, and before you know it they're in a shouting match."

"When did the deputy show up?"

"Must have been quarter of an hour."

"That's just about right," Lamb volunteered. "Turned out he was up at the gas station."

"Last time, you told me that Gwynn said something about the boy, Parker's son," Allaben went on.

"No, that's not what I said. Couldn't be, because that's not what Mr. Ponytail said, was it, Mac?" Simon looked to Lamb for corroboration.

"Don't ask me," said Lamb. "I had better things to do than listen to them."

"Well, I didn't have no choice but listen, seeing as how they were right next to me," Simon countered. He lifted the bottle and drained it. Then he turned to Allaben. "You good for another?"

Allaben nodded, and Simon rapped the bar with his knuckles. Lamb answered with a second bottle.

"Now you listen good, Mr. Federal Agent," Simon continued, "like you should've done the first time. It was like this. Ponytail says, 'You could learn a thing or two from your boy.' Mrs. Parker chimes in, 'Keep Donnie out of this.' But Ponytail's not through. 'Your boy's got some respect for the past. Sure as hell he didn't get it from you.

Fact, there's more to him than you'll ever know.' Parker stands up, like he's half a mind to throw one, even though he ain't had that much to drink. 'I don't need you to tell me about Donnie,' he hollers. 'I know my son just fine.' The other one laughs, says, 'Question is, does your son know his father?' Then come a commotion from Parker's missus. Can't stand to listen to their foolishness for a second more. Nothing better than loudmouthed boys playing a stupid game. Her Donnie's more of a man than the both of them. She marches for the door, stops when she gets there, asks, 'You gonna drive me home, or am I gonna find a ride?'"

Allaben glanced at Lamb, who nodded agreement.

"That part I heard," he said. "It's just like Simon says. Parker settled up and followed her out. Never said another word."

"And Ponytail?"

"Sat and watched him go. It quieted down after that. The deputy left, too."

"What time was it?"

Lamb shrugged. "Not too late. Before ten. Because not long after, the Admiral says he's going to get himself home, too, on account of having to get up early Sunday morning to win a bet. Ponytail just raises his glass to that."

"Did Gwynn stick around?"

"He had one more – a brandy, I think it was."

"Offered me one," Simon interjected. "Regular gentleman about it. I said, 'Thank you kindly, but I'll take a beer.' You can never go wrong with beer."

"Did he talk with anyone else?"

"Don't think so," Lamb answered. "He paid his tab and walked out. And I was happy to see him go."

"Any parting remarks?"

"He didn't say, 'I got a feeling someone's going to shoot me' if that's what you mean. He just plain left. I don't believe he had a car."

Correct. Gwynn had left his car at the inn. When he left the bar, he walked back. A guest, Eleanor Miller, saw him at about 10:15 smoking a cigar on a bench by the summer kitchen. So he hadn't made any stops along the way. He turned in at about 10:30. No telephone calls, no note. What did he think about as he lay in bed? Not, Allaben guessed, that this was his last night among the living.

He'd been too full of himself to contemplate his own end, which was already then in sight. He had doomed himself with his own vainglory. On the verge of a great triumph, of good for once bettering evil, he had fallen victim to his own headlong righteousness.

Allaben would not make that mistake – many another, but not that one.

44

It didn't seem that anyone was home at the Parker house. In fact, there didn't appear to be anyone at home in the whole development. Allaben had driven the bird-named streets of Brookside Meadows without so much as setting eyes on a single human being. Except for a cat prowling the lawn next door, there was no sign of life at all. Could it be that everybody was at the re-enactment? Or if not already there, then they were on the roads, for it had taken him half again as long to get here as it ordinarily would've.

No one had answered his call from the Mansfield Tavern, not even a machine, though he'd let it ring a dozen times. Don, of course, would be at the lot, and Donnie would be on the battlefield. But where was the lady of the house? Not at her office, where he had next tried to reach her. She hadn't made an appearance there, nor had she called in. Her first appointment, the receptionist chirped, was at 12:30. She was showing a house in Braddock Heights.

Odd that he'd not got an answering machine. So odd that he'd decided to drive to Brookside Meadows on the chance that Pamela was at home, only not in the mood to field calls. So much the better, as far as Allaben was concerned. But it looked as if he had bet wrong.

The driveway was empty, and the garage was closed up. He

pulled up to the first of the two doors and got out of his truck. He gave the car door a hard shove. The bang would give notice, if there were anyone about to whom his arrival might be of interest. In the two hours since he left the battlefield the sky had turned purplish-gray, the color of an old bruise, and the spanking white vinyl of the Parker house stood out in sharp relief against it. The curtains were drawn. The quiet was eerie; not even a bird to protest it.

He'd stepped to the garage window and peered inside when the phone in his pocket rang. The caller ID notified him that it was Stuart London.

"Yeah, Stuart?"

"Where are you now, Felix?"

"Standing outside what appears to be an empty Parker house. I'm now looking into what seems to be an equally empty garage. No Lexus in there."

"That's because the Lexus – what's left of it – is at Carson's Body Shop on Motter Avenue. But if it's Pamela Parker you're looking for, her you'll find at Frederick Memorial."

"What the hell?"

"Had a little accident a few blocks from her office this morning. Slammed into by a good size SUV, just as she was getting out of her car. She got clipped."

"I'm on my way. Is she all right, do you know?" Allaben asked as he jogged back to his truck.

"As of ten minutes ago her condition was stable. The docs say she's pretty banged up, though."

"Was it an accident?"

"Well, that's for you to find out, isn't it? I'm just dealing in facts here, Felix. I can tell you this: the SUV didn't call 911 and stick around. I'd hustle if I were you."

❧

Frederick Memorial Hospital, where Allaben had been a recent guest, was about twenty minutes away on an ordinary Saturday morning. With all of the traffic, it took him thirty on this one, despite taking every shortcut he knew. In his effort at haste, he would be spared a beating from his own conscience, at least for awhile. He couldn't drive and kick himself in the pants at the same time. Self-reproach would have to wait. There would be plenty of time for that later.

As he pulled into the hospital parking lot, he saw the Parkers, father and son, leaving the building. They walked side by side, heads down, as if studying the asphalt for clues to their misfortune. Allaben stayed in the truck and kept out of sight until they climbed into a black sedan and drove away.

Within five minutes, Allaben was showing his credentials at the nurses' station and getting a doctor's reluctant permission to visit the patient. Mrs. Parker was going to be fine. But he should keep it short, as they'd just now administered sedatives and pain killers, which would soon take effect. Mrs. Parker had been through a lot. He should keep that in mind.

Pamela Parker's bed was in a corner of the room. Hospital curtains were pulled closed around it. She had no immediate neighbors and no other visitors.

"Mrs. Parker?"

No response. He walked to the foot of the bed, gathered an edge of the curtain, and peeked in. A slice of Pamela's face was visible above the hospital gown, a slice that was swollen and badly discolored. Her eyes were closed. Allaben cleared his throat.

Her eyes opened. She turned and looked at him, wearily and without a great deal of interest.

"May I talk to you, Mrs. Parker?"

She turned away, but Allaben was already inside the tent. He pulled a chair to the side of the bed near her shoulder. An IV tube was laced through the stainless steel bed rail.

"How do you feel, Pamela?"

"Like a dog that's been hit by a car. How do you think I feel?"

"Did you see the driver?"

"No."

"Are you sure?"

"What kind of question is that?"

"Do you really have to ask?"

Five seconds passed. A monitor beeped on the wall above her. He wondered if she'd fallen asleep.

"Pamela?"

"Why don't you leave me alone?"

"You know the answer to that, too."

She turned to him. Her eyes were lackluster and bloodshot. "What do you want from me?"

"Just tell me the truth," he said.

"Hard to do," she replied wearily. "Didn't I say that to you before?"

"Now's the time, Pamela. Before it's too late. If you don't help me, I can't help you."

She pushed a button on the side of the bed, and slowly rose to a position eye-level with Allaben. "What do you want to talk about?"

"Let's start with Curtis Gwynn."

"Curtis Gwynn." She reached for the container of apple juice on the tray on the side of the bed opposite Allaben. She took a long, slow sip through a straw. "What about him?"

"Why did you ditch him?"

"He was a shit – a devious, scheming bastard. Just like …" she trailed off.

"Just like who?" Allaben knew she was lying.

"Just like all of you. There's not one of you can be trusted."

"Who? Ex-cops? Skirt-chasers? Men in general?"

But she wasn't listening. She took another sip of the juice.

"Did Curtis betray you," Allaben asked, "or was he about to?"

"Curtis was a nobody," she sneered. "How could he betray me? Let's change the subject. I'm sick to death of Curtis Gwynn. You don't count for much in this world, dead or alive, unless someone cares about you. Nobody gave a damn about Curtis Gwynn. If it wasn't for you, he'd be old news by now."

"Somebody else figured the same way."

"I didn't kill him."

"I know you didn't."

"And I don't know who did."

"That I'm not so sure about."

"If I did know, I wouldn't tell you. I'm glad he's dead. He was nothing but trouble, the biggest mistake I ever made."

"The biggest? I don't think so."

She studied the juice box she was still holding, then returned her gaze to Allaben. Her expression was sullen, almost defiant. Allaben knew what she was thinking. But he would wait, let her worry.

"You thought Curtis was only interested in you."

"He was."

"At first he was. You whistled and he came running. He never thought to ask what a woman like you could see in him. He'd think no further than his crotch. How long did it take him to start asking questions about your brother?"

She shrugged.

"It surprised you, didn't it?" he pressed on. "You thought – or Mason thought – you had him right where you wanted him."

"Between my legs," she said airily.

"Where you could keep an eye on him for Mason. But he turned the tables on you. It was a real cozy arrangement – Mason using you to keep tabs on Gwynn, and Gwynn using you to get the goods on Mason. That's some brother you've got, Pamela. And some boyfriend."

"You don't know my brother, Inspector. You have no idea."

"I think I do have an idea," Allaben said.

A kind of cynical amusement came into her eyes.

"What?" she asked. "What do you know? That Mason is ruthless? That he's hard and selfish? That nothing is more important to him than his career – even his sister and her virtue? What do you know?"

"I'll guess that he just tried to have you put in the hospital, or worse, for one thing."

That brought a noise something between a snicker and a snort. "Hah. And for another?"

Allaben pulled from his jacket pocket the sheet of photos of Donnie Parker and handed them to her. She looked at the photos, then at Allaben.

"I told you, Allaben, that I won't have my son involved. Drag me down if you want, but not Donnie."

Allaben didn't like the tone in her voice, but it was now or never. There would never again be a time when she would be this vulnerable, when the logic of the situation would press so heavily to a full confession.

"Is that what you said to Curtis?" he asked.

"I'm tired. I need some sleep."

"How did he find out?" he pressed. "Did you tell him? Late one night after you'd had one too many drinks? Did he promise it wouldn't go any further?"

"'An educated guess' is what he called it."

"And he kept after you – wouldn't let go of it."

She nodded lazily. The sedative was doing its work.

"And he promised it wouldn't go any further."

Another drowsy nod, then a wan smile. "You're not going to give up on this, are you?" It was not a question.

"No, Pamela, I'm not."

"Because you're a cop."

"I used to be a cop."

"What are you now?"

"I'm the obstinate bastard who's going to nail your brother to the wall."

"Even if the hammer hits me, too."

"I don't want to hurt you. That's why I'm here."

"What about Donnie?"

"I'll do my best to keep him out of it."

"No matter what happens?" Her voice was beginning to trail off.

"I'll do my best."

"Promise?" Nearly inaudible.

Allaben nodded. She managed a second listless smile. "Ironic," she whispered. "I guess I'll have to trust you, now."

Rubber soles sounded on the tile floor. Allaben pulled aside the curtain to see a nurse approaching the bed. Her mission was clear. The interview was over. But Pamela had already ended it, and by the time he had risen from his chair, she was fast asleep.

He looked out the large, wide window closest to the bed. The sky was swollen, the color of graphite. It was going to rain.

"Families," he thought. With families, it's the luck of the draw, and Donnie Parker had been dealt a truly lousy hand. Allaben picked up the sheet of photos and studied the boy's face. He'd given Pamela a promise and now he'd have to keep it. The question was, How?

45

A steady rain was falling on Sharpsburg when Allaben finally finished negotiating the battlefield traffic and reached the Mason Greer campaign RV. It was parked along the main street just a few blocks past the road to the Visitor Center. Wick Mallory stood beneath the canvas overhang attached to the RV's side, the *MASON GREER, THE MAN FOR OUR TIMES* side facing the street. Allaben pulled into a space next to the sheriff's red-and-white cruiser, which was tucked next to a polished black Lincoln town car. No sign of a Range Rover with Kentucky plates. He slid his hand over the cruiser's hood as he walked past: still warm.

"Any news?" Mallory asked.

Allaben shook his head. "She's asleep now. The doctors say she'll survive."

Mallory looked grim. A delicate beading of perspiration had formed on his forehead, just below his hairline.

"Mason's on the phone," he said, then turned to lead Allaben up and into the RV.

They stepped in. Mallory dutifully wiped his boots on a mat just inside the threshold, and Allaben followed suit. Mason Greer was the RV's only occupant. His back was to them; a cell phone was pressed to his ear.

Allaben quickly took in the room: a desk, sofa and chairs, two television monitors, three laptops, one of them resting on the couch. A sideboard stood to the right of the entrance, on it a cluster of framed photos, a tray of liquors, and a wooden humidor, the exact duplicate of the one in the Fish & Game Club.

Greer had not spoken. When he turned, his face radiated vexation. He looked like a man with much on his mind and little at hand to relieve it. He set the phone on the desk.

"She's resting. That's all I can get out of them," he said.

"The doctors told Felix she'd be okay," Mallory commented.

"Have you spoken with your brother-in-law?" Allaben asked.

"Yeah," Greer replied. "He's already been to the hospital. My nephew, too. Pretty shook up, the two of them." He looked at Mallory. "No point waiting," he said. "Let's get going. You in the lead, Wick. We'll get there quicker."

He took a few steps toward the door but stopped when Allaben failed to budge.

"Where's your wife?" Allaben asked.

"She's at a luncheon. Battlefield preservation. Why do you ask?"

"And your daughter?"

"With her mother. Is that okay with you?"

Greer turned to Mallory. "What's with your friend, Wick?" He didn't wait for an answer. "My sister's laying in a hospital bed, and he's taking attendance."

Once again he stepped toward the door, and once again Allaben stood his ground.

"This is no game, Greer, and you're not going anywhere. Not yet."

"Felix, you sure you know what you're doing?" Mallory asked.

Greer retreated to the desk, perched on a corner.

"What were you talking with Pamela about, Allaben? Did she run off at the mouth, like she does sometimes? She's liable to say anything. Obviously, she's not the most stable person in the world. And she's just had quite a scare. We'll get her through this, though. Patch her up. And then we'll see she gets the insides of her head treated. Send her someplace to dry out, someplace quiet. Which is what we should have done years ago. I'm as much to blame as anyone," he added contritely.

Allaben laughed at this.

"What's the hell's so funny?"

"I've known some real heels, Greer, but none of them could hold a candle to you. 'Put her someplace quiet.' Yeah, getting T-boned will do that."

Greer bridled. "I don't have to take this from you! Throw him out, Wick."

Mallory cast an exasperated glance at Allaben.

"We've got to get to the hospital, Felix," he warned. "There's no time for this now. If you have business with Mason, you can take it up with him later. Come on, let's go."

"I'll take it up now," Allaben replied, "with him *and* with you. I'm not letting either of you near Pamela Parker, not until I tell you both how things stand."

"What's that supposed to mean?" Greer blustered.

"Felix? Are you serious?" Mallory asked.

Allaben looked the sheriff straight in the eye. He slowly drew his automatic from its holster, then slowly lowered his hand until it came to rest against the seam of his pants.

"This is how serious," he said. "Now sit down, Wick."

Mallory stared at him. He stepped to a chair and sprawled there.

"I hope you're not expecting a confession," he drawled.

"What in God's name are you talking about?" Greer barked.

"He knows," said Mallory.

"Knows? I don't care what he knows," Greer snorted. "He doesn't have anything. And don't you forget it."

Allaben ignored Greer. He kept his attention on Mallory.

"It had to be you, Wick. Greer called you that Saturday night, right after Pamela called him. She told him about the argument, and about the meeting at the creek Sunday morning. She told him and he told you. It was an opportunity that couldn't be allowed to pass. Curtis Gwynn was now a serious threat, not to you but to him, your ticket to the big time."

Greer started to break in, but Allaben was not going to yield the floor.

"You see, Wick," he went on, "Gwynn had learned something that could bring Mr. Mason Greer down, and with him his entourage, you included. So you had to act quickly. And you didn't mind so much, either, did you? After all, Pamela had taken him into her bed, this loudmouthed ex-cop who'd ratted on his fellow officers. You were out of her bed and he was in it. That had to hurt, Wick. Besides, you owed Mason one. I'll bet he reminded you of it."

"Don't say anything, Sheriff," Greer warned. "He doesn't need our help to make an ass of himself."

"Funny thing is, Wick," Allaben continued, "it was Mason who told me about you and Pamela. Made sure I heard it, too. I guess he wanted to give me something to think about. But I should've heard it from you."

"He's talking through his hat," Greer sneered.

Allaben pressed on, looking straight into Mallory's eyes.

"You got up very early on Sunday morning and drove over to Roger Irwin's house. You flattened the tire on his Jeep. Not very original, but it worked. Then you drove down to the battlefield and tucked your car someplace, not too far from the Bridge. It was early. The sun was just coming up. So far, so good. You hadn't seen anyone. And if you did see someone, no problem – you'd just turn around and take your leave. No harm done. Who's going to question a uniform? But where was Gwynn? His car wasn't in the parking area. You walked to the overlook, and there he was, in Union blue, walking into range.

"From that point on, it was easy. You went back to the car, took a rifle out of the trunk – maybe a sniper's rifle, one of the weapons in the gun club arsenal – and you slipped into the woods that run down to the creek. Perfect cover. Gwynn couldn't see you – no one could see you – but you could see him as plain as day, standing there cooling his heels while he waited for Irwin. A pot shot. It would take less than a minute to get into position, take aim, pull the trigger.

"Now you were in danger, but not much. In a couple of minutes you were out of the park and heading away from the Pike and from Irwin. What were the chances you'd be seen at that hour?"

Allaben paused. He had not taken his eyes from Mallory, who sat completely still through the whole of Allaben's little speech. Now Mallory glanced at Greer, who shook his head in disgust, before turning once more to his accuser.

"Are you finished, Felix?"

"No," he said, "I'm not finished. But you are, Wick. And your patron, too. Because your luck finally did run out. Someone *did* see you driving away. Hal Snyder was walking toward the creek, and he saw a sheriff's car, probably in the distance. He didn't give it a moment's thought. In fact, he forgot about it until the next day. But you saw *him*, and you didn't forget about it.

"You knew what you had to do. But to do it, you had to learn his movements, his habits. You had your deputy talk with his wife and with the other rangers. That's how you found out that Hal always stayed late at the battlefield, climbed the tower by Bloody Lane at sundown. And maybe you knew, too, that he liked to take a bottle with him. A nice set-up for you. So you walked to the battlefield that Monday evening and you watched the tower. You saw Snyder go up, and a few minutes later you saw Poole go up after him. In due time, Poole came down. You waited until the coast was clear, and then you climbed the tower. And you pushed Hal off the observation deck.

"That second ranger those kids saw up on the tower wasn't a ranger at all. It was you. They saw the hats and assumed rangers. One of those hats was Snyder's. The other one was yours. It couldn't have been Poole. Poole doesn't wear a hat. He never wears one – not in the morning, not in the evening, not atop the Observation Tower."

Mallory shifted in his chair, lowered his chin, then raised his eyebrows at Allaben, as if to ask if there were more to come. There was.

"Here's where it comes apart, Wick. Gwynn's murder I can understand. He was playing with fire, and he knew it. You might even say that he was asking for it. I'd have a hard time saying that he wasn't. It wouldn't make it right, but it would be understandable.

Snyder, though – that was different. Hal was an innocent. All he did was take a walk in the morning. He happened to see something, something that for all he knew meant absolutely nothing. Sure it troubled him, when he remembered what he'd seen, enough so he was going to talk to me. But he didn't have a notion of the danger he was in.

"As it turned out, he did as much harm to you dead as he would have done alive. Whose idea was it, anyway, to put an end to Snyder? Was it yours alone, Wick?"

"He's bluffing, Wick," Greer snorted. "This isn't a case. It's pure fantasy."

Allaben responded to Greer. "Wick killed Gwynn because you convinced him that Gwynn had to be put away. The real question is, why did *you* want Gwynn eliminated?"

"Now, wait a minute, Allaben. You just wait a minute. It's bad enough you're accusing the sheriff of a capital offense …"

Allaben didn't let him finish.

"I wonder if Wick knows the real reason," he went on. "Did you ever tell him? My guess is you didn't. You fed him a story about Gwynn threatening your career, told him that Gwynn knew some things about you – maybe your ties to the PRL – and knew some things about Wick, too. Things that could sink your ship if it got out. And poor Wick would go down with you. Besides, as I said, Wick owed you one."

Greer broke in. "A lot of hogwash. You're spinning your wheels."

"You're right," Allaben admitted. "It *is* hogwash. But it kept me off the real scent. You probably had your patsy of a brother-in-law or some other hireling arrange to have those thugs try to scare me off. Make a point of showing me a coiled snake. And pointing me right to a dead end. Right, Mason? So long as I followed that lead, I'd get nowhere. You told me so yourself in your office. Said it would take a lot more than a story like that to derail you. Might even gain a few votes by it."

Mallory swiveled to Greer. Greer shook his head sadly.

"He's blowing smoke, Wick. Another hired gun. When he's gone, there'll be another. Out to get me."

He turned to Allaben, his face twisted with scorn. "Why don't you just finish your business here and leave. Say your piece and get out. You haven't got a leg to stand on. You're bluffing, Allaben, and it's not going to work. Come on, Wick. We have to go."

Allaben looked from Greer to Mallory. The sheriff's face was in profile, his jaw tightened in concentration. He didn't know. Allaben was sure of it. And if there were any doubt, a glance at Greer was enough to dispel it – that studied carelessness gave him away for the liar he was. Rain spattered against the windows, danced on the roof. From far away a siren sounded. Mallory tilted his head ever so slightly. He'd heard it too.

There wasn't much time. Allaben gathered himself, tried to put out of his mind everything but the three breathing creatures in this room. His own breath came short and quick. He tightened his grip on the gun. Yes, the safety was off. If he was going to go through with it, it was now or never. He turned to Mallory.

"Gwynn did know about the PRL. That's what he was there for, to infiltrate the club, to check into their doings. But he found out something else, something he hadn't bargained for, a secret that could bring down Mason Greer for good. And Mason Greer couldn't allow that. Until Gwynn stumbled upon it, only one other person besides Greer knew about it, and that was his sister. For years he worried that she'd give it away, let it slip when she'd been drinking. And she was drinking more and more – she was almost out of control. The only thing that stood between Greer and the statehouse. Because, Wick, she knew that Donnie was not her husband's son – not Don's son – but *his*."

Allaben nodded at Mason Greer. Mallory's forehead wrinkled in puzzlement.

"What? What did you say?"

"It's true. Gwynn found out. Maybe from Pamela, late at night, in the bedroom. Or maybe she only confirmed what he'd convinced her he knew, knew from comparing photographs, suspected from her hatred of her brother. But in any event he knew, and Mason knew that he knew. Gwynn made sure of that. So he had to be stopped. But you couldn't be told the real reason why."

Allaben paused to gauge the effect of the shell he'd just launched. Greer coolly scratched the side of his face with his ring finger. He slipped off the desk and crossed the narrow room.

"Mason?" Mallory demanded. He was out of his chair now.

"What am I to say, Wick? I've just been accused of knocking up my own sister! To say nothing of conspiracy and murder. What next? I won't dignify these outrageous slanders. I won't descend to his level. I'm going to smoke a cigar and wait for him to leave. Unless you come to your senses and hurry him out of here."

He lifted the lid of the humidor and selected a cigar. Allaben spoke to Mallory.

"Remember, Wick, what I told you about Simon? That he heard Gwynn say something to Parker in the bar? Here's what he said: 'Does your son know his father?' Parker didn't get it, but Pamela did. She was scared. She probably called her brother the moment she got home, told him what Gwynn had said and about the meeting with Irwin by the creek. Then he called you."

Mallory studied Allaben for a moment. Greer pulled open the bottom drawer of the humidor, where the cigar cutter was stored.

"Jesus Christ, Mason. You. Pamela. My God! He's telling the truth." Mallory's face was red.

Greer's answer was curt. "Think before you speak, Wick."

Suddenly Mallory was in motion, turning away from Allaben, drawing his .45. It made no sense to Allaben, who automatically crouched in shooting position, until he heard the bang of another gun. He realized as he swiveled toward it that the whine that he'd just heard was a bullet whizzing over his head.

Greer was aiming a shiny silver automatic at his chest, and would have got off another round if a locomotive in the form of a .45 bullet hadn't plowed into him. The force of the impact rocked him backward. He stumbled, and backed with a thud into the sideboard. The cabinet shuddered but held. He folded to the floor, his back pressed against the wood. Mallory stalked toward him, his gun extended in a police grip. Greer watched him come. His breathing was labored. Suddenly, it stopped.

Mallory stood over Greer.

Allaben kept his voice as sure and as calm as he could. "Wick," he said, "let's put an end to this now. Put your gun down."

Mallory straightened, turned, stepped toward Allaben. He stopped four paces away. His gun hung in his hand. Allaben did not lower his. It was pointed at the sheriff's heart.

"Put it down, Wick."

Mallory did not seem to have heard.

"Are you sure about this, Felix? You're not making it all up about Pamela?"

Allaben nodded his head.

"I was crazy about her, from when we were kids in high school," Mallory mused. "But she wanted a lot of things, things I wouldn't be able to give her."

They listened together to the siren approaching. Mallory smiled.

"That will be my faithful deputy," he said. Then the smile faded. "Sorry, Felix, but no freakin' prison for me. Say goodbye to Pamela."

He raised his gun.

Allaben fired.

46

There were a half-dozen up-market cars clogging the semicircular driveway of the Froehling house when Lester Dawson drove up. It had been a forty-minute, traffic-snarled slog of a drive, but, preoccupied with the sudden news and how to manage it, Dawson had hardly noticed. He parked the Range Rover under the canopy of a huge sycamore by the curb. The house was set back a good fifty yards from the street. As he strode toward the front door, he noticed his shadow, Stetson and all, keeping him company. The departure of rain and the arrival of sun that afternoon was good news indeed for all the visitors and re-enactors who would congregate at Antietam battlefield that afternoon. Mason Greer was dead, but life would go on.

Dale Froehling, who'd been expecting Dawson, opened the door before his visitor had the chance to remove his hat and knock.

"Christine's book club has the downstairs commandeered," he said. "Let's scoot through to the back porch." He led the way first through the foyer, through a short hallway lined with antique prints, then into the great room. There, a handful of women sat on facing sofas, refreshments and drinks on the glass coffee table between them.

A quick hello to all and a few words passed with Mrs. Froehling, who whispered of her shock at the news about Mason Greer. Then Dawson followed his host past the dining room and study to the screened veranda.

"It's terrible, simply unbelievable!" Froehling pronounced once they were settled into a pair of Adirondack chairs. "Mason Greer dead! Damn it, Lester, what happened?"

Dawson placed his hat on the end table beside his chair to free up his hands. "I don't know much more than you. The sheriff's dead, too. Wick Mallory. My understanding is that Allaben, the federal agent – you know, the one at the barbecue – was there, too. He's alive, though. I hear that he shot Mallory."

"What the hell's been going on, Lester?"

"That's the question of the hour, isn't it? Greer must've been holding out on us. I don't know if we'll ever know what. Or why."

"This is bad, bad all around."

"Yes, it's bad, but there might be an opportunity here, Dale, a way to move forward."

"For whom? Greer was perfect for the part."

"For us. For our cause. It begins with you, Dale. Forget your campaign."

This drew a puzzled look from Froehling.

"Forget the campaign? Okay, suppose I do. Where you going with this?"

"I'm going to ask you to make a somber public statement announcing that, for the good of the country, you're going to withdraw your candidacy for the state senate and run for attorney general in Greer's place. You're an attorney, Dale. You've served in elective office. You've got the experience. And best of all, you're on our side. It's a good fit. Run for state attorney general. And win."

"I don't know, Lester. This comes out of the blue. Let me think on it, talk to my wife."

"You do that. You could be a hero, Dale. Trust me. I'll get Mason's wife to stand up for you, help you tug at heart-strings from here to Baltimore. As far as the senate seat goes, if, as you say, you've got the goods on your opponent, then we shouldn't have much trouble rustling up someone to replace you. Someone who'll beat her just as easily as you would've."

"Maybe. I need time to consider this, Lester. I'll talk to some of our people. You just might be onto something."

Confident that he'd piqued Froehling's interest, Dawson raised his hands as if to frame a picture. "I can see the billboards already, he said. *'I'm for Froehling. I'm for Freedom.'*"

Froehling rose from his chair and began to silently pace the length of the veranda. Back and forth, back and forth, his hands clasped behind his back. Dawson let him pace. He knew his man, knew that with every step Froehling took, he drew nearer to sealing the deal. Attorney general of the state of Maryland? In a minute or two he'd be claiming the idea as his own.

Suddenly Froehling stopped. He turned to Dawson, uncertainty in his eyes.

"What about tonight?" he asked. "Are you still going through with it?"

"I've already given the go-ahead. It's set for 10:00."

"Is that wise, Lester?"

"In light of Mason's death, you mean? Absolutely – now more than ever. We'll avenge the loss of one of ours."

"But the other thing …" Froehling paused to frame it correctly. "The other operation," he finished.

"Unfortunately," Dawson conceded, "I think we have to put that one – the big one – on hold. Too many distractions and Feds sniffing around. Besides, it demands its own news cycle. It's best to wait for a quieter time."

A loud burst of laughter arose from within the house, distracting Froehling momentarily.

"Yes," he resumed, "Let's wait at least until I've formally declared. Ideally, wait until after the election."

"When you'll be wearing the mantle of the law," Dawson chuckled. "Our man."

Another burst of laughter from inside. Froehling smiled.

"Let's go see what that's all about."

Dawson rose to follow him back into the house. He was smiling, too.

47

Allaben waited in the gray flourescent light of the baggage claim area. He stood next to the carousel that would receive Miranda's luggage when her flight from San Francisco landed. According to the arrivals board, the flight was on time. She would be on the ground in a couple of minutes, and the first thing she'd do is call him.

Livery drivers stood idly by, each holding a name card in one hand and a cellphone in the other. Travelers passed by pulling carry-ons, mothers and fathers passed by with children in tow, girls reunited wth boyfriends passed by – all headed toward the glass doors that led to the gloomy arrivals platform, where a steady stream of vans, taxis, and passenger cars stopped and started up again.

An oversized duffel sat all by itself on the baggage carousel, tagged but unclaimed. It put Allaben in mind of Mallory's body, lying in a lifeless heap on the floor of the RV. Greer's had been in a sitting position, slumped in the direction of the doorway.

Allaben was tired. He'd endured hours of interviews, first with State Police detectives, then with a duo of FBI agents, and finally in an after-hours phone conversation with Sam Folliard.

It was only when Folliard had asked the inevitable question

that Allaben decided to keep the truth to himself. It didn't belong to him; it wasn't his to share. Two others knew it, but each had a good reason to safeguard it: Stuart London, to honor his pledge, and Pamela Parker, to shield her son. There was no telling what Folliard would do with it if it were in his possession. Allaben could see nothing to be gained by offering it up.

"Why? To shut him up, Sam. Gwynn had the goods on Greer, something that directly linked him to the PRL. And just to make sure that nothing was left behind, they torched Gwynn's apartment."

He waited. Would Folliard buy it?

"Whatever he had on Greer must've been hot," Folliard said. "I think I'm going to pull Irwin out of there."

"He won't like that."

"He's been compromised, Felix. We can always smuggle another agent into the ranks of the PRL, here or in another chapter. And they've lost their knight in shining armor. It's back to the trenches for them, at least for a while."

"Greer probably thought his best chance was to take me out. There would be questions for sure, but there would be answers, too. A man with his spotless reputation, and the county sheriff to back up his story. He thought fast."

"I'm sorry about Mallory." Folliard was gruff.

"Wick wasn't smart, Sam. It was a risk shooting Gwynn, but he figured his uniform would tilt the odds in his favor. Besides, who would care about Curtis Gwynn? He and Greer had no way of knowing that *you* would. They thought it would be their investigation to lead, and to lead nowhere. It must have been quite a surprise when I showed up."

"We had to find out what happened," Folliard said. "It couldn't be Irwin who did the finding out."

"It might have been him who engineered the shooting."

"I had to find out," Folliard repeated.

"It was a dirty business, Sam."

"Of course it was. I thought it must be, or I'd have had someone else look into it."

"Thanks. In you I've got the boss I deserve."

"You're welcome," Folliard said. "You did good work. Too bad it turned out the way it did."

"Like Antietam."

"How so?"

"Lots of blood spilled, ugly, and not much gained."

"Screw it, Felix. We do the best we can. Keep our heads down and live to fight another day. Give me a veteran any day. There's no glory in dying young, even if it's for a good cause."

"I'm too old to die young."

"Me, too. And good for us, I say. Now write it up so it's 100% official, and send me the report with your bill. That's the best kind of closure I can offer."

Closure? Not likely, at least in the professional department. No, if he was going to find closure, he would have to seek it on the domestic front – with Miranda, with Carolyn, with his dead wife.

Maybe Carolyn was right. Maybe he shouldn't try to do this on his own. Maybe Miranda needed someone else she could learn to trust, trust in a way that she could never allow herself to trust him. Carolyn had volunteered to accompany him this morning – for moral support, she'd said. But he knew as well as she did that it was merely a gesture on her part, an overture of sorts.

"It's not the time, Carolyn," he'd said. "Let's let things settle down, get her back to school and her friends. She's fifteen. She gets more nourishment from them than from me."

He knew he was talking to himself. So did Carolyn.

"I like the 'let's,'" she said. "*Let us.* You and me."

A warning horn sounded at the next carousel; a few seconds later, it clattered to life.

Allaben walked to the arrivals board. Miranda's flight had landed. He pulled out his phone.

What would he say to her on the drive back to Frederick? He'd been rehearsing all afternoon. "Yes, I killed a man today, a man I knew, and I was almost killed myself. But I'm fine, Miranda. Everything's going to be fine." He could see the look on her face: skepticism laced with angst.

His phone rang. He looked at the screen. It was Folliard. Again?

"What now, Sam?"

"Where are you?"

"At the airport, waiting for my daughter."

"Sorry, Felix. I forgot. I just thought you might want to know."

"Know what?"

"Does a tower on the Antietam battlefield mean anything to you?"

"The Observation Tower?"

"Yes, a stone observation tower."

"Sure. It's at the foot of Sunken Road, what they call Bloody Lane. What about it?"

"Well, it's not at the foot of anything anymore," Folliard explained. "It's been bombed. Leveled. Happened within the hour, at 10:00 on the dot."

"What? The Tower?"

"That's not all, Felix. A kid was there. Got killed in the explosion."

"A kid?"

"A boy. Sneaked in, I suppose, after closing time at the battlefield."

"Has he been identified?"

"Yeah, but it's not official. This just happened, and the familiy hasn't been notified. Name's Parker. Danny Parker."

Allaben stared at the carousel. The gray duffel bag hadn't budged.

"Are you there, Felix?"

"Donnie."

"What?"

"It's Donnie. Not Danny. Donald Parker, Junior. "

"Okay. Donnie Parker. Know him?"

"Yes, I know him. My daughter knows him, too. He's Greer's nephew, his sister's kid. I've spoken with him. I liked him."

"Sorry to hear that, Felix. I guess an expression of sympathy is in order."

"Another boy dead at Bloody Lane. Will it ever end, Sam?"

"It doesn't look like it."

"Has anyone taken credit?"

"No, but they left a calling card – a banner with a blue cross on a red field, the Confederate battle flag. It was planted in the ground nearby."

"The war goes on."

"Yeah, but it could've been worse, much worse."

"Worse? A kid was killed. A kid I happened to know."

"I'm not saying it's not a tragedy. That's the spin the media will likely put on it. But this bombing was a gesture – a violent one, it's true – but still a symbolic one. I don't think whoever did this meant it to be murderous. In fact, it's a sideshow compared to what we thought might be coming."

"I'm having a hard time with 'symbolic' Sam. And what do you mean by 'might be coming'?"

"Listen. Those photos you took at the Fish & Game Club? We had them enhanced. We've got guys that are good at that – enhancement."

"I couldn't make out anything."

"One of them shows what looks like the business end of a rocket launcher. A rocket launcher, Felix. Either being loaded onto or taken out of that truck. Think Gaza. Think Israel. This is a whole new order of craziness."

"There were also assault rifles, boxes of ammo, body armor, plastique," Allaben returned. "Irwin knew this, so you must've. Why the hell didn't you do something about it?"

"We were keeping an eye on them, but the timing wasn't right for a raid. I'll tell you this, though – assault rifles don't fire rockets. That rocket launcher gave us pause. They're lunatics, Felix. We can't put anything past them. Want to guess the distance between the gun club and Camp David?"

"Seriously?"

"Serious as a heart attack. Easily within range. I've been on the phone with the White House. Turns out the Vice President was planning a stay there. We've got a team on the way to the gun club right now, though I expect that those responsible for the bombing are long gone. Probably the weapons, too. I'm coming up myself tomorrow."

Folliard paused. Allaben knew what was coming next – an invitation to join him in tracking down lunatics. Another assignment.

Just then he saw Miranda stepping off the escalator, a bag slung over her shoulder and a cellphone at her ear. She walked like her mother, as if she had just graduated from finishing school. Had she learned about Donnie? It would be the breaking news on every TV monitor in every waiting area and every bar she'd just passed as she made her way from the gate to the baggage claim.

"Sorry, Sam," he said, "I've got to go."

"Felix?"

"Miranda's here. I'll call you tomorrow."

He watched Miranda tap her phone to end a call, then tap it again to make another one – to him. She looked up to get her bearings and saw her father. She hadn't time to arrange her face. Exhaustion, grief, disgust with the world. Yes, she knew about Donnie.

She walked up to him, fumbled for words, dipped her chin, began to cry. Allaben folded her in his arms, as if to shield her from the treachery of the world.

He clenched his teeth in a no-cry hold, asking himself even as he did so why he didn't just let go and weep. God knew he had reason enough.

His daughter's face was pressed against his chest.

"Let me look at you," he said.

"No," she whispered.

"Let me look at you, Miranda."

She drew her face back and gazed up at him. He kissed her forehead.

"It's late," he said. "Let's go home."

THE END

29306080R00195

Made in the USA
Middletown, DE
14 February 2016